LORD EDGINGTO

BOOK 2

# A BODY
## AT A
# BOARDING
# SCHOOL

A 1920s MYSTERY

# BENEDICT BROWN

# COPYRIGHT

The entire 'Lord Edgington Investigates...' series is dedicated to my much-missed father, but this book is also for my mother Laraine and all the other inspirational teachers who read this.

# OAKTON ACADEMY PARENTS' DAY 1925

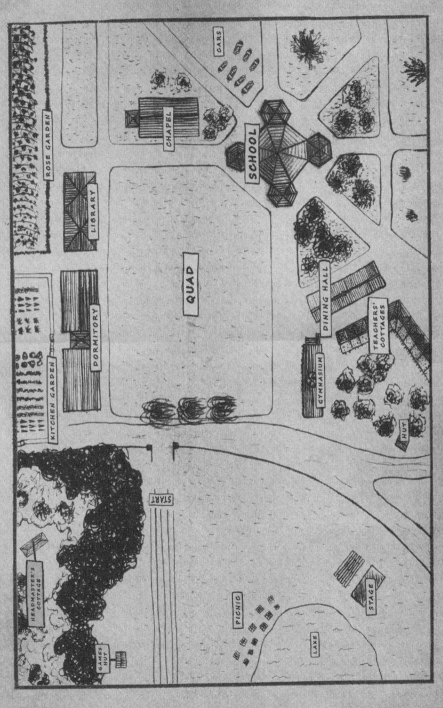

# AUTHOR'S NOTE

**All Readers**

Welcome back to another 'Lord Edgington Investigates...' mystery. This book is set in England in 1925, but I've tried to use language which is easy to understand in context. Even so, I've included a list of unusual vocabulary at the back of the book which might help.

One thing that has surprised early readers is that "sixth form" in the old British school system was the last two years of high school. It is not the same as sixth grade in America. This makes Christopher and his friends aged sixteen to eighteen.

**New Readers**

This novel is spoiler-free so you won't find out the killer from the previous book, though a few of the suspects may be mentioned. I will eventually revisit some of those characters from 'Murder at the Spring Ball', but for the moment, I'm trying not to give anything away.

# CHAPTER ONE

I'd never seen any point in running. It's too much like having a long, drawn-out heart attack, but with no light at the end of the tunnel. I finally came to see its benefits on the day that the Marshall brothers chased me out of Latin class, screaming, "We'll bash your head in, Roly-Poly!"

Zooming along the sixth-form corridor, like Harold Abrahams winning the sprint at the 1924 Olympics, I was an absolute rocket. I shot down the stairs and out of school before they could catch up. I knew that I only needed to reach the toilet block, and then I could lock myself away until lunch was over. While this meant that I would be going without food for ten whole hours (in a row!), Oakton Academy's lunches were about as appetising as a plate of mud with a sprinkling of parsley on top.

As I sped across the quad, there were no other boys in sight. I could see the entrance to the toilets not fifty yards away, and a feeling of joy swelled up within me. For one fleeting moment, I thought, *Yes, I'm actually going to make it. I might not die today after all!* But then I spotted Marmaduke Adelaide rounding the corner behind the Marshall brothers, and I knew I didn't stand a chance.

Marmalade, as I tried not to call him to his face, was the fastest and fiercest pupil in the history of Oakton Academy. Every last boy in the school lived in perpetual dread of him. The instant I realised he was on my trail, I jumped behind a row of bushes and hurried towards the chapel instead. My only hope was that the three terrors hadn't spotted me, and I could slip away to that holy sanctuary unnoticed.

As I entered through its lofty wooden portal, I was momentarily concerned that our brimstone-loving chaplain might be there. After a few nervous seconds, I was confident that the church was empty and dashed down the aisle to hide between the pews.

I'd always found the chapel to be a calm, relaxing place and loved the way the golden beams of sunlight struck through the stained-glass window of Saint George and the dragon each morning. My friends and I used to hide in there to get out of playing rugby, but any solace the church had once offered was forgotten when I heard the brothers' voices outside. I held my breath and waited to discover my fate. I have to admit this was an awfully silly thing to do as I had to let it back out again at the very moment that the door swung open.

"We know you're in here, chubby," Edward Marshall stomped in to yell.

His brother Percy emitted a thunderous laugh. "If you've come to say your prayers, you're too late."

I could see their muscly legs pounding down the aisle towards me. They walked in single file and, from my vantage point on the floor, it looked as though an elephant had invaded the chapel.

Everything about the Marshalls was menacing. At sixteen years old, they already had beards longer than my grandfather's and held the school record for giving out the most twisted nipples and barley sugars in one academic year. I'd done a sterling job of staying out of their way over the last decade, but as their footsteps thudded closer, I knew my luck had run out.

"You can't hide from us, Prentiss." Percy's voice echoed up to the rafters and back. The heavy door opened again behind them, but I thought nothing of it. "You're the size of a bus and this is a very small church."

I hadn't been so scared since I'd stayed up reading 'Dracula' and had to light an extra candle to help me fall asleep. My breathing had taken on an unusual whistling sound and, if that didn't give me away, my amplified heartbeat surely would. It was so loud that I was certain our headmaster, Mr Hardcastle, could hear it up in his office on the other side of school. My only hope was that my unfeasibly sweaty palms would make the floor around me so slick that my attackers would slip over before they could get their hands on me.

Sadly, that wasn't to be.

"There he is!" Edward exulted, as he pulled apart the pews on either side of me, so that the two spotty monsters could peer down with glee.

"Get ready to be-"

Before he could announce the exact form of torture he had planned, Edward's head went thumping into his brother's. There was a resounding clack, and the two mini-Minotaurs reeled from the impact. Percy fell to his knees as though he wanted to repent for his sins, and his brother instantly started sobbing.

A mass of freckles and ginger curls let out a high-pitched "Hurrah!" and my saviour reached down to pull me to my feet.

Instead of running away, I stayed rooted to the spot. "You're not here to help them?" I felt it necessary to check, but Marmaduke Adelaide had already spun on his heel.

"Evidently not, Chrissy." His answer echoed about the church.

"And you're not going to give me a black eye?"

He paused in the arched doorway to glance back. "That neither. But if you don't get a move on, Edward will rise from his slumber and finish the job."

He was right. As we'd been talking, the grim brothers had staggered to their feet.

Marmalade was through the door by the time he shouted, "Run, Chrissy. Move your legs, now!"

As I staggered from the church, all I could think was, *More running? What have I done to deserve this?*

# CHAPTER TWO

"Well, I had a nice life," I told my new friend in the dining hall – which was known unaffectionately by all Oakton pupils as The Pig Trough. "Plenty of chaps die before their sixteenth birthdays. I'm lucky I made it this far."

Marmaduke Adelaide was busy attempting to identify the bowls of slop that Doreen the dinner lady had served up and did not look worried. My three best friends William, Will and Billy were there too, but hadn't uttered a sound since we'd arrived. They sat staring at Marmalade as though he were a rare, ginger-haired rhinoceros, as their hot gruel got cold.

"Don't be so dramatic, Chrissy." Marmalade took an exploratory sniff at the grey sludge on his spoon. "It's the last day of term tomorrow. If you can make it through parents' day without being court-martialled by the Marshall brothers, you may yet live."

His words filled me with hope and fear in equal measure. On the one hand, another twenty-four hours didn't seem like too long to get through, but tomorrow was *parents' day*. Parents' day was the joyous occasion when our loving families – who normally paid Oakton Academy to keep their sons away from them – were invited into the school to hear horror stories of our poor behaviour and limited scholastic ability. They even got a chance to marvel at our lack of sporting prowess in a series of torturous races and events. It certainly gave a bittersweet taste to the end of each year, though the fact that my grandfather would be in attendance was almost enough to make up for it.

"Why did they want to kill you in the first place?" Marmalade asked with the dubious nosh now deposited in his mouth. The three Williams still hadn't said anything and were about as animated as the gnomes in the headmaster's garden.

I let out a nervous sigh. "It wasn't my fault. It was the pigeon's."

My former bully gave me a look which said, "Pigeon? What pigeon?"

"The pigeon on the windowsill in old Mr Balustrade's class. He kept smiling at me and it made me laugh."

This was enough to knock Billy from his stupor. "The Latin master was smiling at you?"

I shook my head. "No, the pigeon." The four of them sniggered at this, so at least my imminent death had brought them some happiness. "Well, it looked like he was, which is why I laughed."

I stopped talking then as there was a crash from the kitchen. Doreen the dinner lady had dropped a vat of beans and, to cover her mistake, threw her ladle at the nearest second-former and screamed, "Blessed kids, always distracting me." The line of blue-blazered students who were still waiting for their lunch froze until the storm had passed.

Such outbursts from Doreen were a rather common occurrence, so Marmaduke soon continued with our conversation. "So why did your reaction to a friendly pigeon upset the Marshall brothers?"

I pushed my hair from my eyes and searched for the right words. "Well... you see, Edward was standing at the front of the class, failing to recite the future passive form of *destruere* when I spotted the pigeon."

Though by all accounts unrelated, when dressed in their matching school uniforms and identical black glasses, my three best friends looked like triplets. There were times when even I couldn't tell them apart. I know that it was William who spoke next, as he was the only one of us who was any good at Latin.

"*Destruar, destruēeris, destruetur...*" He could have gone through every conjugation of every verb in the language.

Somewhat mercifully, he was interrupted by Marmalade. "Sorry, Chrissy, but I think I'll have to leave you to their mercy after all. There's no chance of me protecting you if Edward Marshall thinks that you think he's stupid. Though I admit he possesses the intelligence of a recently bludgeoned trout."

"But *why* did you protect Christopher in the first place?" Will, who is distinguishable thanks to a small mole on his right thumb, suddenly looked very nervous and attempted to rephrase the question. "By which I mean... if you don't mind telling us, Marmaduke... or rather, Mr Adelaide..."

The towering ginger nut gazed down benignly at his short, stocky inquisitor. "Chrissy helped me out of a spot of bother with the police a few weeks back."

"You mean the murder?" Billy prompted.

Marmaduke smiled over at me. "That's right. If it weren't for him, I would have ended up in gaol for a crime I didn't commit. I owe him my life."

He was exaggerating, of course, and my cheeks turned as red as his hair. "My grandfather was the one who saved you. He's the detective, I'm just..." I wasn't entirely sure how to finish that sentence.

He ignored me and continued. "Anyway, it's lucky that I'd nipped out of Latin when old Balustrade wasn't looking. I was lounging in the corridor just as Chrissy shot past, pursued by two bears. I thought I'd better keep an eye on the situation and... The Marshalls are here."

I was still shy from my time in the limelight. "Well, that's not exactly what happened, but-"

"No, Chrissy." Marmaduke twisted my head around to look at the door where my twin tormentors stood. "They're here now."

My friends bundled me under the table. The floor was sticky and there were fragments of beer bottles dotted about. It reminded me of a rumour that was going around school about wild parties in the dining hall each night. I'd dismissed the idea as nonsense and there was no time to reconsider as, just then, the two-man elephant approached. They could hardly fail to miss Marmaduke. He was as tall as a lighthouse and twice as bright.

"What have you done with him, Adelaide?" Marshall number one grunted. "We're not here for you. We want Roly the runt." To be honest, I'd heard worse insults. Poor "Stinky" Simon Speight had never got over the shame of his nickname and rarely emerged from the school library except for lessons.

"I've no idea what you're talking about." Though I couldn't see his face – as I was busy cowering at his feet – the light-hearted tone Marmalade adopted proved that he was not afraid of them.

"Christopher Prentiss," Percy clarified. The two brothers normally shared duties in a conversation and split their responses most democratically. "You know the chap; he looks like a blister. We thought we'd do the honourable thing and pop him."

This was enough to get on Marmalade's wick, and he rose from his seat. "If you lay a finger on Chrissy, I'll make sure that you never-"

He was interrupted by the head prefect, who strutted over to wield his authority.

"I'll have no fighting in my dining hall," Dominic Rake vociferated, and the room fell silent. "What's going on?"

"That's none of your concern," Edward responded. He and his brother had turned their attention to the new challenger, so I stuck my head out to watch. "Why don't you run along and find some first-formers to intimidate? No one's scared of you here."

I was scared of all the prefects. They were identifiable by their black, double-breasted blazers with golden buttons and a large yellow letter P sewn on the lapel. Dominic Rake was the leader of this military faction and was not much more pleasant than the Marshall brothers. Tall, gaunt and as thin as a pole, he suited his name rather well.

A tense silence had set in as they stared each other down. It was only when Doreen dropped another dish in the kitchen that the stand-off finally relaxed.

"What do you say, boys? Can we make it to the end of term without anyone getting killed?" Rake tried to sound cheerful as Percy Marshall pushed past him.

Edward lingered to deliver the last words. "I'd say the chances are slim."

# CHAPTER THREE

I stuck to Marmalade for the rest of the day like he was made of… ummm… jam. My friends were slowly warming to him too as, when he wasn't trying to punch or strangle anyone, Adelaide could be quite good company. For perhaps the first time in all our years at Oakton Academy, we prowled those halls like we weren't afraid of some beast coming to pick us off. With Marmalade next to us, we walked like lions. Though it's true we were only heading to our final, and so potentially most excruciating, history class of the year, we held our heads high and puffed out our chests.

Dr Steadfast is one hundred and thirty-seven years old and started working at Oakton in the eighteenth century – approximately forty years before the school was even built. And while nothing in that sentence is true, I can promise that an hour spent with Oberon Steadfast felt like decades had passed.

In truth, he probably wasn't more than fifty and was forever dressed in a mortarboard and mud-brown jumper. He had the jowls of a bulldog and the wet nose to match. He stood behind his desk in every lesson, shouting out dates and slapping the blackboard with his yardstick whenever a boy hesitated over an answer. I suppose it was fitting for a man with such an old-fashioned demeanour to teach history, but this did nothing to make his classes more bearable.

"Tompkins! 1642?"

"Outbreak of the civil war, sir."

"Palmer! 1666?"

"Great fire of London, sir."

"Geoffries! 1812?"

Tom Geoffries looked panicked and the immense ruler landed on the board with a resounding "smack". It did nothing to jog his memory, and he searched around his classmates for help.

"Tchaikovsky, sir?" he attempted, in a voice so small it was amazing that the bumbling chap at the front caught the words.

"I beg your pardon?"

"The composer, sir. He wrote his overture then."

There was a gentle tittering from the rest of us, which led to three more smacks of the yardstick. I had to feel a little sorry for the poor, innocent blackboard.

"This is not a music class, my boy, but if you are capable of telling me the particular event in history which inspired said composer's said overture, I might find it in the goodness of my heart to let you off." Steadfast leaned forward to make Geoffries even more nervous.

I couldn't stand seeing the fellow suffering like that, so I decided to give him a clue. I performed a silent dance with my legs kicking out under the table and my hand tucked between the buttons on my shirt.

His eyes flashed with joy and he yelled, "Napoleon's doomed invasion of Russia, sir."

Steadfast's long, drooping chin scrunched tighter. "Very impressive, Geoffries." He nodded approvingly, and the whole class let out a sigh. "But you and Prentiss will come back here this evening to write lines. Geoffries, you will write the phrase, 'I must not copy from my classmates when I am ignorant of the correct answer' one hundred times." And Prentiss, how about, 'I am neither a Cossack nor a nineteenth-century French emperor'?"

This received another laugh and another bang on the board. "Moving on, boys," Steadfast continued with a morose smile. "Campbell! 1879?"

Our professor's classes consisted of three distinct parts. First came the years, then the events, and last of all he'd shout out specific dates he expected us to know. Having been in his class for half a decade, I'd had the knowledge machine-gunned into me but still dreaded every moment.

The call-and-response would have continued the whole hour, if Dominic Rake hadn't come knocking at the door.

At first, the bulldog at the front ignored it.

"Prentiss! The twentieth of March 1815?"

Oh, yuck. The beginning of the nineteenth-century always stumped me. It was almost certainly linked to agriculture in some way. Or the Napoleonic wars again. Or perhaps...

"Yes, sir," I began, stalling for time. "That's an easy one, on the twentieth of March 1815-"

The door opened and the stern prefect marched in. "Excuse me for interrupting, Dr Steadfast, but Headmaster wishes to convene the sixth form for an assembly."

Our teacher looked thoroughly disappointed by this development and opened his top drawer to extract a cigar. "Very well, boys. Have a summer and come back ready for more classes in the autumn."

There was no word missing in this sentence. He did not wish us a good, stimulating or pleasant summer, just a summer in itself. We packed our books away, but he hadn't quite finished with me. "And, Prentiss, when you come back at six o'clock, you can write an extra hundred lines which say, 'On the twentieth of March 1815, parliament passed the Corn Bill.'"

He crashed down in his seat, with his cigar piping out smoke, and had a good smirk before we moved on to our next injustice.

There was something rather stifled about my classmates as we trundled along the dark sixth-form corridor. The end of term was supposed to be a time of carefree hijinks, but forty minutes with Steadfast had extinguished our candles. We needn't have worried though, things were about to get worse.

"I won't be having it!" Hardcastle bellowed as soon as we were sitting down before him in our neat rows.

The Marshalls were just a few seats away. I had to thank my lucky stars and all the saints for the fact we only had one class together. They looked like they literally wanted to eat me.

"Do you hear me? I won't be having it!" Our headmaster was yet to explain exactly what he would not be having. He stood at the immense, wrought-iron lectern, twitching with his usual nerviness. To his left were a selection of unsavoury characters. Rake was there, of course, his eyes registering every raised eyebrow and curled lip for signs of disobedience. Next to him was our matron; a gorilla-human hybrid with a hunch-back and a drooling lip. She made a low humming sound, even when she wasn't speaking.

To contrast with these unique specimens was the actually quite lovely Mrs Hardcastle, known affectionately to us boys as *Mama*. How the perpetually irate Mr Hardcastle had wooed such a placid and pretty lady was the question which every Oakton boy went to bed puzzling over. It was not just that she was so stunningly beautiful that we all fell in love with her, it was that the only other women in school were Matron and Doreen the dinner lady. Unlike her husband, that pastel princess was softly spoken and had a warm smile. She was simply wonderful, and we weren't the only ones to notice.

The final figure on that creaking wooden stage was our chemistry teacher, Mr Herbert Mayfield. Herbie was the softest of all our teachers, and we were terribly fond of him, just as he was fond of Mrs Celia Hardcastle. It wasn't as though he discussed his feelings with us boys, but it was hard to avoid this conclusion as he emitted a long, romantic sigh whenever she was near. Which is exactly what he was doing when Mr Hardcastle explained why he'd called us to the hall.

"I know that, traditionally, the last day of the academic year is a time for pranks and jokes, but I won't be having it." He shook his shiny oval head. Much like on his first day at Oakton, a few years earlier, I couldn't help but marvel at how perfectly egg-shaped it was. "If I hear of a single stone hurled at the staff room window, a trace of toilet paper suspended from a tree, or one lower school pupil hauled up by his britches, I'll show as much mercy as the emperor Caligula did to... to... to whoever it was that Caligula didn't like."

Old Mr Balustrade wouldn't be impressed by the headmaster's classical knowledge, but no one said a word. The only person there who looked unconcerned by Hardcastle's fury was Marmaduke Adelaide, and I'm fairly certain that the assembly had been called in his honour.

"There will be no repeat of last year when one of you emptied a bottle of whisky in the staff room tea urn. Nor do we want the sort of behaviour that occurred two years ago when Matron ended up in her own infirmary. And the less said about 1922's debacle the better!"

Marmalade had been responsible for all of these incidents and more.

"I think we can do better," he whispered to me without moving. "In fact, I already have something incredible planned."

"Adelaide!" I can only assume that the reason Mr Hardcastle was given the job as headmaster was that he had preternatural hearing and, much like a bat, could home in on his target. "What do you have to say that is so important it cannot wait until after school?"

Marmalade wore an innocent smile. "My apologies, sir. I was merely commenting to my colleague how jolly excited I am for the summer holidays."

The brick-built gentleman before us did not immediately reply. I could tell that he was weighing up his response by the way he chewed the inside of his cheeks in a slow, steady rhythm. "You have one year remaining at this institution, Adelaide. If you're not careful, it will be a particularly unpleasant one."

"I'm dreadfully sorry, sir," he replied, emphasising his faux regret a little too strongly. "I solemnly promise that I will never make a sound in front of you again."

"Enough cheek, young man. You know, it's not too late to call your father to pick you up a day early."

The abundance of self-assurance, which had previously shone out of Marmaduke, disappeared in the time it takes to flick a light switch. Though some claimed otherwise, every last boy in school was scared of Mr Hardcastle. He was not merely a demon with a cane, but possessed the singular ability to call our parents at a moment's notice and inform them of our misdeeds.

Seeing the fear he'd struck into my neighbour, our headmaster looked rather pleased with himself and addressed the audience once more. "To recapitulate, no nonsense today or tomorrow and, if anyone in this room so much as scratches his name on a desk or runs in the corridor, I've devised a special end-of-term punishment."

Our immense Matron laughed her deep, growling laugh at this and added, "You really don't want to find out what he's got in store for you, boys." I could see from her face that this was no idle threat. It made me rather woozy.

With his last word spoken, Hardcastle narrowed his deep blue eyes and darted his gaze down to us. After approximately twenty seconds of silence, the head prefect decided to intervene.

"Is that all, sir?" Rake enquired. "Only there's still five minutes left until the next lesson and... well, it is an assembly."

Hardcastle searched about for a solution. "Yes, you're quite right, boy." He shot his hand out and pointed to Herbie without looking. "Mr Mayfield, lead the boys in a hymn or some such. I'll be in my office."

Hardcastle stalked off the stage with his good lady wife following meekly behind. Poor Herbie looked entirely crestfallen, as she smiled apologetically. His pain at seeing the woman (I have to assume) he was in love with drifting from the room, like a balloon on a summer's day, was compounded by the fact he would now have to sing in front of everyone.

There was only one thing for it.

"All things bright and beautiful…" I began, hoping beyond hopes that I would not be the only one. "All creatures great and small." I paused then as my nerves got the better of me. I'm no soprano and my voice came out in a particularly reedy tone.

Marmalade punched me on the arm before saving me for the second time that day. "All things wise and wonderful, The Lord God made them all."

"Each little flower that opens,

Each little bird that sings." My whole class had joined in by now and, though the three Williams made a point of singing at far too high a pitch, like castrato choir boys, it actually sounded rather nice.

"He made their glowing colours,

He made their tiny wings."

By the end of the second verse, the whole sixth form were singing as one. We launched back into the chorus with great gusto, getting faster and faster as we went. We wouldn't have done this for just any teacher and dear Herbie looked overjoyed. Even that prig Rake was singing, and I doubt he'd ever made a sound before that wasn't in some way critical of the boys around him.

When the song was complete, we gave ourselves a good clap and Matron stepped up to the lectern.

"Right, that'll do. Now back to class."

# CHAPTER FOUR

There were only two hours left with Herbie (and some lines to write) before I could say that my scholastic investment for the year was complete. Not even the thought of Dr Steadfast telling my parents that I'd helped another boy cheat or, my maths teacher, Mr Arthurs, complaining about my near total ignorance of algebraic formulae could dampen my mood.

"No matter what the other teachers might say about you, boys," Mr Mayfield began when we were clustered around him in the chemistry lab, "I think you're just great."

"Three cheers for Herbie!" Tom Geoffries exclaimed, and we banged our feet on the floor in celebration.

The cheerful teacher lost his smile for a moment and calmed us down. "You'd better not make so much noise or Mr Balustrade will be up here to complain." He was a small, delicate man with fine, gold-rimmed glasses and hair in a side parting that looked like it might slide from his head at any moment. He was forever dressed in pale colours – as though he were trying to blend in with the whitewashed walls – and spoke in such a soft voice that we rarely made a sound in his class for fear of missing an important instruction.

He stood up and pulled his white coat on.

"Now, I've got a bit of a surprise for you today." The very best thing about Herbie, though, was that he managed to make learning about chemistry a real pleasure. I was no scientist – or mathematician, historian, geographer, linguist… Well, there are a lot of things I hadn't quite mastered, in fact, but Herbie helped me to understand his lessons because he was simply so passionate about what he was teaching. Sadly for us boys, he was an exception rather than the rule.

He turned on a Bunsen burner and raised a bottle of pink liquid to the very hottest part of the flame. The substance quickly turned green and let out a puff of smoke. We boys cooed in response, as this was truly the most exciting thing we'd seen in school all year.

"That's just for starters. Next, I'll need a volunteer and I'm going to choose him."

"Well, then he's not a volunteer, is he, sir?" Marmaduke replied.

"Yes, you are, Mr Adelaide. Up you come." Both teacher and student smiled broadly, knowing that the skit they'd just performed could have come straight from a variety performance.

Herbie disappeared off into the supply cupboard and came back with a trolley covered in flasks of glowing substances, gently dancing creatures in petri dishes and large pieces of apparatus which we weren't normally allowed to touch.

"Now…" Herbie began a lot of sentences with this exclamation. "…we know that Mr Adelaide here has an impressive head of hair, but I think it could stand out even more."

Facing the class, with our teacher behind him, Marmalade looked quite nervous. Herbie waved a wand over the boy's head, and his bright red locks stood on end. As we laughed at the reaction, a violent look crossed the boy's face and I was reminded that this was the same chap who had given me a black eye just one month earlier.

"Ummm," he finally said. "I don't like this. Do you mind telling me what you're doing?"

Between passes of the tubular wand that Herbie was holding, he rubbed it on his woollen trousers. "It's static electricity. I'm creating a charge on this tube with the friction from the material in my trousers before transferring the electricity to the strands of hair, which causes them to rise."

"I thought electricity was deadly sir?" one of my less-than-brainy classmates called out.

"Not in small quantities and the charge we're creating here is very small indeed. Would anyone else like a turn?" Every boy in that room put his hand up.

Herbie couldn't hide how much he was enjoying himself as he made ordinary objects glow in the dark, turned a small bottle into a rocket and showed us any number of exciting explosions. The lesson finished with a homemade firework display and, throughout the two hours, he calmly and clearly explained the science behind everything we were seeing. It certainly beat shouting out dates with Dr Steadfast or Mr Balustrade's endless Latin conjugations.

At the end of the class, Herbie stood at the door to shake hands and even used an adjective in his farewell. "Have a wonderful summer!"

I was sure that any one of us boys would have run to London and back to buy him a sandwich or dashed off a five-thousand-word essay if he'd asked. We simply loved him.

"Any plans for the holiday, Prentiss?" he enquired, as I'd dawdled putting my things away and the other boys had already gone.

"Yes, I know exactly what I'm going to do," I said with some enthusiasm. He perched on the corner of his desk and waited for me to explain. "Actually, I misspoke. I haven't the faintest idea *what* I'm going to do, but I know that I'll be spending it with my grandfather."

"Lord Edgington?" Herbie sounded rather impressed, and I nodded proudly. "No wonder you're excited. The man is a legend." He smiled to himself in that way old people do when thinking back on their childhoods. I couldn't tell you Mr Mayfield's exact age, but he was thirty if he was a day. "I remember when I was a boy I used to read all about the great Superintendent Edgington in 'The Boy's Own Paper'. He was forever fighting crime and bringing villains to justice. I actually considered becoming a policeman myself because of him."

I didn't like to interrupt his nostalgia, but felt I had to show off a little. "He's coming to parents' day tomorrow, I'll bring him to see you."

Herbie's eyes almost popped from his head. "Do you mean it? That would be marvellous. I'd absolutely love to shake hands with him before I leave."

Still in his reverie, he apparently hadn't noticed the bombshell he'd dropped. "Leave, sir? Are you not teaching us next year?"

He cleared his throat a little affectedly, and cast his eyes to the floor before answering. "I'm afraid not. You see, I'm off to explore new horizons, but it's been an absolute thrill to teach you all and I really will miss your class."

He peered out through the windows to the quad, where a number of boys were already unleashing merry hell.

I didn't know what else to say, so I closed my bag ever so slowly, dragged my chair back into position and finally decided on, "Well, I wish you weren't going." I realised that was far too soppy a sentiment for an Oaktonian boy to utter and made up for it by running from the room on the brink of tears.

Down in the yard, Rake and the other black-garbed prefects were failing to control the sixth-form firebrands. The Marshall brothers had got hold of two younger boys and were riding them around the quad like donkeys. Henry Castleton had found a tin of paint from somewhere and was writing a lewd message on the wall for Hardcastle to find – though I'm almost certain there's no Q in knickers – and skinny Peter Jarvis was running in circles singing, "Run, run as fast as you can. You can't catch me, I'm the gingerbread man."

He turned out to be wrong on that score. Matron soon picked him up, slung him over her shoulder and dropped him in a bush.

There was one notable abstention among the mischief makers. Marmalade was sitting on a bench in the middle of the chaos, doing nothing. With my three best friends alongside him, he sat with his legs folded at the ankles, looking quite peaceful. It was only when Mr Hardcastle turned up to get everyone under control that I understood what was happening.

We watched as the real heavies of the school (Dr Steadfast, Doreen the dinner lady and our headmaster himself) set to work rounding up the troubled youths. The Marshall twins didn't stand a chance against Doreen, who picked them up by their collars, one in each hand, and dropped them into a nearby rubbish bin. Though slow and heavy footed, there was no getting past Steadfast either. He had the wingspan of a pelican and walked across the playground with his arms out to capture fleeing culprits, like a one-man game of red rover.

Once the majority of the boys had been rounded up, it was time for the headmaster to blow his shiny top once more. "What did I tell you? What did I tell any of you?" He didn't wait for an answer, and no one was desperate to provide one. "I will personally make sure that every boy involved in this debacle is given a severe dressing down in front of your parents tomorrow."

Such threats no longer seemed so frightening when compared to the delights of that afternoon, and several prisoners chirped out their resistance. The little man used the steps into school as his soapbox. He was nervy and indignant, even by his standards, and he spat fragmented sounds rather than whole words, as he waited for calm.

"So much for the *special punishment* he's devised," Marmalade muttered, and Mr Hardcastle managed to sense his insolence from forty yards away. Perhaps he could read lips.

"Don't think you're getting off so easily, Adelaide. I know you're up to something. I've got my eye on you."

The headmaster's comment might have been felt more deeply had Derek McGeorge not chosen that moment to go running across the quadrangle with no clothes on, shouting, "Long live Oakton Academy for nincompoops and bootlickers!"

Hardcastle scowled more fiercely, but Marmalade just smiled and waved.

# CHAPTER FIVE

I trundled back to the sixth-form corridor for my final detention of the year, and it was enough to sap all the excitement from the day. To be fair to Dr Steadfast, at least he was no fan of corporal punishment. Though perhaps a few whacks with the sole of his shoe would have been less painful than being bored to death by two hundred lines. I did the old trick of writing all the first words, then all the second and so on, but it still took half an eternity.

Dr Steadfast sat on the dais at the front of the class. He had his feet up on his desk and smiled at Tom and me the whole time, until Geoffries got to leave halfway through the slog. I suppose that's the definition of sadism; thrilling in the pain you inflict upon others. Whether it was with a cane, a leather strap or, indeed, pointless brain-numbing repetition, old Steadfast was a rum sort in my book.

To add a little variety to my imprisonment, there was eventually a knock at the door and he bumbled off to see who it was. He stuck his head out into the corridor, had a bit of a shout, along the lines of, "I'm busy and you shouldn't be disturbing me here anyway," then nipped back inside. I couldn't hear who he was talking to, and what had unsettled him to such an extent.

My torment came to an end when Steadfast settled back down in his seat and swiftly fell to snoring. I finished my final line, put two hundred full stops and, feeling as free as a wandering antelope, sneaked from the room. I'd missed supper by this time – which is exactly why my diabolical history teacher had called me to his room at six o'clock. I knew that the boys would smuggle out some bread and butter for me. Though hard as an iron doorstop, it was the only thing Doreen served that anyone wanted to eat.

"No more funny stuff tonight!" our resident Doberman bellowed as I entered our floor.

"Of course not, Matron. I'm going straight to bed."

Standing at her post like a sentry guard, she scratched her chin and watched me with a gimlet eye as I passed. She was a large, charmless woman with seemingly no motherly instinct beyond her near hourly insistence that we wash behind our ears. It was difficult to comprehend why she'd chosen such a career, though perhaps there'd been no vacancies for slave drivers at the time.

I was happy to slip into my pyjamas and get into bed, knowing that, however disappointed my mother would be in me the following day, my grandfather would be there to cheer me up. It was odd to think that he'd been absent for two-thirds of my existence. He'd shut himself away in his suite for the last ten years. Now that he had emerged, it was impossible to imagine a world without him.

I couldn't decide whether to continue 'The Pickwick Papers' or crack open Shakespeare's 'A Midsummer Night's Dream' to mark the end of term. Instead, I nodded off with thoughts of my family in my head and would have slept through until morning if it hadn't been for a voice in the middle of the night, waking me from my slumber.

"Chrissy, it's time to go. Come along, wake up, wake up." I could tell from the depth and insistence of the voice that it was Marmaduke Adelaide. He was hidden in the darkness at the end of my bed.

I thought about throwing my pillow at him, but knew he wouldn't give up.

"What do you want?" I mumbled, before a pleasant thought entered my mind. "Are we having a midnight snack?"

In the faint light that was peeping through the curtains beside my bed, I could make out a curl of his hair and the unimpressed look on his face as my eyes adjusted.

"Do you ever think about anything except for food?"

"Of course I do. I like birds and-" I was about to give him some examples of my other interests, but he interrupted.

"Get out of bed this instant. I have the most devious plan, and I need your help."

Is there anything more painful than having to emerge from a warm, cosy blanket in order to go on a fruitless mission which is bound to get a boy in trouble? Well probably, but it was difficult to imagine just then.

Yawning like I'd just had double Latin, I swung my legs from the bed and stabbed my feet into my slippers. Marmalade looked far more awake than I was and now wore a contented grin.

"What have you done?" I asked in a whisper to avoid waking our classmates or, far worse, Matron herself.

He let out a titter but didn't say another word until we'd tiptoed outside into the moonlight. "Just wait, Chrissy. This is the prank to end all pranks." We walked over to the main block. "The prank de résistance. The prank du jour. The prank de…" He'd never been very good at French.

"Yes, but what is it and why did you go waking a fellow at this preposterous hour?"

He didn't reply but excitedly tapped his Roman nose. As he did so, there was an unexpected crinkling sound and I could tell that he was hiding something under his red and blue checked pyjamas.

"If Hardcastle catches us, you know what will happen," I complained. We were halfway across the quad now, and I could see that there was no sense trying to reason with him.

"How would he catch us?" He scoffed at the idea. "It's one in the morning and everyone is tucked up in bed. Matron is snoring away, Steadfast will be having sweet dreams in his cottage and Hardcastle will be in the arms of his loving wife. This is a guaranteed plan. No chance of failure."

He snickered once more and sneaked across the grass like a particularly clever fox looking for his dinner. Inside the school, it was as quiet as a library.

"Just get on with it. I was having a lovely dream about getting married to my one true love, Alice-" I stopped then as I wasn't entirely sure what my one true love's surname was.

His grin colonised new territories on his cheeks. He kicked open the door to the hall and took a deep breath, to savour the moment. "Stand here and tell me if you hear anyone coming."

"You said that they're all asleep!" My voice got a little squeaky then. "Hardcastle is going to flay us."

I lingered in the doorway as Marmalade sprinted the length of the hall to jump onto the stage.

"Don't exaggerate, Chrissy."

"I'm not!" I whispered as loudly as I could. "If anything, I'm under-exaggerating. When Hardcastle finds us, he's going to pull our toenails out one by one and send them home to our parents with the bill for our school fees."

"That's ridiculous." He was up on a chair behind the stage curtains and had pulled something small from his pocket.

"Yes, entirely ridiculous," a voice at the back of the room rumbled. "I'll make sure that your parents have paid up well before I touch a hair on your heads." Hardcastle stepped from the shadows, and a sliver of light rebounded off his perfectly smooth dome. "I knew you were planning something, Adelaide. Now tell me what it is or you'll be sorry you ever heard the name Tobias Hardcastle."

I thought my anarchic friend might point out how desperate the headmaster clearly was to have spent the night prowling the halls on the off chance his students were causing trouble, but no. In fact, Marmalade could not move a muscle; he looked like a sculpture on a plinth.

"Prentiss?" The headmaster's voice had become gruff and lupine. "What about you? Are you going to tell me what you're doing here at such an hour on the last night of the summer term?"

The only sound I could produce was a clicking in my throat. No words would come and I was also having trouble breathing. In my whole life, the headmaster had never once had to address me directly. I'd done my absolute best not to stand out, but on my first day spending time with Marmaduke Adelaide, I'd been caught red-handed in this dubious enterprise.

"I..." I tried again. "I don't know anything about it." This was almost entirely true.

Hardcastle allowed his gaze to wander back to Marmalade, and I managed to gulp down some air.

"Follow me, boys." He turned to exit the hall and lead us up the stairs to the staff corridor. The fact he didn't grab us by the ears and pull us there was somehow more frightening.

"Whatever you're carrying, get rid of it now," I told Marmalade once he'd caught up with me, only for Hardcastle to lean back around the doorframe.

"Yes, that's a very good idea, Adelaide." Even for our disgruntled headmaster, he was unusually aggressive and I once again had to wonder what had inspired his bad mood. "Why don't you hand over whatever it is you're hiding, and maybe I'll go more easily on you?"

Marmalade extended one hand and unfurled his fingers to show a clutch of thumb tacks.

Hardcastle narrowed his eyes and seized the offending articles. "I'll take those, thank you."

He waited for us both to pass and I knew how cows must feel being herded into an abattoir. My legs were heavy as we ascended the stairs and I had to cross my fingers that I was safe in my bed and this was a figment of my slumbering imagination.

It would have made a lot more sense if it was a dream. I was Christopher Prentiss, famed for not being famous. Master of no subjects, winner of absolutely no scholastic prizes, certificates, or badges of merit in my eleven years at school. I wasn't the type to get up in the middle of the night in some exciting plot that our bulldoggish headmaster would discover.

*Definitely a dream,* I told myself as we navigated the dark corridor past the staff room. *Definitely a dream,* I thought as I breathed in the smell of stale cigarettes and cups of tea. *Definitely a dream,* I tried one final time as we got to Hardcastle's office and he pulled a ring of keys from his pocket with a jingle.

"I bet you wish you'd stayed in bed, don't you, boys?" He let out a laugh as he ushered us inside and I came to accept that this was not in any way, shape or form a dream and that I was about to get my first patented Hardcastle beating.

Every wall of the office was covered in shelves, each of which held a unique display of artefacts. There were African masks and golden nautical instruments, monkeys carved out of coconuts and old flintlock pistols. It lent the space the look of an untidy museum or Uncle Sol's shop in Dickens' 'Dombey and Son'. It was certainly far more interesting than I would have imagined from our staid headmaster, but there were more urgent matters to think about just then.

Marmalade looked more terrified than I felt and was sucking down sharp, noisy breaths. "It was nothing bad, sir. Just a bit of last-day fun."

Hardcastle had dipped behind his desk and was searching for something. "In which case, you won't mind telling me what you had planned."

My accomplice didn't have an answer and turned to me for assistance.

"We..." I attempted. "We were..." I managed to land upon a rather clever explanation. "We were going to put those pins on old Balustrade's chair so that, when he sat down, he'd get a bit of a shock."

Our headmaster had slammed his cane down on his desk but

continued his search. "No, you weren't." He poked his head over the table to eye us again. "Adelaide was standing on a chair when I caught you, so I know that's not true."

"If… When…" It was Marmalade's turn to stutter.

Hardcastle lit the lamp on his desk and stood back up.

"Come over here, boy." He pointed a stubby finger at my companion.

Whatever Hardcastle had found was well hidden behind his short legs. Marmalade took his first steps over to the flogging block in the corner, and the headmaster's face was reshaped by vicious glee.

"You needn't worry, Mr Adelaide." His eye was twitching again and I could see how agitated he was. "With all the thrashings I've given you over the years, I doubt you have much feeling left in that region."

Marmalade knew the routine and knelt down in front of the block. It was small, wooden and had two steps for the victim to lean over. It rather reminded me of an Olympic podium.

"Last chance, boy. Tell me what you had planned or you're going to get it."

My new friend shot a defiant look at his tormentor. "I'm not scared of you."

Hardcastle positively roared with laughter. "Well, you should be. You very much should be."

Marmalade closed his eyes to prepare for what was next. I'm certain that our headmaster wanted me to bear witness to the cruelty he was about to inflict. He raised the cane in his right hand and, with a whistling swish, brought it down firmly on Marmalade's pyjama bottoms. I had to wonder whether the soft, flannel fabric would be as resistant as woollen school trousers, but my friend didn't cry out. He screwed his eyes tighter and braced himself for more.

With a hyena's smile on his face throughout, Mr Hardcastle delivered four more swipes of the cane, and I had to hope that was the worst of it. I could tell that he was disappointed in the impact he was having; silent tears were not enough. I stood beside his desk, feeling complicit in the savagery, but powerless to intervene.

"You're something of a sportsman, aren't you, Adelaide?" He paused between words, like he was trying to build up strength, that nerve in his eye twitching the whole time. "Tell me, boy, are you a fan of cricket?"

He dropped the cane to the floor and raised his other hand which held a broad wooden bat. Maintaining it in the air for the briefest of moments, it gave me just enough time to intervene.

"It's up his shirt!" Even as I said the words, I knew that Marmalade would have preferred the beating. I sacrificed loyalty for the sake of his unbroken bones. "I don't know what the plan was, but he's got something hidden in his pyjamas."

Marmalade opened his eyes and I'll never forget the reproachful look that he beamed across the room. Hardcastle yanked him to his feet, then tugged up his pyjama shirt to reveal a long roll of paper which was wrapped around his body. The headmaster pulled on one end so that Marmalade went spinning on the spot.

With a hurried intensity, Hardcastle laid the glued-together reel out on the floor to discover Marmalade's plan. From where I was standing, I couldn't make out what was sketched upon it, but our headmaster let out an unimpressed huff as I moved around to see.

"Very funny, Adelaide. Yes, very droll. It's a shame you didn't put as much effort into your schoolwork as you put into your art."

I managed to catch a glimpse of the charcoal drawing before Hardcastle rolled the paper away. In the centre of the image was a perfect caricature of the man himself, in all his egg-headed glory. Poised just behind him, Dr Steadfast's oversized boot was about to make contact with the headmaster's engorged bottom.

Matron was even more terrifying than in real life and dwarfed poor Celia Hardcastle, who looked on in shock. Herbie was there too, staring at his beloved with hearts for eyes, Doreen had launched her ladle at the indignant head's head, and, in the background, countless pupils watched in amusement. It was quite the masterpiece. Marmalade must have been working on it for weeks.

"I suppose you planned to hide this behind the curtains to reveal it during the parents' day closing ceremony. Am I right?" Hardcastle screamed with newfound vigour. "Back on the block!"

Marmalade had spotted the cricket bat in our headmaster's hand and hesitated. His eyes jumped over to me, but there was nothing I could do to save him. I'd never seen that titan among schoolboys look so scared before, even when he'd been caught up in a murder investigation. I felt physical pain inside me at the thought of the great

Marmaduke Adelaide being brought down to earth.

"It was only a joke, sir," he breathed out, and his sobs became audible.

"I'm sure your father will find it very amusing when he comes to see me tomorrow." He spat as he spoke. "Now, kneel down."

"You don't have to do this," I tried, and Hardcastle's cerulean eyes flashed in my direction.

"Don't worry, Prentiss. You're clearly not to blame in this matter. We'll put it down to the corrupting influence of a wicked boy and you can go back to your room."

"I'm not leaving." I surprised myself with the resilience in my voice.

"Stay and enjoy the show then, but you'll be next." His fingers curled around the handle once more, and he eyed his prey hungrily as he raised the bat for the second time. "I should have done this years ago, Adelaide. Maybe you'd never have become such a tearaway."

"Mr Hardcastle, stop!" The words roared out of me, but no one could dissuade him from his course.

"Tobias, what are you doing?" No one but his wife, that is. "Put the bat down this instant. You could kill the poor child!"

Standing in the doorway, Mama had saved us. She was dressed in a peach satin negligée and looked entirely out of place in such a scene.

Her husband still held his hand in the air, and his face was covered in sweat from the fury he'd worked himself into. "Celia, you don't understand. Go back to bed and I'll be along shortly."

"I'm not going anywhere until you let these boys leave." She came closer to show she really meant what she was saying. We watched Mr Hardcastle to discover what he would do next, but his resolve had faded.

"It has to be done, Cece. Boys must learn." His fire had died down, and I could see him for the petty bully he was. "They must be taught a lesson."

Mama didn't need to say anything else to prove him wrong. She put her hand out to Marmalade and he jumped up faster than a choirboy at the end of mass. I followed along just as quickly, in case the headmaster went for me instead.

"I'll make sure they get back to the dormitory safely," Mrs Hardcastle told her husband, and, as we left his office, the last thing we heard was the sound of the cricket bat crashing to the floor.

# CHAPTER SIX

A bright summer's day dawned the following morning to burn away the darkness of the night before. At breakfast, Marmalade was back to his jocular self and spurned his usual empty-headed friends to sit with me and the three Williams again. He was joking and doing impressions of Doreen the whole time, though, in the brief moments of quiet, there was a reticence about him which I'd never previously noticed.

The school itself was alive with pre-holiday excitement. Every member of staff and prefect was bustling about to prepare for our parents' arrival later that morning. Mrs Hardcastle had cut roses from her garden and placed them in bouquets in every room. I was sure she must have been up with the dawn to get the school looking so pretty.

An "Oakton Academy Parents' Day – 1925" banner had been hung above the main entrance and colourful bunting in red, white and blue was strung from the trees along the drive. It was all very jolly and reminded me of the St Mary-Under-Twine village fête.

It's strange to think how I set the events of the night before so easily from my mind. I thought little of the trauma we'd experienced – perhaps dismissing it as nothing but a nightmare after all. The only thing in my head that morning was the chance to see my family. Though I'd visited Grandfather a few days earlier, a month had passed since I'd seen my mother and I was feeling rather homesick.

I went outside to wait for them and was thrilled to spot my Grandfather's Silver Ghost tourer gliding down the drive. I thought he might have come in something sportier, but was sure that my mother had changed his mind. And, besides, they needed the extra space. Along with our chauffeur, Todd, there were a couple more unexpected guests on board.

"Christopher!" Grandfather's booming voice seemed to echo even in a wide-open space, but he was not the first to reach me.

His golden retriever Delilah came bounding over, full of the joys of summer. From the way she jumped up on me and let out a good old bark, you wouldn't have thought I'd been playing with her in Cranley Hall just that weekend. Perhaps no one had told her where she was going and it came as a surprise. I made a good fuss of her and ruffled her ears, but there were more people still to greet.

"Wonderful to be here, my boy," my grandfather told me, and my insides felt as though they were smiling. "Halfway through sixth form already? You'll be a grown man before we know what to do with you." He was dressed, as was his custom, in his dove-grey morning suit and was formally accessorised that day with his silver cane and top hat. It was hardly summer attire, but then men of my grandfather's age and standing are usually forgiven for such eccentricity.

"Darling, I'm so proud of you," Mother announced, as she pulled me in for a hug. "Another year of school ticked off. I remember bringing you down here when you were a tiny boy. It's incredible to think that-"

I had to interrupt her as she would have got all soppy and I didn't want any of the other boys hearing tales of little Christopher Prentiss in short trousers. "What's Cook doing here?" I felt the question was overdue and watched as my grandfather's most esteemed servant busied herself removing wicker baskets from the car.

Grandfather took a step closer. "Remember, Christopher, I attended The Oakton Classical and Commercial Academy for Distinguished Young Gentlemen myself when I was a boy, and I know what the food is like here. I thought I'd give you a treat by bringing Henrietta along to prepare lunch in the kitchen just for us."

I didn't like to think how Doreen would receive this invading force and wasn't entirely sure that our cook's offerings were a huge improvement. Though Cranley Hall's long-serving chef possessed all the skills required to work in such a distinguished house, her experimentation often led to dubious results. I could only imagine the boiled strawberry pâtés and iced cabbage we would soon be eating.

She smiled over affectionately and I waved back. Todd looked similarly pleased to see me and offered a quick, "I hope you haven't got into any trouble this year, Master Christopher," as he waited to move the car.

"I managed not to burn the school down." I can't have looked too comfortable as I made this joke. Arson or otherwise, I was still worried that Hardcastle would tell my mother of last night's misadventure.

"Before we go in, my boy," Grandfather began, then dashed back to his car to extract a canvas from the back seat. "What do you think of this?"

His eyes creased up with expectation as he held out a blotchy painting for my inspection. I didn't quite know what to say. "Oh, yes, Grandfather. It's... Well, it's a painting."

The positivity drained from his face. "I know it's a painting. I'm the one who painted it." He regarded the work proudly. "It's my new hobby. I've always wanted to have a stab at expressing my artistic instincts. So, what do you think of it?"

My mother looked on sympathetically as I stuttered out an answer. "Yes, I... You know, it's quite the prettiest sunset I've ever seen. I doubt that Vincent van Gogh could have done a better-"

"It's a field of poppies," he interrupted. "And you are a terrible liar."

"I think it's a wonderful first effort, father." My dear sweet mother is a much better fibber than me and took the old man's arm to guide him inside. "You'll be making a name for yourself as an artist in no time."

Grandfather was appeased by her response and smiled once more.

The skittish school receptionist offered us the parents' day running order and map. First came the meetings with teachers and then were the sporting trials. Neither filled me with joy, though the picnic that was laid on after was normally a cheerful affair. The day would finish up with prize-giving, then the closing ceremony in the hall, where Mr Hardcastle would deliver the end-of-year reports.

"I still remember my time here," Grandfather informed us, though he did not choose to reveal whether the memories were positive ones.

It was certainly a grand old building. Once the estate of some long-since impoverished family, Oakton Academy's main block looked more like a castle than a school. It was tall and narrow with four turreted towers set back within the building and crenellations all around. I'm sure it would have been a rippingly fun place for boys to occupy, had it not been for Hardcastle and his ilk setting the syllabus. Rather than focusing on the negatives though, I felt invigorated by my family's arrival and the thought that, in just one year's time, I would be leaving Oakton behind and heading out into the world as a man.

"Lazy, muddleheaded and not particularly bright!" This was Dr Steadfast's assessment of me when we funnelled into his office in the staff corridor. I thought he was surprisingly restrained in his assessment. "Just yesterday he couldn't tell me what happened on the twentieth of March 1815. A date which any student of history should have seared into his brain by the time he reaches the sixth form." He waved his hands around angrily, as though he were conducting a very poor orchestra. "How will he contribute anything to society if he cannot retain basic information such as this?"

There was a moment of silence which Lord Edgington would break. "Well, I don't know what happened on the twentieth of March 1815, and I think I've contributed rather a lot to this fine country." His voice was a hammer, his stare a drill.

Old Steadfast couldn't do much but jabber out, "The passing of the Corn Bill," and he suddenly looked rather nervous. I was surprised that he hadn't made more effort to dress up for his visitors. He leaned against the wall in a typically grubby ensemble. His ugly brown jumper was flecked with stains and chalk dust, though the board was clean and I could tell he hadn't written anything on it for days.

My mother's tone was a little more conciliatory than her father's, but she was equally unimpressed. "Can you tell us anything about Christopher's engagement with the subject? He's forever reading old books on any number of topics, so he must have gleaned some of his passion for the past."

Steadfast quivered like a plucked bow, but could produce no response.

Grandfather's eyes went for a wander around the room and he took in the shelves of musty brown books that covered every wall. "I had a history master like you. He spent every class shouting out dates that he expected us to memorise. He turned the very concept of the past into something unbearable. Instead of fostering a love for the subject, he made learning a bore. It is only in the last decade that I've discovered how fascinating history can be. I have read great sagas of the ancient Greeks, Romans and Egyptians, delved into the bronze, dark and middle ages, explored the agricultural and industrial revolutions, and all of that was *despite*, not thanks to, my old teacher Mr Brandish."

His tale was told, and he sat politely waiting for my flabbergasted teacher to respond.

"Well," the inflated football stuttered back, "Well, quite. Yes, indeed… In fact, yes."

My mother is generally the most diplomatic member of our family, but even she chose to let the man stew in his own juices.

Steadfast's jowls were shivering, so it was down to me to smooth things over. "I did know the date of Napoleon's invasion of Russia, sir."

He gratefully emerged from his tongue-tied trance. "That's right. And I was most impressed." He wracked his brain for some further evidence of the good he'd imparted. For a moment, I was worried he might compliment me on my Cossack dancing. "Not to mention the lines he wrote for me yesterday evening. I consider myself something of a graphologist and, truly, I have never seen such neat handwriting. Incredible looping Ys that reminded me of the script of the late Duke of Blackpool. Elegantly crossed Ts of which Queen Victoria herself would have been proud. And, let me tell you, there was not one spelling mistake in all two hundred sentences."

I had never expected to feel pity for my boorish professor. Before the might of my grandfather's intellect, he had turned into an earthworm and had more wriggling yet to endure.

"You gave the boy two hundred lines for forgetting an insignificant date like the signing of the Corn Laws?" A selection of glass ornaments on Steadfast's desk rattled and clinked as Lord Edgington's voice soared. "I doubt there was a less stimulating day in world history than the twentieth of March 1815! And then, rather than educating my grandson, you saw fit to waste yet more of his time by making him write out the same uninvigorating sentences over and over again."

"No," Steadfast countered, sitting up straighter in the chair as though he were the schoolboy.

"No?" Grandfather turned those two letters into as eloquent a retort as you could find in any work of William Shakespeare.

"Or rather… yes." Steadfast's whole body was shaking by this point.

"Well, there you go." My grandfather's immense moustache jiggled from side to side as he stood up to leave. "Unlike you, I don't enjoy insulting other people's intelligence, so I think it's time we were leaving. Your insight into Christopher's educational development has been truly…" He paused to ruffle his beard. "What's the word I'm looking for?"

"Lacking," Mother replied and smiled at her father before the three of us headed towards the door.

I did not look back to witness the horror on Dr Steadfast's defeated face, though I rather wish I had. I felt terrible for my classmate Austen

Naunton and his parents, who were waiting for their turn outside. If Steadfast hadn't melted into a puddle by this point, they would certainly have a rough ride of it.

"The man's a total imbecile," my grandfather announced, once we were out of earshot. "Now, where are we off to next?"

# CHAPTER SEVEN

I was happy that Herbie's lab would be our next port of call. As a more recent arrival at Oakton, he'd never been awarded an office of his own, so we trekked off to the fourth-form corridor.

"It is a genuine honour, sir," he rushed to tell my grandfather. "And you, Mrs Prentiss, of course."

"I already like you more than the last chap." Grandfather let out a hearty laugh and so began a brief, but enthusiastic, meeting of minds. My academic achievements were soon forgotten as Grandfather fired off questions about recent scientific discoveries that he'd read about in journals. Mr Mayfield got in a few queries of his own on former Superintendent Edgington's illustrious career, and my mother seemed to enjoy herself quite as much. It was apparent from the points she raised that she was just as knowledgeable about stellar nucleosynthesis and Dr Einstein's theory of relativity as the two men. Personally, I could barely spell half the concepts that were discussed. Overall though, we had a lovely time and everyone was thoroughly disappointed when our allotted time with Herbie was over.

Our trips to see my other teachers were less agreeable. There's no need to go into any of the hurtful things that my geography teacher, Mr Anders, had to say about me – though the phrase "wilfully dozy" stays in my mind for some reason – and I was very happy when we arrived on the school field for our final meeting.

My games master, Mr Bath, kicked things off by declaring, "Christopher clearly does not agree with the concept of physical education," and it went downhill from there. "I see no reason for him to come to this school."

Grandfather managed to restrain himself from throttling the man, and it was my mother's turn to raise her hackles.

"How dare you!"

"All I'm saying is that I don't understand why you'd send a boy to Oakton who doesn't want to play rugby." The lithe, bearded fellow looked at me as though I were some bizarre abnormality. An albino donkey, or perhaps a two-headed sheep.

My mother's gaze hardened. "So you're saying that the only reason we'd send our son to one of the most famous schools in the country is so that he can be battered by a team of fifteen louts while chasing after an egg-shaped ball?"

The uncouth chap cleared his throat before answering. "Those aren't the words I'd use, but the basic message is there."

"How dare you!" she said again, and my grandfather had to intervene. "Thank you for your time, Mr Bath. It's been... enlightening."

Mother was furious and had to be tugged away from the games hut.

"Of all the ignorant, ill-mannered people I've met in my life, he may well be the worst."

Grandfather looked at her in that disapproving way of his. "Learn to pick your battles, Violet. Men like that are best ignored."

She couldn't be calmed down so easily and continued to hiss out steam. "But to say such things. As though physical strength is more valuable than learning to read and write. You'd think it was the dark ages." I couldn't hold in a giggle, and they both turned to look at me. "You don't seem particularly upset about it, Christopher."

I laughed louder and finally confessed, "Mother, he's been saying the same thing to me for years, and I've lost very little sleep over it. I didn't tell you because I knew that you'd react just like this."

She gave me an affectionate slap around the arm. "I should never have sent you to such an old-fashioned institution as this one. It's all Walter's fault."

She looked sad that my father wasn't with us. And though I wished my dear daddy hadn't had a prior engagement, his ingrained philosophy from his own days at Oakton would have caused him to agree with everything the teachers said. So at least we'd avoided a few arguments.

"Daddy sends his love of course." Mother smiled for my benefit.

By this time, other parents were congregating on the field for the second event of the day. There was a stage set up – as our headmaster clearly didn't enjoy being viewed at regular height – and he was already there to announce the commencement of the sporting events. Mrs Celia 'Mama' Hardcastle sat blank-faced alongside him, and I had to assume she had forgiven, if not forgotten last night's drama.

"Lord Edgington..." he began, with a literal nod to my grandfather. "...ladies and gentlemen, if you could all gather round, I'd like to say a few words before our sporting programme gets started." He waited for the noise to die down and I was interested to see which of the teachers had bothered turning up for the speech. Herbie had joined us but was immediately called away by an announcement over the school's Marconi speaker system.

Old Balustrade, my Latin master, had found a comfy spot to lie down in and put his straw boater over his face. Matron was there too, hovering at the edge of the congregation like a security guard and, as he was in charge of the main event, Mr Bath really couldn't get out of it.

"It is such an honour to be here to open Oakton Academy's athletic trials." Hardcastle's endlessly twitching eye gave the impression that everything he said bordered on the sarcastic. "I trust that you have come away from your interviews encouraged both by your sons' educational enrichment and the commitment of our staff."

Well, that had to be sarcasm!

"Our physical education specialist, Mr Bath, will be starting the events presently. All that remains is for me to wish you a very pleasant day with us, and best of luck to the boys." Despite these conclusive words, he managed to bore everybody for another five minutes. I was worried that Mrs Hardcastle would nod off in her chair.

When the speech was finally over, there was an unenthusiastic mumble as parents dispersed and Hardcastle climbed down from the stage with his wife's arm for support. He began to mingle with his guests, only for another burst of sound to break from the loudspeakers, which were supported on high poles around the school.

"Could Mr Hardcastle please return to his office?" I recognised the uneven voice of the school secretary, Jonathan Greeves. "That's Mr Hardcastle to the headmaster's office at once, please."

The boys around me tittered as we realised that Hardcastle had just been sent to his own office. He cursed under his breath, apologised to the father he'd been talking to and stamped back towards the school, leaving Mama in his stead.

With this slice of entertainment concluded, my mother turned her attention back to me. "You won't hurt yourself in the race, will you, Christopher?"

I looked down at the ground to pretend that I didn't like it when she babied me. "Do stop fussing, Mother." I glanced about in case the other boys had heard. "But, as it happens, yes, I probably will hurt myself. I've got about as much interest in running six and a half miles across hilly terrain as I have in eating the mouton tartare that Cook made for lunch last Sunday."

Grandfather bristled at this. "A ridiculous comparison, my boy. Mutton in all its forms is delicious and Cook prepared it exquisitely."

I let out a painful sigh of remembrance. "It wasn't the meat I had the problem with; it was the sheep's skull in which it was served. The eyes kept looking at me."

Clearly unswayed, my grandfather grunted, but Mother still looked concerned about the race. "You will be careful though, Christopher? You've never been the sporting type and I worry you'll pull a muscle."

I was more worried about passing out dead after my imminent physical torment, but I tried to reassure her. "I'm sure I'll… live."

To my annual horror, sports day was compulsory for all students. We didn't even get to choose which event we participated in. When I'd first started at the school, I'd been allowed to jump along cheerfully in the sack race or even have a go at the egg and spoon, but being in the sixth form meant that I would be a competitor (of sorts) in Oakton's cross-country quarter marathon. I spotted the three Williams over by the starting line and was about to leave my family behind in the spectators' stand when Grandfather decided I needed some encouragement.

"Let me just tell you this, Chrissy." He put his hands on my shoulders and looked at me intently. "I don't care one iota what position you come in this race. I don't even mind if you finish."

"I know, Grandfather, the most important thing is to take part."

He was apparently rather confused by the statement. "No, not at all. I was about to say that you clearly don't have a runner's physique and that what you're about to do is terribly foolish. Why should we value a person more highly because of the velocity at which he can move his legs?"

I didn't know how to respond to this. I suppose he'd set out to spare my feelings, before they were inevitably crushed, and… well, it left me oddly animated. For the first time in my life, I actually wanted to run somewhere.

"Thank you, Grandfather. That was quite inspirational."

He looked puzzled again. "Well, jolly good. Now go out there and win, lose, come somewhere in the middle or give up halfway. It won't reflect on your worth as a human being in the slightest."

He smiled, and I wondered whether, had Mr Bath delivered such a speech when I'd started at Oakton, I'd have turned into an all-action, sprinting strongman. Either way, I dashed over to the beginning of the course, unzipped my nice, warm cardigan and removed my long trousers – I'd come prepared and had shorts on underneath.

I barely noticed Marmalade sidle up alongside me. I was taking deep breaths and geeing myself up for what was ahead.

"Chrissy, I'll forgive you for last night if you do me a favour." This rather broke my concentration.

"You'll forgive me? I practically saved your life." I turned to face him, and he did not look happy.

"No, that was Mama. You told Hardcastle where my drawing of him was and now he's going to show it to my father whenever he turns up." If I'd been worried about how my mother would react to poor reports from teachers, I could only imagine how desperately frightened poor Marmalade would be once the notorious Horatio Adelaide made an appearance.

"But, if I hadn't told him, he'd have broken your back." My voice got squeakier the more I said.

He looked askance. "Oh, please. The old fellow was having us on. He would never have used the bat on me. And that's why you have to go to his office and get my drawing."

"His office? In the staff corridor? Which is strictly out of bounds to students?" Having somehow got used to the idea of a long, gruelling run, he'd thrown an even more unpleasant scenario in my path. "But Hardcastle is there. I'm bound to get caught."

"Don't be ridiculous." He sounded very blasé about the whole thing. "This is his big day, he'll be back in a jiffy. All you need to do is peel off from the race when we turn the corner at the games hut. From there you can take the path among the trees and then cut through the kitchen garden without anyone seeing."

"If it's so easy, why don't you do it?"

He huffed impatiently. "Because everyone would know it was me, and I'd get in even more hot water."

I wondered if the correct phrase should be *even hotter water*, but

I didn't dare correct him. And, besides, I was having trouble forming sentences.

"But… Why don't… What happens if…" Hot, sweaty and supremely breathless, I felt like I'd already run the race.

"Thanks, old chap. I knew I could count on you." He slapped me on the back. "This will give me the perfect alibi."

"Here we go, boys." Mr Bath arrived, holding a small, black gun. It turned out that it was just a starting pistol, but it added an extra jolt of fear to the proceedings. "If you approach the line, we'll get the race under way."

There was some cheering from the stand and I heard Grandfather issue a shout of, "Remember, Chrissy, the result is irrelevant!"

"On your marks," Mr Bath began. "Get set. Go!"

# CHAPTER EIGHT

The more athletic sorts shot off to the front, leaving William, Will, Billy and me to plod along behind. I would have used that first stretch of the race to consider whether to go through with Marmalade's plan, but I was soon distracted.

"Hello, Chrissy baby!" Edward Marshall fell back from the main group to run alongside me.

His brother did the same, so that I was flanked by the twin trolls. "Adelaide isn't around to protect you this time." Percy was right. I could see Marmalade striding off into the distance at the front of the pack.

The three Williams couldn't do much either, so they ran a little faster to avoid any trouble with Marshall and Marshall. It was a cowardly act by my three best friends, but I didn't blame them. I'd most likely have done the same in their place.

Mr Bath had taken it upon himself to report on the race through a metal speaking trumpet. "There's some movement at the back as William Batty, William Keder and William Williams catch up with the main group."

"As soon as we're out of sight past the games hut, you're going to get the hiding of your life." Edward spoke through gritted teeth.

I swallowed hard, which was rather difficult to do when already puffing my lungs out. "Couldn't we just forgive and forget, eh chaps? It's the last day of term, the whole summer is ahead of us. No one will remember what happened by the autumn."

"I will," Percy snapped.

I tried to convince them one last time. "But I was laughing at the pigeon!"

"Did you hear that, Edward? He just called you a pigeon!"

"What? Plump and hungry? You've got some nerve!"

Throughout this conversation, our pace had been falling off and this gave Mr Bath something else to focus on. "Prentiss is taking up the rear now, with the Marshall brothers jockeying for position. Edward Marshall is falling back a little... now Percy... now Christopher. It's a real battle for last place out there."

As ridiculous as this scenario was, it had given me an idea. I slowed down further, but the Marshalls copied me. For the crowd, it must have looked like we were a trio of centenarians bumbling to a public house. We were barely walking, our eyes on one another's the whole time.

"Nice try, Prentiss." Edward's face curled up in a wicked smile. "But no matter how slowly you amble, we'll get to where we're going in the end."

He had a point.

"You can feel the tension, ladies and gentlemen. I wouldn't have picked young Master Prentiss as the competitive type, but he clearly has his heart set on losing this race and won't let his two rivals claim the prize." Mr Bath had really fired the crowd up with his reportage, and they were about to lose all decorum. "He's at an almost total standstill!"

I stopped entirely and doubled over, clutching my stomach.

"I think..." the games master continued. "Yes, ladies and gentlemen, it's quite clear. Christopher Prentiss has a stitch, we're sending medical assistance."

I looked back to see Matron bounding across the field as the Marshalls ran on the spot beside me.

"Come on, Percy," Edward said with a growl. "This is getting ridiculous. We'll nobble him after the race."

They started to accelerate and Percy shouted another warning back to me. "You can't avoid us forever, Roly!"

I was relieved to see them go, but now had the never-maternal Matron on my trail. I waited until the brothers had turned the corner, then waved back to her to show that I was all right, before recommencing the race. She looked rather disappointed that she wouldn't get to use the contents of her medical bag on me.

I reached the games hut at a fine pace, then cut through the woods to get to the kitchen garden. Slowing down just a touch, I ran between two rows of cabbages – an everlasting source of sustenance at Oakton – and came out by the dormitory block. I almost ran into Dr Steadfast, who was puffing along the path towards the field. I ducked behind the fence and spotted the head prefect, Dominic Rake, following some yards behind. He looked dreadfully anxious about something, but there was no time to worry about him; I was on a mission.

Once they had gone, I darted along the side of the buildings like a military spy. I made it around the quadrangle in seconds! Perhaps it was the adrenaline of that very slow race, but I'd lost my fear of being caught. I eased the door to the main block open and, crawling low to the floor, I passed the reception where Jonathan Greeves always sat.

It was awfully exciting, I can tell you. If I'd known what fun it could be to break school rules and plunge myself into dangerous situations, I'd have done so years before. I knew my objective; I had a relic to retrieve that was more powerful than any amulet in a children's story. The treasure I was seeking had the ability to save a boy from his father's strap.

As I hadn't spotted Hardcastle anywhere, I had to assume he was still in the building. I approached the staircase, but then my bravery deserted me. I heard a terrible grunting sound and nearly left my skin behind as I bolted up and away. My fears that the school had been overrun by wild boar were set to rest when this noise was followed by an equally intimidating voice coming from one of the rooms further along the hall.

"You'll do as I tell you, or live to regret it." It almost certainly belonged to Doreen the dinner lady, but the reply, when it came, was too quiet to make out. To be perfectly honest, such a statement was very much in character from the school cook, so I hurried onwards.

I took first one flight of stairs, then the next, working my way up to the staff corridor, floor by floor. As I did so, my heart beat louder, but I pressed on. It was only as I reached the top level of the building that the tension caught up with me.

Memories of the night before had invaded my head. I could picture our headmaster's bitter snarl as he prodded us along that corridor towards his room and hear the terror in Marmalade's voice as he knelt over the block.

I tried to clear my mind. After several deep breaths, I put my hand against the door. My eyes involuntarily read the "No students permitted" plaque as I carefully turned the handle. There was no sign of life inside. No snoozing teachers or even a grumpy cleaner. I was clear to continue, but no longer sure whether I had it in me. I was moving more slowly than I had on the field, barely shuffling my feet along the smooth marble floor.

There was one more door to tackle. A thick wooden jobbie, with a sign screwed to it, which said, 'Mr T. B. Hardcastle BSc MA'. I tried to listen through the keyhole, but all I could make out was a faint hissing. The thought of pushing it open with the headmaster still inside was almost paralysing, so I thought up an excuse to be there.

I raised my hand to knock, just as a rather impressive bang resounded from within. I forgot my pretence altogether and barged straight through the door.

The room was full of smoke but, as it cleared, I started to make sense of what I was seeing. Hardcastle was propped up with his back to the flogging block. There was a flask of bubbling green chemicals sticking from his mouth and white residue all over his face.

It was safe to conclude that he was really quite dead.

# CHAPTER NINE

I should have learnt the importance of careful observation at a crime scene from my grandfather, but I was a little shocked to say the least. Instead of taking my time to notice every last detail, I became hypnotised by the poor man's death mask. His face was contorted in horror. His eyes were unnaturally wide and his head was tipped back painfully on the blood-stained block, where so many of my schoolmates had suffered his wrath. Not knowing what else I could do, and with no desire to regurgitate that morning's porridge, I ran from the room.

I suppose it would have been wise to inform the secretary of the situation, so that he could call the police or what have you, but I needed to get back to Grandfather. I needed him to explain what I'd just seen. My thoughts were in a tangle and, even if I hadn't picked up on any vital evidence, as the famous Lord Edgington would have, I'd seen enough to set my mind racing.

I didn't make any effort to hide this time. I ran straight through the school and along the path to the playing fields, dodging late-arriving parents along the way. I thought I could quietly retrieve former Superintendent Edgington from the throng of proud parents, but sadly Mr Bath spotted me.

"Ladies and gentlemen, I'm sorry to break off my coverage of the lower school hurdles, but there's a development in the cross-country quarter marathon which I simply must communicate. Master Christopher Prentiss has sufficiently recovered from his near-race-ending stitch to overtake the whole pack and reappear from the other side of the school. This really is a turn up for the books and I will endeavour to keep you apprised of his progress."

A number of parents, presumably unfamiliar with just how much of a sarcastic so-and-so Mr Bath could be, clapped politely as I headed towards the long rows of spectator's benches. My grandfather had spotted me and was on his feet before I arrived. Mother, meanwhile, looked relieved that I hadn't pulled a muscle and went back to watching the younger pupils fail to jump over the hurdles.

"What's the matter, boy?" He could read me like a headline in The

Times. "Tell me what's wrong."

"Mr Hardcastle's dead." I tried to whisper, but at least one father caught what I'd said and looked over. He didn't seem too concerned and soon turned his attention back to the athletics.

"How can that be?" Grandfather's brows became furrowed.

"I think he's been murdered. Please come."

He didn't need any more prompting. He waved to Mother and strode down the steps to join me. Even before he got there, Delilah had popped out from behind the benches and was wagging her tail excitedly at the promise of an excursion.

"Gun, knife, poison?" Grandfather began, as he increased his pace and charted the shortest route to the school. "What did you see?"

I had to think. "Chemistry set?"

He nodded as though this were an obvious fourth option and didn't say another word until we entered the main block. I could see that, in these quiet moments, he was laying the groundwork for the investigation. I had expected him to ask me why I'd abandoned the race, but such minor details could wait.

Delilah had been happily trundling beside me this whole time, staring up like she thought we were about to feed her. When we got to the main block, she let out an insistent bark as we mounted the front steps.

"What do you mean?" Grandfather asked back. He had the habit of talking to her as though she were a fully rational human.

She replied with a softer moan.

"No, of course you can't come with us. You can see that I have work to do. A crime scene is no place for a dog."

The poor creature sat down with her head on her paws, looking frankly rather miserable. It felt terribly cruel to leave her there.

Jonathan Greeves, the school secretary and Hardcastle's lackey, was in his box near the door.

"Have you called the police?" Grandfather asked in his typically direct tone.

"The police?" Greeves was as flustered as ever.

"Yes, the police. Your boss has been murdered. Why on earth has no one called them?"

I should probably have spoken in the poor chap's defence, but

I'd learnt not to enrage Lord Edgington any further once his temper was excited.

Greeves's sapphire-blue eyes jumped from side to side, unsure which way to look before they finally landed on the telephone attached to the wall. A smile still curled his lips, but this didn't surprise me. He was a curious sort, and his emotions never quite matched the present moment, as though there were a delay in his circuitry.

Grandfather nodded and set off along the corridor. He didn't need directing and shot up the staircase ahead of me. This meant yet more running for me to catch up with him. I have to say, the gently undulating hills of Mr Bath's cross-country race were preferable to those horribly steep stairs.

Halfway up, he gripped the bannister and paused as a concession to his advanced years.

"Grandfather, how do you know where we're going? This building must have been totally different when you attended the school." The old man had any number of tricks for extracting secrets from the world around him, and I wondered if he'd read my mind again.

He smiled. "It stands to reason that the headmaster has his office at the top of the school. He was a suspicious chap and, from everything you've told me this year, I imagine he would have wanted to keep a weather eye over the boys at all times. By having his office on the third floor of the building, in the eastern corner, overlooking the quadrangle, he could create a panopticon."

I didn't actually know what this word meant but was determined to look it up at the first available moment. I had another, more pressing question. "Then, how did you know which room he died in?"

This time, Grandfather really wasn't impressed by the question, and I endured a full roll of the eyes. "Because he was called to his office over the loud-speakers. Now, keep up, Chrissy." He lurched off ahead and I could tell that this short command had more than one implication.

As we reached the next landing, Herbie was coming out of the fourth-form corridor. Grandfather spotted him and pointed back the way that the man had come. "Stay in your room, Mr Mayfield. The police will be here shortly and I think it's in your best interests if I speak to you before they do."

"The police?" My chemistry teacher's tone reached a high C.

"Do as I say, man. There's no time to explain."

I watched as my teacher doubled back towards his laboratory, a look of shock and fear on his face. The detective in me said that any half-decent actor could feign such emotion, but the Christopher in me thought there was no way dear old Herbie could be involved in the killing, bubbling chemicals or not.

We pressed on up to the top floor and, from the "No students permitted" sign on the left-hand door, Grandfather knew where to go without asking. I was coming to see that the mark of a good investigator was, at times at least, to ask yourself the questions which needed answering before relying on other people.

He showed no fear as he pushed on through and speedily ascended the oddly sloping hallway. "I suppose that's his door at the end of the corridor?"

I nodded but said nothing, once more mystified by how he could reach the right conclusions so readily.

The old superintendent prodded the door open with his elbow and looked inside. Nothing had changed since I'd abandoned the room; Tobias Hardcastle was just as dead as when I'd left him. Grandfather extracted a pair of gloves from his pocket, but loitered on the threshold.

He peered at the body and the cascade of pale foam that had poured from the chemical flask. "Bicarbonate of soda, citric acid and some sort of dye I imagine." He took a step closer and sniffed the air. "Other ingredients may have been added to lengthen the reaction. It's little more than a party trick."

There were all sorts of queries I would like to have put to him, but I had ground to a halt in the doorway and decided to watch him work.

He paused before getting too close and made a careful study of the room. In the left corner, there was a spiralling staircase which led up to the astronomy tower. I really should have considered that the killer was hiding there when I first entered. Grandfather peered up through the wooden slats and held his breath for a moment to listen. Confident in whatever he had or hadn't heard, he moved on.

Very little had changed since my visit the night before. There were piles of reports on the headmaster's desk, which would have been handed out in the parents' day closing ceremony. A number of thick books were at hand, no doubt for throwing at unruly boys, and I noticed Hardcastle's cane resting on the floor.

"You don't suppose it was one of my classmates who wanted to stop Hardcastle giving out the reports, do you, Grandfather?"

His eyes now on the victim, he answered without looking at me. "You are entirely correct, Christopher." This made me cheerful for about three seconds before he continued. "I do not think for one moment that he was killed for such a mundane reason. I'm sure that your friend Marmaduke Adelaide has received nothing but bad reports since he started at Oakton and yet, for the most part, his teachers are still breathing."

I thought it would be sensible to stop asking questions after that.

My grandfather bent down to examine the body. I'd been avoiding the grotesque sight until now, but finally accepted that I'd have to look at it once more. The beaker of liquid had lost its fizz, and only a layer of white scum on its surface could speak of the dramatic reaction I'd witnessed. I noticed there was a strip of paper around the outside, held in place by a rubber band, but I couldn't imagine what purpose it served. The contents of the flask were still eerily green and made me think of some alien artefact from the distant planets of H. G. Wells's novels.

"The chemicals didn't kill him of course," Lord Edgington exclaimed as he leaned over the flogging block to examine the back of the man's head. "Looks like he's had a good few whacks with…" His eyes scanned the floor for the weapon and soon located a heavy wooden carving which lay bloodstained and splintered beneath the desk. "…that ornamental monkey."

I might have let out a nervous laugh then, to which Grandfather tutted. "It's not funny, boy." It was a little bit. "Well, perhaps the tiniest bit." He had to suppress a smile himself but soon fell serious again. "I think you had better tell me exactly what happened when you were here before. There was some sort of explosion, I presume?"

"That's right." I refused to ask him how he knew this. I was coming to think he was only making such statements to show off. "I left the race-"

"A wise decision, boy. Very wise."

"I left the race and, when I got here, I heard a loud noise from the doorway and came in. He was just as he is now, only the beaker was bubbling away on top of him."

He didn't immediately react to this information and, in fact, closed his eyes. I wondered what I was supposed to do whilst the eccentric old chap had his nap, but he came around a few moments later.

"The way I see it, the killer would have entered the room before the headmaster, knowing that his victim would be along shortly after."

"But how could he-" I began, then realised that I was falling wide-eyed into the same trap as ever. I stopped myself and turned my question into a declaration. "You mean, it was the killer who called Mr Hardcastle back from the field, so he knew the exact time that his prey would enter the room."

I'd made him smile, and it wasn't out of sympathy for once. "Bravo, Chrissy, that is exactly it. Hardcastle came into the room and got knocked out by the monkey." Neither of us managed to resist laughing this time. "Then the culprit positioned the body on the block here, pushed the head back, so that it was relatively flat, and started the fuse."

"What fuse?" I'm sorry, but I couldn't help it. I was determined not to sound like an impressionable child in awe of the great man, but he kept impressing me!

He pointed at the wooden floor behind Hardcastle's supine form. "Over here. Only the burnt remains are visible of course, but the killer left a cracker – or some sort of indoor firework – with a long fuse."

I didn't say anything then. I really wanted to; the words were on my lips, fighting to get out, when he looked up at me expectantly and said them for me. "But why?"

"Yes, why?" My voice went higher. "I was just about to ask the same thing."

"It's simple, isn't it?" He waited for me to agree with him, but sadly I couldn't. "The killer wanted to draw attention to his crime. If you hadn't been here, perhaps someone else in the building would have come looking. He set the fuse – well, two fuses in a sense. The piece of damp paper wrapped around the neck of the flask prevented the reaction from occurring until the substance on top had fallen through. All that gave the killer time to get away and distance himself from the crime. If you'd been a couple of minutes earlier, you might well have caught the blighter."

This idea failed to excite me. In fact, I was rather shocked at the possibility and didn't like to think what impact the ornamental monkey would have had on my own tender skull.

"Do you see anything that might tell you who was responsible?" I thought this a far more sensible question than my previous efforts. Grandfather must have agreed, as he began to examine Hardcastle's clothes.

There were traces of the *caput mortuum* which had overflown from the beaker. White foamy residue covered his cheeks and had dripped down to stain his suit jacket. Grandfather poked his fingers into the man's top pocket and pulled out a long wooden splint. I recognised it as the type we used in chemistry class for stirring substances.

"Hmmm," Grandfather intoned, but I would not take the bait this time and refused to ask what he was thinking.

"Grandfather," I began instead, "I don't suppose the killer would have worn gloves?"

He was rifling through the other pockets now. "I very much think he would have. Why do you ask?"

"Oh, nothing really. It's just that there's a white pair on the floor beside the bookcase. It looks like they might have some spots of blood on them." I pointed and his whole face became serene.

"Fantastic observation, Christopher. I saw them myself when we came in of course, but I'm glad to see you spotted them."

I didn't entirely believe him but felt encouraged by the compliment. "Doesn't that mean we've got our man?"

From his expression, I knew that I'd misspoken. "Why on earth would you say that?"

"Well, fingerprints, of course. If we take the gloves down to the police station, the experts there can search for prints and we'll know who's to blame."

It was his turn not to say anything, so I continued. "What? That's how they do it, isn't it?"

He shook his head morosely. "I'm afraid they'll struggle to extract much from pure cotton."

# CHAPTER TEN

We finished up at the scene of the crime but found no clear smoking gun. It was something of a disappointment. I'd rather hoped to have the case tied up by lunchtime so that we could enjoy the school picnic.

Still, there was a killer on the loose and it was no time to be thinking of food. The fact that he'd been murdered with a statue of a monkey made out of a large hairy coconut, did not make it any less serious – well, perhaps the tiniest bit.

In my attempt not to look excessively ignorant in front of my brilliant grandfather, I resisted firing off a whole list of questions, which I will reproduce here for the sake of my sanity.

- **Why did the killer wish to draw attention to his crime with the firework?**

- **Why go to such lengths to stage a tableau featuring a beaker of fizzing chemicals and then rely on whatever murder weapon came to hand?**

- **Was it because the killer thought murdering someone with a monkey was funny?**

I could go on, but these were a few of the doubts that were playing on my mind as we once more descended the staircase to speak to the school secretary. I suppose this led me to another question which was, why didn't we speak to Mr Mayfield first to save having to trek back upstairs after? Had I made such an enquiry, my grandfather would surely have told me not to let my lazy limbs get in the way of our investigation.

"What's the secretary's name?" Grandfather asked as we arrived on the ground floor.

"Jonathan Greeves. He's rather an unusual chap; extremely nervous and unsure of himself. It's a wonder he got the job in the first place. Hardcastle never seemed happy when he was around, and Greeves was a wreck as soon as the headmaster entered the room."

He considered this for a moment but said nothing more as we approached the small reception.

"The police are on their way, Lord Edgington." Greeves spoke unusually quickly, perhaps to prevent my grandfather from telling him off again. "And, may I say, how honoured we are to have you here to assist with the investigation."

Peering through the unglazed window into the incredibly neat cubbyhole of an office, Grandfather eyed the man suspiciously. "If you must."

Greeves looked nervous again. "Oh… well, then we are most honoured to have you here to assist with the investigation."

Lord Edgington nodded his thanks. "Very good. Now, the calls for the headmaster and Mr Mayfield which came through the loudspeakers outside; That was your voice, wasn't it?"

He moved his head in a trembling motion which passed for a nod.

When the man furnished no further reply, Grandfather demanded. "Well, why did you make those announcements?"

Greeves's words came out in a torrent. "I was just following orders, sir. When I came back after making some tea this morning, I found a scrap of paper on my desk telling me to call Mr Mayfield at twelve o'clock and Mr Hardcastle ten minutes later. I was simply doing as I'd been told." This last sentence would go perfectly on the young chap's tombstone.

Dressed in an ill-fitting tweed jacket with an inappropriately flamboyant white dress shirt underneath, his clothes gave the impression of a man who had got dressed blindfolded from someone else's wardrobe. He wasn't typical Oakton material.

"And you didn't think it was strange that whoever wrote the note failed to sign it?"

The cold fish turned to me. Perhaps he hoped I would provide him with the answer, but he was barking up the wrong boy there! "Um, no."

"And you didn't question who wrote it?" Grandfather sounded quite mystified.

"Well, no. I didn't."

The former officer's lips pursed together so that his moustache formed a semi-circle in the middle of his face. I really thought he was about to lose his temper when Greeves added a word of explanation. "But only because the handwriting belonged to Mr Hardcastle."

Grandfather froze for three heartbeats before he stretched his arm through the large, glassless window. "Show me, please. In fact, wait."

He flipped the hatch up and entered the miniscule room which served as Jonathan Greeves's anchorhold. With his gloves still on, he picked up the note that Greeves was pointing to in the wastepaper basket.

"I threw it away as I didn't think it was important."

"Not to worry, young man." Grandfather adopted a somewhat warmer tone. He had recently taught me the importance of charm in a detective's toolkit, and he used it to good effect. "Do you happen to have a sample of your employer's hand?"

He ruffled through a stack of papers in a small drawer and produced an unsent letter. "Will this suffice?" He was frowning at that moment, and I had to assume his smile would turn up before long.

Grandfather responded with an absentminded bob of the head, as he was already comparing the two documents. "Very interesting."

The vagueness which the great Lord Edgington employed at such moments usually triggered his faithful assistant into action, and I couldn't resist the obvious question. "What have you found?"

"It's a good copy, but far from exact. The letters are a little too tall, their tails a tad flamboyant and the dots of the Is and Js are excessively weighty. This note was not written by Mr Hardcastle and so we have another level of theatricality to the crime." He let out a huff of disapproval and put the two pieces of paper down on the tiny desk. "I must say that I don't hold with murder being such a complicated matter. There are far simpler ways to kill someone without being apprehended."

Greeves seemed to agree. His face fell and, staring out through his squint of a window, he said, "Yes, I always thought the best way would be to take your victim up somewhere high and push him over the edge. It's your word against his that it was an accident and he's not going to say much if he's dead."

Grandfather glanced at me then. For once, it was clear what he was thinking. "Thank you for your insight, Mr Greeves."

The skinny fellow let out a fluted laugh. "Of course, of course!"

"Now, I've been wondering about something." The old man paused to let us both consider what it could be. "Were you sitting here at your desk from twelve o'clock onwards?" Greeves nodded in acknowledgement. "Then I imagine you heard the explosion upstairs in the staff corridor?"

"Why, yes. It was quite dramatic in fact." He did not act as though an explosion in school was anything to worry about.

"In which case, why didn't you leave your post to investigate?"

Our suspect – as, it was abundantly clear, that is what Greeves was – squirmed like a fish in a bucket. "I... Well, you see..." He pulled at his striped, blue and white tie. "I saw Master Prentiss running into the school and assumed that he was playing an end-of-term prank."

"How is that possible?" I couldn't help shouting. "I ducked under your window. How could you possibly-"

Grandfather interrupted my sceptical ranting. "All right, Christopher. You're not particularly good at making yourself small. We won't hold it against you." He turned back to our suspect with a darting look. "For the moment, I only have one more question for you. Who was in the building after Mr Hardcastle entered and who has since left?"

That inappropriately jubilant smile seized Mr Greeves's face again as he listed our potential culprits. "Dr Steadfast stopped to talk to me. He often likes a bit of a chinwag and he said he was off to see the cross-country. You already know that Mr Mayfield had been called back and Scuttlewell the caretaker was here this morning. He was locking up rooms that were no longer needed, but I think he might have left already. Oh, and that boy was about the place somewhere. You know, the head prefect. He's a strange young man."

That such words would come from Greeves's mouth said a lot about Oakton Academy's top boy.

"He's called Dominic Rake." I gave them the name and the two men turned to me. "I won't deny that he's an odd character. Only, he idolised Mr Hardcastle, and I can't imagine him being involved in the murder."

"That's the chap," Greeves twittered, and then I had another thought.

"Wait, you forgot someone. I heard Doreen's voice as I mounted the stairs. The dinner lady was talking to someone in a room further along the corridor."

The old man's stare ground the chap down, so that he responded with a nervous, "Oh, you're quite right. She was here collecting supplies to make lunch."

Lord Edgington cleared his throat. "And that's the lot? No one else could have been in the building at the time?"

Greeves reflected on the question for a long, quiet moment and then burst back into life. "Not unless they're still hiding in here somewhere and I never saw them enter."

Something seemed to fade in my grandfather then. He took a few steps out of the cubbyhole and might have floated on down the corridor if I hadn't put my hand on his arm to stop him. This seemed to knock him out of his stupor and he turned back to the secretary.

"Thank you, Greeves. You must stay here until the police arrive. We'll be back to talk to you before long, no doubt." He didn't wait for a response, but spun towards the stairs before his oddly blank expression returned.

Grandfather explained what he was thinking without me having to ask. "I feel we are falling into someone's trap. It's too early to say for certain, but everything I noticed about the body appears to have been arranged for the police to discover."

He seemed almost nervous about this possibility, and I sought to reassure him. "You'll still get whoever's responsible, Grandfather. That's what you do."

"Maybe, Christopher. Maybe." He paused again when we reached the lower-school classrooms. For a moment he looked all of his seventy-five years, and I worried he would give up entirely. "We're going to speak to your teacher now. Mr Mayfield must have been here when the murder occurred and was called back to the school just like the headmaster."

"That doesn't mean he's to blame," I began, unable to hide my emotion. "If Herbie was going to kill someone, he wouldn't plant a bubbling beaker of chemicals on top of the body. He might just as well have left a big sign saying, 'The chemistry teacher is the murderer.' Surely you can see that?"

My grandfather bit his lip for ten whole seconds and, when he finally spoke, I could see the red mark where his teeth had pressed against the skin. "You're right, boy. You're quite right. Only…"

Even by his own opaque standards, Grandfather was less than forthcoming that morning. He struggled on up the stairs and allowed me to lead the way towards the laboratory.

# CHAPTER ELEVEN

With everyone else on the field for sports day, I'd rarely seen the place so free of life. When we found Mr Mayfield, he was motionless at his desk. He looked a little like that famous sculpture of a man sitting thinking – I can't remember its name.

He jerked to attention as we came through the door. "What in heavens is going on?"

"Sit back down, Mr Mayfield." Grandfather had rediscovered his assertiveness. It was as though he had pulled his policeman's uniform on the moment we entered the room. "I'll tell you everything in good time, but please stay exactly where you are."

Grandfather extracted a chair from under a desk and positioned it in front of our witness. It was far too small for him, but he didn't complain and was primed for the interview.

He paused for several ticks of the clock above the backboard and sized the man up with a long, hard stare. "You must tell me from the start, did you do it?"

Herbie's eyes were near totally white right then as he tried to make sense of what he was hearing. "Do what? You still haven't told me what's happened." His mouth remained dangling open for some time after the words had escaped.

Now, I know I've never worked for the police – or studied the implications of body language and the minuscule changes in the tone of a suspect's voice which would inform a more experienced detective whether a suspect were lying – but I was fairly certain that this lovely chap was as honest as they came.

"I'm afraid to say that the police will not believe you," Grandfather continued, turning his head to gaze out of the window, to where a line of boys were jumping in sacks on the field. "The vast majority of officers look only for the simplest solution. And, you must concede, you are the obvious suspect."

"Please, Lord Edgington." Herbie's voice shot louder as he begged for mercy. "Please tell me what has happened. I solemnly promise that I haven't the faintest idea what you're referring to."

Grandfather gave him another searching look. "Christopher found

Mr Hardcastle in his office. He's been murdered." Another pause, another slight adjustment in the angle of his head, like a magpie waiting to swoop. "I have a number of reasons to believe that you are responsible for his death, and I predict that the police will be here any minute to arrest you."

Herbie had been sitting with his hands palm down on his knees. He suddenly clasped his fingers together so that his pale linen suit scrunched together. He was normally far more casual but had dressed up smartly for the influx of bothersome parents.

"I didn't… I mean, I couldn't. Why would you think that of me?" He spoke in little more than a whisper now. His tone no doubt matched the erratic fluctuations of his emotions.

"As I said, I have any number of reasons to suspect you of murder, but that's not to say that I think you're guilty."

I felt terrible for poor Herbie and decided to show him a little of the mercy that my grandfather clearly wouldn't. "I'm sure you'll be able to clear this whole situation up, Mr Mayfield. There's no chance you were involved."

My more experienced companion did not look as though he agreed. "I need you to tell me exactly what happened after you were called from the field."

Herbie shook his head disbelievingly. "I… Well, I came back here to my lab. As you can very well see."

"Not exact enough." I'd seen my Grandfather interview suspects before and he could be as soft as a rabbit. He clearly wasn't employing that technique today. "I need to know your every movement from that moment until now. Come on, man. There's no time for dillydallying."

Herbie took a deep breath and focused on his answer. "I left the field and went into school, as requested over the public address system."

"Did you see anyone on the way?" I was quick to ask, desperate to add another name to our rather paltry list of suspects.

"Well…" He thought for a moment and his natural smile emerged for the first time since we'd arrived. "Yes. Dominic Rake was giving his minions some instructions on the quad and then he went into the building ahead of me. Oh, and Dr Steadfast was smoking one of his awful cigars out by the entrance when I went inside."

"Very good." My grandfather had adopted a tone which bordered on civility. "So what was the message when you arrived?"

I knew he already knew the answer to this question. Whether Grandfather knew that I knew that... no, hang on, I've got a bit muddled there. Never mind.

"Jonathan – the secretary Jonathan Greeves – was in his usual spot, but didn't know anything more than that he was supposed to call me in at twelve o'clock. He was as befuddled by it as I was. It looked like the headmaster's writing, but Mr Hardcastle was over on the field just then. I decided that either a delayed parent would be up here wanting to speak to me, or the headmaster had decided to wish me well on my last day of school. Either way, I thought it best to wait. Hardcastle isn't a man who bears defying."

Standing beside the two men, like a referee before a bout, I saw the slightest flicker of acknowledgement on my grandfather's face as he realised the same thing I had. Herbie had spoken of his recently deceased boss as though he were still alive. It seemed to me that, were I to plan and carry out a murder, I'd be likely to think of the man I'd killed as being deceased rather quickly.

"And then?" Grandfather looked at the faded equations on the blackboard as he asked the question.

"When I got up here, I killed time tidying the stock cupboard and I'm fairly certain that someone had been messing about in there. I didn't think too much of it, especially after that firework went off. Boys will be boys, don't they say?"

I kept my gaze fixed on Mr Mayfield. The youngest of all the teachers, he had only worked at Oakton for a few years but had quickly become a favourite. There was something warm and winning about him that we boys adored.

"Was there anything missing from your cupboard?" By the time Grandfather had finished his question, he'd already changed his mind. "I should look for myself."

Herbie gave his assent with a wave of the hand. Shooting from his tiny wooden chair, my grandfather looked as though he'd suddenly grown up. The three of us made our way to the door in the corner of the room which was stocked full of wonders – well, to a sixteen-year-old boy it seemed that way at least. There were big glass jars filled with interestingly named chemicals, containers with skulls and crossbones marked on them, and boxes with the word 'flammable' stamped in large red capital letters. It was every arsonist's dream.

As Lord Edgington inspected the shelves, Herbie explained what had happened. "I spotted some white powder on the floor, though I imagine it was only bicarbonate of soda. I assumed one of the boys was planning a joke, it's traditional at this time of year. You know, a volcano of foam in the tea urn at lunch perhaps, or a nice loud explosion during the closing ceremony." He grinned at this, then remembered the news we'd brought with us and fell serious again.

Grandfather sniffed the air in the musty cupboard in quite the same way as Delilah when she picked up a scent. Without revealing what he'd discovered, he asked another question.

"When was the last time you were in here?"

"In the cupboard?" Mr Mayfield had a bit of a think. "Yesterday evening. I was packing up a few of my possessions."

Grandfather didn't react but knelt down to touch a wet patch on the floor then rubbed his fingers together.

"That was from a bottle of sulfuric acid one of the boys dropped last week." Herbie gave another smile and then another frown.

"Then why does it still feel wet?" Grandfather shot the words up to us, and I had to question why he was treating Herbie in quite such a hostile manner. I put my hand out to him and he returned to standing. "Now listen. There was a beaker of some chemical mixture placed on top of the body and the explosion you heard was in fact a small firework that was set off in the headmaster's office." He selected one of the small, black crackers that my teacher had used in our final class. "For that reason alone, the police will suspect you."

"I told you, I had nothing to do with this." My teacher was beginning to sound nervous.

"Is there anyone else in this school who would have access to fireworks at this time of year?"

"No, but clearly someone was in here and-"

Grandfather flew from the cupboard, apparently unconcerned for the man's plight. "This is doing no one any good. We're going around in circles. All I know is that, if you aren't the killer, somebody certainly wishes it to appear that way."

Herbie collapsed onto his green, leather swivel chair. "I have no enemies here. I get on well with all the other staff and the boys too. I doubt one of the parents would go to such extremes to incriminate me in a murder."

Grandfather took up his thread. "In which case, you're not seeing the wider picture. I have to admit, with this being my first trip to Oakton in many years, I am limited in my knowledge of the place. What I can tell you is that nothing is ever quite so rosy in a boys' school. You'll have rubbed someone up the wrong way, I can tell you that for a song."

Mr Mayfield's tenor voice reached its high note once more. "I'm telling the truth. I like working here and don't go out of my way to upset people."

As my grandfather loomed over the poor chap, I felt my loyalties stretched between these two influential figures in my life. A moment passed before my words jumped out of me and I immediately wished I hadn't said anything.

"Then why are you leaving your job?"

# CHAPTER TWELVE

The atmosphere in the room felt as though it had been frozen by liquid nitrogen. Or do I mean liquid oxygen? I'm sorry, but as much as I enjoyed Mr Mayfield's classes, I rarely retained much of what he was talking about.

"That's neither here nor there." Herbie's light tone was suddenly absent. His calm had disappeared. "The fact I'm leaving my job does not mean that I murdered a man."

Grandfather restrained himself from further accusations and it was down to me to speak. I say, *speak*, but it was little more than a throaty whisper. "Is it because of Mama?"

Herbie spun his chair away from me and marched to the window. With his back to the two of us, he ran his hand frantically through his short blonde hair. "You shouldn't be speaking of such things, Prentiss. You're too young to understand."

After my teacher's half-admission, Grandfather stepped forward to speak. "Perhaps I, on the other hand, am old enough to comprehend what the boy is referring too. I imagine that Mama is the name the boys call Mrs Hardcastle?"

We could only see half of Herbie's face and his eyes appeared to be fixed, not so much on the world beyond the window, but the glass itself. They connected with nothing as he uttered a single word. "Indeed." My kind-hearted teacher needed more time to find the courage he was missing. "Right, very well, I am in love with Celia Hardcastle. It's not as though it's a secret. Half the school knows."

Grandfather launched a new question straight back at him. "And did Mrs Hardcastle return your affections?"

"There was a time when I hoped that might be true. I used to visit her each afternoon as she attended to the rose garden. With the gentle way she spoke, I came to believe she might care for me, but no words of love ever passed between us."

"Something changed?" Grandfather asked, reading between the lines.

"Yes, she made it very clear that she had no interest in me. I was a fool to devote my heart to a married woman, but as Antony said to Cleopatra, 'There's beggary in love that can be reckoned'. Celia was my Juliet. Though, to her, I was merely a face in the chorus."

Lord Edgington did not appear charmed by his lyricism. "All right, man. That's enough Shakespeare. Love may have made a fool of you, but it needn't transform you into a poet."

My teacher had tears in his eyes and it was terribly moving. I felt rotten for the poor chap, which, I suppose, was the last thing that he wanted.

"I know what everyone thinks of soppy old Herbie. That's why I'm leaving. Not so much for my broken heart as how ridiculous it all feels. There are boys in the lower school who give me sympathetic looks every day. One likes to say, 'Chin up, sir,' whenever he comes to class. I'm the laughingstock of the school."

Grandfather let out a soft breath before responding. "So what you're saying is that you had a motive as well as the opportunity and expertise to murder Tobias Hardcastle."

Herbie turned to look at the man who, a short while earlier, he'd spoken of as a hero. "You can't possibly believe that."

"What I believe is irrelevant, that's exactly what the police will think. You've no alibi! As I've been trying to tell you since we arrived, you need to prepare for the worst."

"If you're saying-" He didn't finish that sentence as the door to the laboratory swung open and Inspector Isambard Blunt of Scotland Yard was standing in the doorway with a grim smile on his face.

"Terribly violent place Surrey has become. Barely a week goes by these days without an upstanding member of the local community being hacked to death. I don't suppose you had anything to do with it, did you, Edgington?" The shabby little man stepped into the room with two more reticent officers in his wake.

"Starting as you mean to go on, I see?" My grandfather did not have the smoothest of relationships with his ex-subordinate. "Perhaps you could make the effort to catch the killer this time without my help."

The two men enjoyed a brief staring match which, inevitably, the ratty fellow in the gabardine coat lost.

Blunt's lip flared involuntarily and he tried to get it under control before making another accusation. "Then what about your grandson?" He didn't look at me as he spoke, which is lucky as my eyes were darting about suspiciously. It had just occurred to me that I was as much a suspect as Herbie himself. "I hear he was the lucky chap who found the body. That'll be the fourth he's seen in a month. Bit of a coincidence, don't you think?"

The inspector clearly had his heart set on arresting as many members of my family as possible, but Grandfather was having none of it. "Don't be ridiculous, Blunt. I suppose you've visited the scene of the crime?"

The inspector nodded.

"So then you've seen the beaker with green liquid in it and the foam that spilled out all over the dead man whose head it is still resting upon."

"Yes, and?"

"And clearly Christopher had nothing to do with it."

Blunt folded his arms over his chest, unimpressed by the defence. "And why's that?"

"Because my grandson is hopeless at chemistry, everyone knows it. Just ask his teacher."

I appreciated my grandfather's support, if not his assessment of my academic ability. We turned to look at Herbie who was silhouetted against the bright blue sky through the window. He gave an awkward shrug of concession.

"Mr Mayfield, I presume." Blunt looked reluctant to give up on his initial theories, but now that he had a new suspect in his sights, he was clearly warming to the idea. "You were my next candidate. The chap at reception has been telling us all sorts of interesting stories about you. I think we'd better go somewhere quiet to discuss what's really been going on here."

Blunt raised his arms as though the man would attempt to get past, but Herbie was no fighter and meekly showed his empty hands. "There's no need to arrest me, I'll tell you whatever you need to know."

"You can't! This isn't right." Why am I always the one who ends up shouting such statements? "Mr Mayfield has done nothing wrong. If he was going to kill Hardcastle, he would have made it look like someone else did it."

Blunt was smiling so much I could see his crooked yellow teeth. "Pipe down, boy. This has got nothing to do with you. This is police business."

I thought Grandfather might intervene, but instead he put his hand on my shoulder to calm me down. Even Blunt was surprised at this subdued reaction and narrowed his eyes warily.

"And that goes for you too, your lordship." The inspector turned these last two words into an insult. "Try to remember that you're not on the force anymore and to stay out of my way."

I wanted to run after the halfwit inspector and set my teacher free, but I knew it was hopeless.

"Why didn't you do something?" I found myself shouting once more, when we were alone.

At first, Grandfather didn't respond. He sat down in Mr Mayfield's chair and put his hand to his long, snowy beard to think.

"The truth is…" Even when he finally answered, he took his time over his words. "The truth is, I don't think there's anything more that I can do." He straightened his back and peered up at me. "We're looking at one of two scenarios. Either your teacher is a murderer and will be punished accordingly, or the real killer has done such a good job of making it look like that's the case that it will be very difficult to prove Mr Mayfield's innocence."

I was already bristling before he'd finished his summary. "He can't be the killer. It doesn't make any sense. He's not the sort for one thing, but it's completely illogical that he would have incriminated himself. If the chemicals had poisoned Hardcastle, you might argue that Herbie was the likely culprit, but they served no other purpose than to make the scene look ghoulish."

He gently rocked the chair from side to side. "You must be able to see by now that a murderer making himself such an obvious suspect that the police would rule him out is a clever tactic." He paused and waited for his words to have their effect. "But I can't help agreeing with your thinking, Christopher. Perhaps it's foolish to say that your favourite teacher is a good egg and he couldn't have killed his rival, but I was very much coming to that conclusion myself."

He stood up sharply and pulled down on his dove-grey waistcoat. "Come along, Chrissy. We have very little evidence and even less time, but we have to start somewhere."

His sudden change in attitude alarmed me. He was already marching from the room as I stuttered out, "Where… where are we going?"

"It's lunchtime. Where do you think?"

# CHAPTER THIRTEEN

The Oakton end-of-year picnic is a real highlight of the school calendar and it was just about to begin. Once we'd collected our golden retriever from the entrance, we had to stop at the kitchen on the way.

Doreen the dinner lady wasn't in the best of moods. "I don't care about your hoity-toity *cuisine*. I know what my boys like eating and that's good, honest nosh."

Henrietta, the cook from Cranley Hall, looked horrified. She was standing beside Doreen at the range, peering into a gigantic pot. "I was only suggesting that you add some herbs to your *soup*." She pronounced this last word as though she wasn't entirely sure what was bubbling in front of her.

Doreen emitted an unimpressed grunt. "It's not a soup, it's lamb's brain purée. The boys love it on a bit of bread." From experience, I can tell you that boys wouldn't love lamb's brain purée if it was smothered on a bar of chocolate.

As this conversation was taking place in front of us, a line of lower ranked prefects, dressed in their stark black blazers, were collecting trays from the kitchen hatch to transport them out to the field. There was a cornucopia of delights on offer, from charred sausage rolls to cod liver vol-au-vents. As they collected their charges, each boy gazed at the culinary offering with a mixture of befuddlement and disgust.

"Excuse me, ladies," my grandfather finally interrupted. "I'm sorry to intrude upon your colloquy, but I was hoping to speak to Henrietta." His eyebrows slowly raised up to their peak and suspended there for some seconds as he awaited the reply.

"Yes, milord." Our cook gave a half curtsey.

Doreen, meanwhile, did not turn to look at Lord Edgington. She suddenly became very busy and rapidly stirred the mashed brains with a wooden spoon, as though she wished to manufacture a tornado. Grandfather regarded her with some curiosity, before leading Henrietta away to the door to the teacher's dining room.

"I need your help, Cook," he began. "I'm afraid to say that the headmaster has been murdered and your colleague over there was in the vicinity when it occurred."

Cook took the information in her stride. "I knew it the moment I set eyes on her, I did. I said to myself, *Henrietta, this Doreen is a wrong 'un if ever there was one, and she's not to be trusted.* I could tell from the way she rolled her pastry, you see. You can tell a lot about a person from the way they roll pastry. I've always-"

I was worried that Grandfather was too polite to interrupt, so I did it for him. "We need to know how long she left the kitchen for after twelve o'clock."

"Ooh, now let me think..." She did as she'd suggested, then pointed to the windowsill where an impressive selection of hourglasses in different sizes was on display. "Well, the timer for the minestrone finished at twelve fifteen, and Doreen left to pick up some bags of flour from the storeroom soon after. I'd say she was back by a quarter to one, when I was putting the final touches to the roast vegetables."

As Grandfather computed this information, I was stunned by the fact that Cook was making such very normal food for our lunch. I could only imagine that, before it was served, she would add some truly unappetising ingredients to make the dishes her own.

"You can't be any more certain than that?" he enquired.

She shook her head sadly. "I'm sorry, milord. I was a bit busy myself at the time, but it would have been around then."

"Thank you, Henrietta." He bowed solemnly. I had often noticed that my grandfather held great respect for the woman who prepared his victuals. "Oh, and one more thing." A mischievous smile shaped his face. "Is our lunch ready?"

We carried our picnic basket out to the playing field, much to the envy of the other parents. I watched Billy's father experimentally putting a piece of brain toast into his mouth as we strolled past. He did not appear satisfied with the outcome.

Delilah was yapping at the basket the whole way there, surely aware that there were delights in store for her. When we arrived, Mother had found a place on a blanket beside the lake and was talking to Marmaduke Adelaide's father Horatio.

The somewhat infamous semi-reformed criminal had been shunned by most of the parents there and was bordered by a large space on all sides – lest his wickedness be infectious. My mother had no such fear, and the two were happily chatting away as Grandfather's cherished canine bounded up to demand some affection (and food).

"Horatio," Superintendent Edgington greeted his old nemesis respectfully. I was yet to hear the full story of the two men's past connection during my grandfather's days at Scotland Yard, but I was certain it would be interesting. "What a pleasure it is to see you again."

"Oh, thank goodness you brought food of your own. I just tried one of the sausage rolls and thought I'd chipped a tooth. The drinks they've been handing out are the only thing worth consuming. I'm on my third champagne cocktail already." He raised his sparkling glass in the direction of a makeshift bar that had been set up beside the running track. It was staffed by several harassed looking prefects who seemed to be shouting at one another at all times. "It's really quite tasty, you must have one."

Grandfather was not persuaded by the recommendation. "Perhaps later, we are in something of a hurry."

"Oh, Daddy," my mother proclaimed. "You're not *on the job* are you?"

Horatio's dark eyes sparkled with glee. "Not another stiff to spoil the party?"

Grandfather did not look comfortable with the discussion. "Keep your voice down, I don't want everyone to know yet."

Marmaduke's father would not take the hint. "Has the headmaster snuffed it? I haven't seen him about for a while." He didn't wait for an answer. "Oh, he has, hasn't he? That's simply too wonderful. Odious fellow, always calling me up whenever Marmaduke got into trouble or begging for donations to the school. I never liked him."

"Enough." The old man's temper flared and our lounging companion stopped jabbering. "I just came to give you the hamper and now I'm off to tell his widow the sad news." He clearly didn't appreciate Horatio's levity.

"So we're not going to have lunch?" I might have allowed a hint of disappointment to show in my voice.

"Don't worry about us," Horatio continued, leaning over to the picnic basket to extract the various dishes and a bottle of Veuve Clicquot champagne. "We'll get everything ready for your return."

My mother looked uncertain whether she should accompany us or stay where she was. Delilah had no such dilemma. She launched herself into the air, to snatch up whatever tasty bites Horatio would throw to her, as her master hurried off.

The sun was high in the sky and beat down on my bare arms and legs with great ferocity as I raced to catch up. It was a perfectly wonderful summer's day and I longed to lie down on the grass with a pork pie and a chunk of Red Leicester to have a nap. I knew that such a plan was pure fantasy.

We tiptoed between the blankets towards the spectators' stand where Mrs Hardcastle was awaiting the end of the final races. She was smiley and bright, looking on cheerfully at the boys still competing.

"May we have a word, Mrs Hardcastle?"

The Mama of Oakton Academy looked a little shocked by my Grandfather's presence and launched into an apology. "If this is about last night, I can only say how sorry I am. I don't honestly believe that Tobias wished the boys any harm. It was really quite out of character of him. He was trying to teach them a lesson. Though he didn't go about it in the correct-"

As she was speaking, Grandfather's gaze fell on me momentarily. I could see that he was putting the pieces together in his head and did not need any help understanding what had occurred. The fact I'd sneaked off to Hardcastle's office in the middle of the race and the knowledge of the headmaster's actions was enough for him to fill in the gaps.

He acted as though he knew just what she was referring to. "As shocked as I was to hear of your husband's behaviour, that is not why I wish to speak to you." He caught sight of Inspector Blunt's men emerging on the far side of the field and his pace increased. "I'm afraid I have some bad news to impart. I had hoped to take you somewhere quiet, but that is no longer an option."

Her voice came out in a whisper. "What bad news? What's happened?"

He paused before answering and took her arm to lead us beyond the stand, out of sight of the crowds. "I'm truly sorry to tell you this, but your husband was found dead a short time ago. We believe he was murdered." This was about as delicate as my grandfather could be. We knew full well that the man had been murdered, but he'd chosen his words to soften the blow.

And what a blow it was. I'm amazed poor Mama remained on her feet.

"No…" I'm not entirely certain this is the word she used as it came out in a strangled, dipping tone. Her eyes were instantly hollow and she held on to me for support. "He can't be dead. He just can't be."

Grandfather steered her further into the shade. "I can only tell you how sorry I am to darken this sunny day with such tragedy, but I must ask you one question before the police arrive. Do you know anyone who would have wanted to harm your husband?"

She put her arm around my shoulders then as she clearly didn't have the strength to stand on her own two feet. She smelled like violets and rose petals to match her pretty pink floral dress. It was easy to see why Herbie had fallen in love with her. Though I calculated she was at least two and half times older than me, I would have run through fire if it eased her pain the slightest bit.

She discovered some composure as she sought an answer to my grandfather's harrowing question. "I can't claim that Toby was loved by all, but he had no great enemies. He was a good headmaster, he ran a good school." I thought this an odd topic for her to focus upon at such a moment; as though his efficiency at work should have prevented his demise. "There were pupils who didn't agree with some of his more aggressive punitive methods, but I don't think for one second… No, it couldn't be one of the boys."

"I think the police will agree with you on that matter. But you mustn't mistake their theories for facts. Please promise me you'll keep an open mind."

The vagueness of his language panicked her again and she flung her free arm in the air with unexpected fury. "You know something more, don't you? Please tell me. I'd much rather all this came from you." I'd never noticed before, but she had an Oxonian quality to her voice. She sounded awfully like my brother's friends from university, in fact.

Grandfather sighed and gave in. "I believe the police have surmised that Mr Mayfield killed your husband out of jealousy. There is some evidence which would point to his involvement, but, at present, I believe that it is only circumstantial."

She almost smiled then as the possibility sunk in. "Herbert? They think that Herbert killed Tobias? That's ridiculous. Poor Herbert wouldn't hurt the tiniest of creatures. He once told me he had chosen not to study biology because he couldn't stomach the dissections. There must be some mistake."

Her brief spark of cheer faded away and another wave of sorrow hit her. My grandfather might have expanded further had the two uniformed policemen we'd spotted in Mr Mayfield's lab not arrived at that moment.

"Madam." The first officer, a local boy from St Mary-Under-Twine, could barely raise his eyes to look at her. "I'm afraid we need you to come with us."

I imagine that her anguish was mirrored in my own countenance. She pulled me in close before she left, as though I were the poor soul who needed comforting. Stricken dumb, I looked on as she was escorted away.

Grandfather put his hand on my shoulder where her own had just been. "All deaths leave their mark, boy, but murder is a truly terrible thing. No matter how many cases I have investigated, I never fail to notice the destruction such wickedness leaves behind." He'd slowed his speech to deliver this soliloquy and allowed a few moments of silence to punctuate the remark.

"We should keep going, shouldn't we? For her sake." I only said this so that he didn't have to sound heartless and beckon us on to our next point of investigation.

"Yes, boy. You've never said a truer word."

# CHAPTER FOURTEEN

Instead of heading back towards the school as I'd been expecting, we wandered back towards the swimming lake. Mother didn't look much more cheerful than either of us, despite Horatio Adelaide's attempts at humour. Grandfather sat down on the blanket beside them but said nothing. He had that oddly distant look on his face and I could tell that his mind was somewhere far away, deeply engaged in the puzzle he had to solve. He watched as the swallows or swifts or what have you flew low across the lake in search of flies. They skimmed the surface of the water like skipping stones.

I'm afraid it was far too good an opportunity to pass up and I helped myself to a plate which I quickly loaded with food. I could only assume that Cook's time spent with Doreen had inspired her to keep things simple. There was barely a hint of star anise to the fish ball I scoffed, and the roast beef and orange sandwiches were the definition of sumptuous.

"Eat slowly, Christopher," my mother scolded. "One death is enough for today. We don't want you choking."

I attempted to respond, though the words came out a little crumby. "With Grandfather, I can never be sure when I might eat again. I have to make the most of my opportunities."

She couldn't help smiling at her darling son's witty and insightful retort.

"A boy should have a healthy appetite," Adelaide said, still sipping his cocktail. "Speaking of which, here comes Marmaduke." He pointed to the final stretch of the race where his son was a good furlong ahead of the second-place finisher.

Mr Bath, the games teacher and part-time racing caller, had seized up his metal speaking cone once more. "Adelaide is in the lead. Young Derek McGeorge is unlikely to catch up with the all-round sportsman at this late stage."

"Wouldn't you like to be there on the finish line?" my optimistic mother suggested.

Mr Adelaide was not the most attentive of parents and waved the suggestion away. "No, no. He always wins these things. If you told me he'd passed a test in mathematics, now that's something that would get me on my feet on a sunny afternoon."

"This year's sixth-form cross-country trial has been a cracking race!" Mr Bath yelled for all to hear. "Filled with fine athletes and that remarkable appearance from Master Christopher Prentiss, who now appears to have given up on the race altogether to enjoy, what looks from here to be, a Scotch egg."

As grandfather continued his meditation, Marmalade crossed the finish line and didn't stop running until he'd reached us. "Did you see me, Father? I think I broke my own best time. Bally difficult in this heat, I can tell you!"

"Yes, I saw." Horatio showed no pride in his son's achievement and gestured to one of the prefects for another drink. My own father wasn't known for sentimentality but looked as soppy as my brother alongside this specimen of fatherhood.

"Congratulations, Marmaduke," Mother said, in her typically warm voice. "It was a marvellous run." She looked at me then, perhaps remembering that I had at least started the race, which was surely half the battle won.

With his father disinterested in the boy's presence, Marmalade turned to whisper to me. "Did you get the drawing? Am I safe?"

I didn't quite know how to answer that. "Oh, yes, you're more than safe."

"So where is it?"

"Well..." This wasn't the easiest situation to explain. "You see, old Hardcastle is dead."

"What?" The word was a sudden eruption. "You took things a bit far there, Chrissy. I wasn't suggesting you murder him."

I rushed to explain. "It wasn't me. It was Herbie. Or at least, that's what the police think. Grandfather's not convinced."

We both turned to the illustrious detective. He was sitting in a rather childish pose – his knees pulled up to his chest and his shoulders hunched – looking around the vast picnic which splayed out in front of us. I can't say for certain whether he was aware of anything his eyes rested on, but they were jumping from point to point quite rhythmically.

I thought, perhaps, he was searching out suspects in the crowd. There was no sign of Dr Steadfast, and Matron had now retreated from her duties, but Dominic Rake had appeared and was barking orders at his subordinates over by the drinks table. The orders were coming in fast and clearly what the younger prefects needed was someone to shout at them. On seeing the anger pour out of him, I had to wonder what Rake had been doing at the time of the murder.

Marmalade had another question for me. "So how did Hardcastle die?"

"He had his head caved in with a coconut monkey and then someone balanced a flask of bubbling chemicals on top of him."

"Chemicals?" He sounded dubious on this point. "You clearly had nothing to do with it then. You're worse at science than I am."

I endured his laughter and was happy when something occurred to distract him.

A new team of officers had arrived, and a sergeant mounted the stage. "Ladies and gentlemen," he began. "I've been asked to inform you that a crime has been committed and a man is dead." None of the parents seemed particularly shocked by this. They continued drinking their cocktails and nibbling at the atrocious offerings from Doreen's kitchen. "Murdered, in fact." The officer was clearly hoping for more of a response. "The headmaster Mr Tobias Hardcastle has been murdered in his office." He injected any amount of drama into the words, but the crowd were unmoved.

"Waiter, could you bring me another milk punch?" A mother in the middle of the picnic yelled, and the policeman looked bemused.

What the sergeant had failed to understand was that the great and good who sent their sons to Oakton Academy were not interested in exactly who taught them. Just as they had no desire to know the names of the maids who peeled their potatoes or shucked their oysters. The only thing that mattered was that their children were kept occupied and away from home for as much of the year as possible. Minor details such as the murder of a teacher were a matter for someone other than them.

The officer had one more announcement to make before he retreated from the stage. "You may continue with the festivities here on the field, but the school will now be closed until further notice."

"Here's to old Hardcastle," Horatio said rather loudly. He raised his glass, and several parents turned their disapproving gaze upon him. It was hard to know whether they disliked him so much because of his criminal connections or the simple fact that he came from *new money*.

Marmaduke tried to snag a cocktail of his own but his father looked like he might belt him, and, just at that moment, Lord Edgington came back to life. Without saying anything, he stood up tall before us, rising from the ground like a phoenix, before pulling both cuffs down confidently.

"The break's over, Christopher. We have a killer to find."

# CHAPTER FIFTEEN

It has often been said of me – by my family, teachers and a number of the domestic staff at Cranley Hall – that I simply don't learn my lesson. On my previous investigations with my grandfather, I'd bumbled along at his side, offering all sorts of useless comments and theories for him to laugh at. I had no interest in being a fool though, and fully intended to do things differently this time around by jolly well learning my lesson.

The first stage to my plan was to keep my mouth firmly closed, not ask too many unnecessary questions and observe what the old man was doing. The only problem with this was that former Superintendent Edgington had an expression of pure steel which was as simple to unpick as any safe in the bank of England.

I had no idea what he'd discovered in his reverie, and he didn't offer an explanation. We crossed the field once more, and I noticed Dominic Rake shooting off towards the games hut, well clear of our path. I was quick to assume that he'd spotted my grandfather and got scared, but perhaps he was just helping to pack equipment away.

As we left the festivities behind, I found that there was a question I simply couldn't hold in. "Who are we going to talk to next, Grandfather? Dr Steadfast is a savage chap. I wouldn't put it past him to murder a rival, but who's your money on?"

"Were Steadfast and Hardcastle rivals, then?"

My grandfather's gaze is an awfully fearsome tool, and I might have stuttered a little when replying. "I… well, no. They always seemed to get on rather well, actually. Two like-minded brutes."

"So be a good boy and stop casting pointless aspersions." He offered an affectionate wink, but this was the only answer he would provide until we'd walked through the kitchen garden – in order to avoid the officers at the gate – and arrived at the dormitory block. "Next, Christopher, you're going to show me your room."

We ascended the stairs up to the large sleeping hall which housed enough beds for all forty boys in the sixth form. There was not much space for our possessions or to make the room our own. All my books, a few photographs and the requisite selection of school clothes were stored in a wooden chest at the end of my bed, which is where my grandfather came to rest.

"I think that it's high time I talked to you, my boy."

"Me? Why me?" I found myself blurting out in the hard-done-by tone of a tot.

He directed his usual penetrating stare in my direction. I wasn't used to being a suspect and did not like it one bit.

"Because you found the man's body, and you were there last night when Mr Hardcastle did something 'out of character'. So would you care to explain your part in all this drama?"

I crashed down on the end of Will's bed which was opposite my own. "If it involves me getting into trouble with the headmaster for something that wasn't entirely my fault, will you be angry with me?"

He shook his head once. Everything my grandfather did was neat and economical. To expend more energy than necessary would have been a waste.

"No, of course I won't be angry, boy. You don't think I know that schools are unjust? You don't think I realise, from everything you've told me and everything I've seen today, that Hardcastle was a tyrant?"

I considered his argument. In as quiet a voice as I could manage, as I still didn't trust him one hundred per cent, I began my tale. I went through every last detail that had led up to our trip to Hardcastle's office and the terror we'd endured there. Grandfather winced at the nasty parts and seemed genuinely relieved when Mama came to save us.

"So you left the race this afternoon to help your friend." He thought about this for a moment. "That's admirable behaviour, really quite admirable."

I might have allowed myself a premature smile.

"But you should never have been so foolish as to find yourselves in that position to begin with." His stentorian voice shook through the floor.

"You said you wouldn't get angry!" I countered, and he waved away the complaint.

"I'm not angry, I'm disappointed. I like to think that you're cleverer than that." He was surely the only one. "You should have realised you'd get caught if the man had it in for you." He sounded more disappointed by the fact that Hardcastle had stopped us than my participation in Marmalade's plan.

"Still, the important thing is that you could yet be an essential witness. Clearly your headmaster was unnerved by something. That must be why he lost his temper so thoroughly last night. He might well have killed young Adelaide if he'd used the cricket bat on him." I wasn't convinced that he was focusing on the right part of the story, but he soon moved us on. "Now, tell me what happened today. You started on the race and, as soon as you outfoxed the others by going slower than the lot of them, made your escape. What happened next?"

"I ran back to school through the kitchen garden."

"Did you see anyone on your way?"

I tried to recall. "Well, yes, I did actually. I saw my history teacher, Dr Steadfast. He was hurrying over to the field. He'd have missed the beginning of the cross-country, though I suppose he might have enjoyed the hurdles if-"

"Focus, Christopher. Did he see you?"

"No, he jolly well didn't. I made sure of it." I both felt and sounded rather proud of myself. "Dominic Rake the prefect was a little way behind him, so I waited until they'd gone past."

"Were the two of them together?"

I considered this possibility. "No. I don't believe so. They were both in a world of their own, and Rake looked particularly anxious. After that, I skulked round to the school. I thought I did a good job of ducking under the hatch past Jonathan Greeves in reception, and I still can't fathom how he spotted me."

"You didn't see anyone else?"

I had another ponder and scratched my skull before the memory popped back into my head. "No, but I heard a noise in the main corridor beyond the stairs. It was a frightening, brutish sound; a struggling, heaving sort of noise that you wouldn't believe. It scared the wits out of me, until I realised it was just our dinner lady Doreen talking to someone."

He regarded me uncertainly. "The ground floor corridor? And that wouldn't happen to be where she keeps her supplies?"

A tiny firework of understanding exploded in my head. "You know, that could be it. Perhaps she was moving boxes or some such thing. She does sound like a car backfiring when she concentrates.

Though I'm not certain her voice was coming from the storeroom."

"It puts her in the school at the right time at least. And the fact that there was someone with her is interesting." A distant look consumed his face and I could see that he was considering who it could have been.

Unless there was someone else in the building we didn't know about, I hadn't a clue. Greeves was in reception, Herbie was presumably in his laboratory, and Mr Hardcastle was upstairs being dead.

I didn't utter these thoughts as I wasn't entirely sure of the facts. Instead, I asked, "So Doreen's a suspect? Isn't it unlikely that a lowly dinner lady would have had much to do with a headmaster?" As I spoke, a door swung open on the landing, but no one came through to the dorm.

"It's unlikely that a wealthy lady would associate with a common butler, yet we know such things have occurred. Now, stop letting your assumptions interfere with our investigation." I thought I heard someone moving around in the corridor again, but, when he stopped talking, the silence remained.

"Fine, but that's the whole story. I went up to Hardcastle's office and there was a big bang. I threw the door open and the beaker of liquid was bubbling away. Then I ran to get you as soon as I'd confirmed he was dead. What I don't understand is why you decided to bring me all this way to talk to me when we could have cleared this up over on the field (where there's more delicious food to be eaten.)" I didn't say these last words, but I was definitely thinking them.

"I didn't come here to talk to you, Christopher. In actual fact, it's time I introduced you to someone. Constance, could you please stop lurking in the doorway and come in here?"

# CHAPTER SIXTEEN

Matron stuck her head into the room and gingerly stepped over the threshold. I'd never seen her look so hesitant before; it didn't last long.

The impressively wide woman thundered over to tell me off. "Christopher Prentiss, what are you doing here? You know boys ain't allowed in here during the day without permission." She directed all her anger at me and didn't even glance at Grandfather. "I'll be telling Mr Hardcastle about this. You wait and see."

"You can drop the pretence, Connie. It must be twenty years, but I could never forget a face like yours."

She still wouldn't make eye contact with Lord Edgington, who leaned back placidly with his elbows propped behind him on the bed.

"I don't know what ya referring to. My name is Constance…" She came to an unexpected stop and looked around the room. "…Constance Mattress, and I've never heard of no Crabb Sisters in my life."

Grandfather smiled at me and explained exactly what Matron was so spectacularly failing to disprove. "Connie and her sister Doreen are two of the best thieves I've ever arrested. The Crabb Sisters could have picked a flea's pocket if they'd put their minds to it. Sadly, thinking was never their strong point, and they ended up serving fifteen years each at Holloway Prison."

"We was let out after twelve for good behaviour," the enormous woman informed me rather proudly, having now given up on her ruse.

"It was Dorie I saw working in the kitchen earlier. She tried to hide her face, but I knew it was her."

"Wait a moment," I couldn't let such revelations go by without comment. "Are you saying that, not only are they both criminals, but Matron and Doreen are sisters?"

Grandfather looked across the aisle at me as though I'd just claimed I could fly or that the King was secretly German. "Of course they're sisters, boy. They look practically identical. How could you have failed to spot that? I sometimes despair, I-"

Matron did me a favour by interrupting his bluster. "Eh, but we've gone straight now. Put our lives of crime behind us and found gainful employment terrifying the youngsters into behaving right."

91

Grandfather stood up to look the giantess in the eye. "Constance and Doreen Crabb on the straight and narrow? I never thought I'd see the day."

Her deep voice growled louder. "Eh, it's true. We hardly never does nothing dodgy no more. I swear it on my mother."

He opened his mouth to respond, then changed his mind. He presumably already possessed enough evidence to refute her claim, but chose not to start an argument. "Well, jolly good. I'm awfully happy you've turned your lives around. It must be quite the relief after your time inside."

Her large, square face became a little rounder thanks to a toothy smile. "That's right. Such a relief."

"It would be terrible to think of the two of you returning to prison. I'm sure you have nightly dreams of the terrors you endured. Nightmares in fact."

Her face squared off once more. "That's right."

"Your very existence must be defined by the squalor and indignity of those seemingly endless years of incarceration."

Her chin dropped down so that her head became a rectangle. "Uhhh, yeah. That's exactly it."

"All the more reason for you to help me find Mr Hardcastle's killer then?"

"Oh. Ummm, yeah." Her voice was little more than a croak, but then she realised her mistake and hurried to cover it up. "Oh, he's dead, is he? There's a turnip for the books. Course, I've been over on the field making sure no boys escaped. I couldn't of been involved."

"And yet your sister was in the school fetching a sack of flour, which took her some thirty minutes to retrieve. Would you happen to know what she got up to during that time?"

The woman's eyes wandered off around the two long rows of concrete-hard beds, as though she'd lost interest in the conversation. "My sister? I haven't seen Dorie for decades."

Grandfather puffed out an exasperated breath. "You just admitted that she's here working in the kitchens."

She feigned surprise. "Is she? Well there's a coincidence. What are the chances of two sisters-"

"Connie, tell me what I need to know or I'll make it my mission to discover whatever scheme you've been operating and get you locked away again." Grandfather was a burning ball of rage. He was the sun on a hot day.

I had never expected to see that colossus of a woman intimidated, but she practically jumped out of her blue pinafore when he addressed her. "There's no need to lose your temper, Superintendent Edgington, sir, milord Highness."

Grandfather urged her on once more. "Who do you think murdered Mr Hardcastle? What's been going on at this school, and how do you two fit into any of it?" I was a little scared of him myself then and flinched as he spoke.

Matron crashed down at the end of the bed and the metal frame rose a good foot in the air. "I'm going to be honest, officer, I really don't know what goes on in this place, but it's definitely fishy. More or less every last teacher is barking mad, and no one liked that Hardcastle. He made every day feel like a funeral. And you can call me a thief, but the way they squeeze money out of them boys is bleeding criminal."

Her speech emerged as one great clump of words, which I only came to understand five seconds after she'd finished speaking. She looked up expectantly at former Superintendent Edgington and awaited his response.

"Who in particular didn't get along with the man?"

"Let me think." She scratched the purplish mole on her chin. "That young one. You know, the pretty fella… Mayfield. Well, he's in love with Hardcastle's missus. And it's hardly surprising as Hardcastle was terrible cruel to her. Practically tied her to the kitchen sink and told her how to breathe. That old so-and-so Steadfast has always been after the top job but only made it to head of sixth form. Hardcastle's secretary chappie was terrified to be in the same room as him and, now that I come to think of it, my sister once told me she wanted to murder the headmaster after he complained that her chipolatas were too crispy."

"So everyone wanted him dead?" Grandfather sounded really quite sardonic.

"That's about the inch of it!" Happy to have said her piece, Matron let out a little whistle.

"What about Dominic Rake?" I interrupted.

She turned to look at me, and her face assumed its typically gargoyle-ish expression. "Prentiss!" she barked. "You shouldn't sneak up on people like that!"

Grandfather got us back on track. "The head prefect, Dominic Rake, was also in the building this afternoon. What do you know about him?"

"Nothing. Why, what have you heard?" Her face turned even grimmer. "I know he's a bootlicker, an eavesdropper and a nosey parker. But if he says anything about me, you're not to believe him, sir, lord, Your Honour." When she addressed her comments to me, they came out as threats, but she appeared to have an innate reverence towards my grandfather.

"How did he get on with the headmaster?"

"Well, Rake was made head prefect, so that should tell ya quite a bit." She bowed respectfully to him then returned to her observations. "Nasty brute he is, though. Always spying on everybody with his little gang. It's hard for a lady to go about her business with his type around."

"And what exactly does your business involve?" I waited for an answer that would never come.

"This is getting us nowhere," my grandfather said. "Although you were on the field when the murder took place, I'll still need to speak to your sister. I know you have a great deal of influence over Doreen, so tell her it's in her best interests to cooperate."

Matron stood up to creep from the dorm without turning around. "Very good, Your Worship, milord. Awfully kind of you to talk to me today." She'd got to the door before her rambling petered out and, with one more bow, ran from sight.

Grandfather let out another harrowed sigh, so I thought it would be acceptable to ask a question. "Do you think her sister is capable of murder? I once saw her whack Terence Peterson around the head with the back of a slotted spoon."

"The Crabb sisters were never known for their violence, but who can say what a person is capable of." His words came to an abrupt halt and he darted up off the bed. "They're not as stupid as they like to make out though, and it does have a certain logic to it. Perhaps Hardcastle got wind of whatever scheme they'd cooked up. Constance has always been the mastermind; perhaps by getting Doreen to do the deed, she hoped to hide her involvement."

94

He stopped halfway out of the room. "Come along, Christopher. What are you waiting for? There are more suspects to interview."

"But I'm sleepy after I've eaten," I complained, and he either didn't hear or chose to ignore me as he paraded from the room.

# CHAPTER SEVENTEEN

"The way I see it," Grandfather began, while motoring across the quad, "there are five key figures we must interview to get to the truth. The prefect, your odious history teacher, the dead man's wife, the secretary and Doreen Crabb."

"So, are they the main suspects?"

He stopped in front of the door to the school. "Well, no… it's not that simple. Mrs Hardcastle couldn't have killed her husband, though she could still be involved. Matron could well be in league with her sister, and Herbert Mayfield isn't entirely ruled out either. In fact, for the moment, we can't say for certain who our suspects are. But we can narrow it down further. This way!"

With these short, sharp instructions, I wondered if he sometimes forgot I wasn't his dog.

"When Hardcastle was killed, Jonathan Greeves was at the main exit to the building," I helpfully observed. "So we know who went in and out."

"Do we?" His eyebrows jumped skywards.

"Um, I think so."

"Interesting. Carry on."

"Then there are two more exits that are kept locked, but there's always the side door."

He nodded encouragingly as we skirted the building in the direction of the patch of ground that had been designated for car parking. "That's right, my boy. And as it happens, I had a man stationed in just the right place."

There were long lines of exquisite automobiles in place. I spotted a Lancia, several Lagondas and a stunning royal blue Armstrong Siddeley Landaulette. Our Chauffeur Todd was sitting in the Rolls with his legs hanging out of the door, reading one of the adventure novels that he enjoyed so much. I have to say, being a chauffeur doesn't seem like such a bad job if one has a book to read. He'd parked the car only a few feet from the building and would surely have seen anyone coming and going, no matter how enthralling his story was.

"Todd," the old man announced our presence in that same clipped tone. "I need to know whether you saw anything suspicious at around twelve o'clock."

He tossed the paperback into the passenger seat and jumped to attention at a military pace. "No, milord."

"No one using this door?"

He thought for a moment. "Only the caretaker, but that was a while before twelve and he walked over towards the field after that. He gave me a proper scowl, he did. I wouldn't want to cross him on a dark evening." He waited for his master to reply and, when he didn't, asked, "Was that any help, milord?"

Grandfather uttered a, "No," then quickly clarified. "Or rather, yes, Todd. Very helpful, but it's not going to solve the case. I may need your assistance later, so stay close by."

Grandfather was already starting back to the building, his eyes fixed on the lowest row of windows.

"Painted shut, Grandfather."

He turned his disapproving gaze upon me. "Your sentence doesn't appear to have a subject. Are you suggesting that I am painted shut?"

Though in many ways an easy-going sort of fellow, Lord Edgington could be a stickler for good grammar. "Urmmm, I... No, sir. I just... I was talking about the windows. The caretaker Mr Scuttlewell had them nailed and painted shut after Marmalade attempted to escape from our mathematics class when we were seven years old. It's awfully stuffy in the lower school corridors in summer, I can tell you."

He clapped his hands together. "Well, that's more like it – though not the lack of ventilation. It's becoming increasingly likely that we can exclude any stray students or wandering parents from our possible culprits and focus on four key suspects. The sooner we can speak to them, the more chance we have of finding the guilty party. I'd like to keep ahead of Blunt as much as possible. He can tie himself up interviewing the wrong man while we get to the killer."

His enthusiasm was infectious, and I found myself grinning as I counted off the suspects in my head. "So you're confident it wasn't Herbie then. That's wonderful. With whom should we start?"

"Who had the most to gain?"

I had to think for a bit, but after some quick calculations, I went with, "Well, his wife. Celia Hardcastle would have inherited whatever money her husband possessed. And Matron wasn't wrong about the fees they charge here. I'm sure the headmaster was sitting on a pretty penny."

"True, but your beloved *Mama* was in front of a crowd of two hundred people at the time her husband was murdered."

"She could have been working with one of our suspects. Perhaps Jonathan Greeves was in love with her and did her husband in at her command. Or Perhaps it was Rake or Steadfast even."

With his hand on the finger plate of the main entrance, he furrowed his brow. "Do you really think the woman has it in her to order her husband's death?

I thought about her tragic expression when we'd broken the bad news and felt dreadful for even suggesting it. "No, of course not. She's a lovely, kind-hearted person who would never do anything so dastardly."

His brow was positively crumpled by now. "Then you're not thinking like a detective after all. Never be taken in by a pretty smile or a show of sorrow." I tried to remember the lesson, but doubted I would, and he soon moved us on to other things. "Now, when we go into the school, I'm going to talk to Jonathan Greeves. I'd like you to enter as you did when you found the headmaster's body. Have you got that?"

I nodded and he swung the door open. I dived to the floor like an Italian Arditi soldier, scrambling behind enemy lines during the great war, while Grandfather created a diversion.

"Hello there, Greeves. I'm looking for Dr Steadfast. Do you happen to know where he is?"

I wriggled along on my belly and made it past the reception by the time grandfather had his answer.

"I believe he's upstairs, most likely in his office or perhaps the staff room."

"I'm much obliged, young man."

I jumped to my feet and peeked into the reception as I didn't want to be rude. "Thank you, Greeves."

Grandfather viewed me with a crease in the middle of his forehead, but he said no more as we tramped upstairs to the third floor, passing several uniformed officers on the way.

"How lovely to see you again." Grandfather was all airs and graces as he knocked and entered the staff room to find that slug Steadfast lounging on a sofa with a cup of tea and a depleted tin of biscuits. He did not look pleased to see us.

"Lord Edgington." He nodded but remained seated. "What can I do for you this afternoon?" His eyes kept flicking past us to the door and I wondered if he was planning his getaway. "Would you like to know more about young Christopher's mastery of historical facts?"

Grandfather pulled a high wooden chair out from the end of the table. It was large and ornate, and I was fairly certain that it had belonged to the headmaster. Pulling it into position in front of my teacher, he took his place as a king upon his throne. I hovered next to him like a servant, or a rather quiet jester.

"I imagine you've heard the dreadful news about Mr Hardcastle?"

"Dreadful is just the word for it." Steadfast did not seem as nervous around my grandfather as he had that morning and met his fiery gaze head on. "The world we live in is a truly wicked one."

Grandfather wore an indomitable expression as he expanded on this topic. "Indeed. It is a wicked world, full of wicked people." He turned his head to one side but regarded the teacher just as keenly. "And would you happen to be the murderer?"

The sudden change of tack clearly got to the shambolic chap, and he had to swallow down his nerves. "Me? I can barely bring myself to kill rabbits. I'm an absolute pacifist."

Grandfather clearly did not give much credence to this defence. From my memory of Steadfast's proselytising about the poetic tragedy of the battle of the Somme and the glorious victory of the allied troops at Amiens, I didn't either.

"Oh, how interesting." The lord of Cranley Hall was a wonderful actor and put across his emotions with conviction. "May I ask what you did during the war?"

Steadfast had already fallen for one of the old man's traps and looked rattled. "Well, I didn't go to the front, if that's what you mean. I worked in intelligence for his majesty's government." He sounded inordinately pleased with himself; as though he'd won the war from the comfort of a Westminster office. "I'd love to tell you more about it, but it's all very hush hush."

Without warning, Lord Edgington stood to walk over to the tea urn in the corner. "Christopher, would you like anything? It's not every day a young gentleman gets to look around the staff room at school, you should make the most of it."

I shook my head but took the opportunity to take in my surroundings. It was the first time that I'd set foot inside that fabled space and, I have to say, it came as a disappointment. The walls were covered with notice boards which held countless papers with Hardcastle's spidery writing upon them. Except for Grandfather's throne, the furniture was worn and old, and the air smelt of tea, dust and Mr Balustrade's terribly strong hair pomade. It was not the palace of wonders we students imagined it to be.

Grandfather had managed to find a surprisingly elegant porcelain cup and saucer and, with his drink prepared, returned to continue the interrogation.

"What type of doctor are you?"

"A doctor of history, obviously." Our suspect looked away, as though such a question were too much trouble to answer.

"Ah, not a real doctor then." Grandfather was a true wag, and the effect of his words was immediate. "You have no background in medicine or chemistry? No scientific connection to the war effort?"

Steadfast assumed his smug look once more. He wore the same expression whenever a boy got a question wrong in one of his classes. "No, not me. I'm no scientist. I can tell you the dates of some significant figures, but I wouldn't know an ion from an atom if you put them in my hand."

"Ah, I see."

"Louis Pasteur – 1822 to 1895," the doctor of history intoned. "Robert Bunsen – 1811 to 1899. Alfred Nobel – 1834 to 1896. The fellow invented dynamite, don't you know?" Who he was trying to impress with these facts wasn't clear, but they had little effect on his interviewer, who swiftly changed the subject.

"I believe you are in charge of the sixth form here at Oakton. Wouldn't that make you the obvious choice for the headship now that Hardcastle is out of your way?"

He put his mug down on the chipped white table beside the sofa. "You know, I hadn't thought of that before, but I suppose you're right." Steadfast was no David Garrick, and I could see through his façade.

Grandfather stirred his tea more aggressively. "You can forget the pretence, Steadfast. I have it on good authority that you were after his job."

"Does that make me a murderer?" His voice rose with indignation. "Just because I didn't agree with the way the fellow ran this school, that doesn't mean I stabbed him."

Grandfather analysed each word the man said with lightning speed and jumped on his error. "He wasn't stabbed, as I believe you are aware. Mr Hardcastle was beaten to death."

"Oh, so now you know exactly what I know? You can read minds, can you?"

I was absolutely inessential to this conversation and could do little more than spectate as my superlative grandfather pushed and prodded the arrogant man. Had I possessed the courage to speak then, I might well have shouted something along the lines of, *Go on, Grandfather! Show him what you're made of!*

"I know that you weren't surprised by my questions regarding chemistry. I've no doubt you will have spoken to Jonathan Greeves and perhaps the police to get the details out of them. I also know that you think you're very clever and that, by mentioning the wrong murder weapon, you hope to allay my suspicions."

I'm quite certain that Steadfast had already finished his tea by this point, but he raised his mug again and drained any drips from it to give himself a moment to think. When he was free to speak once more, he looked terribly hard done by.

"Can you blame me? You've come in here to accuse me of murder on a nice sunny day like this. The famous Superintendent Edgington, the bloodhound of Scotland Yard – throwing your accusations around like hand grenades, picking on whoever you fancy as the killer. Well, I'll tell you this… I won't be framed."

I looked at my grandfather to see what he had made of the response. His expression was unchanged, and he continued with a new line of attack.

"I believe that you left the school to watch the cross-country race?"

Steadfast folded his meaty arms over his chest. "And what if I did? I like cross-country running. There's something noble about the exertion it entails. I may not be an athlete myself, but that doesn't stop me from enjoying the spectacle."

His little finger raised most pointedly, grandfather took a polite sip from his Spode blue cup. "The only thing is, you arrived after the boys had set off and left before they returned. I think it must be difficult to enjoy the spectacle of something without seeing it occur."

This was the moment when Steadfast really lost his temper. His arms and legs went lashing outwards from the sofa as though there'd been an explosion in the pit of his stomach. "I'm not sitting here listening to this. You're not even a real police officer anymore, and I won't be insulted by an old man and a boy who knows nothing of history."

"If he knows nothing of history, it's only because you've been his teacher for the last who knows how many years."

Steadfast pulled himself up to standing, his eyes fixed on his accuser. "How dare you? You've crossed a line, Edgington. I'll be speaking to the inspector about this."

He stomped off, but Grandfather still had time for one more poke at the bear.

"1833." His voice was crisp and clear and Steadfast took the bait.

"I beg your pardon?"

"The year that Alfred Nobel was born. I believe it was 1833, not 1834."

He sputtered, "Why... Well... You're not nearly as clever as you want everyone to believe!" before storming from the room.

# CHAPTER EIGHTEEN

When we next caught sight of Dr Steadfast, he was bending Inspector Blunt's ear in the downstairs corridor. Grandfather neatly steered me in the opposite direction, ignoring the inspector's insistent calls.

"Do you think that Steadfast is our man?" he asked, once we were out in the fresh air. We'd found a shady bench under the willow trees for him to finish drinking his tea.

Continuing with my plan to think before speaking, I didn't immediately answer. I had to consider everything we'd learnt so far. "Well, he doesn't seem to have a scientific background... And he mentioned dynamite but didn't seem to connect it to the firework in Hardcastle's office. So... no?"

He took a sip, which he followed with a satisfied *ahhhh* of approval. "Very good, Christopher. I approve of your thought process. For every ridiculous conclusion you've come to today, you've made almost as many valid points. Your ratio is improving."

"Thank you, Grandfather." I had to hope he was complimenting me, though it wasn't entirely clear.

"You are right to conclude that Steadfast's anger and bluster are not signs in themselves that he's our culprit. Just as Mr Mayfield's helpful attitude and Jonathan Greeves's apparent openness do not guarantee their innocence. Not even the Crabb sisters' lengthy criminal records should be held against them when looking at evidence of a capacity to kill. All of these elements can be explained in different ways. Therefore, until we have definite proof, we must not jump to conclusions."

I dared make another comment. "But if I was going to pick one of them, I'd go with the nasty chap over the nice ones every time."

He shook his head dejectedly. "Yes, Christopher. I understand that this is a natural human instinct, but it is one we must resist as investigators in this case."

"Aren't detectives human, then?"

He considered the question. "In some ways, it would be better if we were not. Though that would present a different set of problems."

He paused what he was saying to look around the three sides of the square in front of us. A month earlier, the ground had been nothing but mud, but Mr Scuttlewell had laid a bright green lawn in time for parents' day. The beds around the quad were chock full of sweet peas, hydrangeas and bright pink phlox and I felt uplifted once more by the promise of the season ahead.

"It really doesn't feel like so long ago that I was here myself, you know." Grandfather turned to look at the dormitory block, and I wondered whether he was searching out his own window from half a century before. "Some of the teachers I had back then were savages, but the headmaster kept them under control. His name was Mr Fulton and, somehow, he made this place feel rather special."

"I'm surprised you weren't taught at home by a governess or something very Victorian like that."

He smiled, and, in that moment, I could see the young man he must have been. "I was until I was eleven. Her name was Assumpta, and she was terrifying. I used to hide under my bed because I was so scared of her. The only thing sharper than the sting on my behind when she took a belt to me was her tongue when she told my parents of any perceived slights. I was desperate to get away from her, and yet starting here was still the most frightening moment of my young life. I thought the older boys would eat me alive.

"Finally, though, it wasn't so bad. This is where I decided what I wanted to do with my life. Where I discovered art, music and literature. Where, despite so many teachers telling me what to believe and how to act, I learnt to think for myself."

He fell quiet with that vaguely elated look on his face, and I tried to make sense of what he had told me. "So you're saying... No, wait a moment. What are you saying?"

He laughed a little and looped his finger through the cup again. "I'm trying to explain that you should be thankful for the education you receive. There are still children in this country who never learn to read or write, despite all the progress that's been made. So, even if it isn't exactly what you'd like it to be, you must make the most of your school. You'll appreciate it in the long term."

He took one last sip and set the cup and saucer down on the bench beside us. I thought he'd shoot back off and criticise me for being slow, but he remained rooted to his seat. Perhaps it was the ever-rising temperature of that vibrant summer's day that had slowed us down.

We might have stayed in that happy spot until the sun set if our next witness hadn't come straight to us.

"Lord Edgington," the secretary shouted over to us when he was still several yards away. "There's something I need to talk to you about." Had our killer been lurking in the bushes at that moment, I could just imagine a shot ringing out and poor Jonathan Greeves falling to the ground with his hand to his chest. Luckily for everyone, that wasn't the way things turned out.

"What is it, man?" Grandfather injected some energy into the scene to make up for our suspect's languid delivery (and my sleepiness).

Shyly and slowly, Greeves inched his way forward and then hung beside our bench, like a coat from a hook. "I should have told you before, but I didn't know if it was the right thing to do." His every word came out in a nervous shudder. "That inspector inside has been bustling back and forth, shouting at me whenever he passes and... Well, I'll be honest, I'm rather worried that he thinks I'm..."

I was well aware that my Grandfather had little time for ditherers but, rather than telling the man to spit out whatever he had come to say, he calmed his own temper and in a soft, understanding voice, said, "You can tell me, young man. Whatever it is, you can tell me, and I'll do what I can to help." I don't know about Jonathan Greeves, but I was certainly reassured.

The trembling chap was so pale that he looked quite transparent in the daylight, and I wondered when he'd last seen the sun. "Maybe it's got nothing to do with what happened to Mr Hardcastle or maybe it changes everything, only-"

"Yes, my son?" The veteran detective had taken his sympathy a bit too far and sounded like a priest.

"I told him, you see. The day before yesterday, I told Tobias what I'd found, and he said he'd investigate the matter. If I'd thought for one moment that my actions would-"

"Get on with it, man!" Upsy-daisy, this was me.

I didn't mean to be so insistent, but he'd been warbling on for so long without getting to the point that I felt it needed saying. Grandfather looked a little surprised; perhaps I had more of his temper in me than anyone had realised.

The secretary glanced down at his hands. "There was money

missing, from the school funds I mean. Since the old bursar died last year, it was normally Mr Hardcastle who dealt with the books, but I noticed some discrepancies and inspected the situation more closely." He came to an unexpected pause then and, when he looked back at us, his eyes were wide with fear. "There are thousands of pounds missing. I really couldn't understand it."

Grandfather studied the man carefully before asking the next question. "What did Hardcastle say when you took him the news? How did he seem?"

"I went up to his office and he wasn't very happy at first. I don't know exactly why, but he was never particularly happy when I was near. I suppose you must have heard that he didn't think much of me, well it was true. I tried my best to do a good job for him-"

"Tell us about the money!" I bellowed again and immediately had to apologise. "I'm so sorry, I don't know what came over me." This was a bare-faced lie. He was quite the wettest individual I'd ever met, and it was awfully difficult to listen to him fail to get to the point time after time.

"Yes, of course, the money." He took several breaths to help himself onwards. "When I brought up the subject, Tobias's whole demeanour changed. He was suddenly very grateful. He patted me on the back and said I'd done a wonderful job."

Grandfather narrowed his eyes to make sense of this. "Did he attempt to offer an explanation?"

"Well… yes. As a matter of fact, he claimed it must be an error at the bank and that he would look into it as soon as possible. I told him that there was money missing here at school, not just in the bank, but he insisted it was nothing to worry about."

"So, why didn't you tell Blunt this?" I was struggling to make sense of Greeves's actions. "Why come to us?"

He transformed back into the jabbering wreck he'd been one minute earlier and, for the first time in my life, I thought about slapping another man about the cheeks to calm him down. Luckily, Grandfather stepped in so that I didn't have to.

"Now, now. There's no need to be agitated. We're here to help you. Just take a deep breath and answer the question."

He looked at my grandfather with a grateful grimace, then did as instructed. "I thought that the police might blame me for the money going missing. The books were kept in my office when Mr Hardcastle wasn't using them, you see, and I had access to the school bank account. I was particularly worried because, when I looked back through them, I noticed that the discrepancies only date from the time that I've been working at the school."

"You did the right thing." Grandfather stood up to put his hand on the man's shoulder. "Don't worry about Inspector Blunt, I'll talk to him if he gives you any trouble. Go back to your duties and we'll visit you later if we need to know anything more."

Greeves looked quite reassured all of a sudden. "Thank you, Lord Edgington. Thank you so much."

Grandfather's smile had a power unto itself. It unfurled like the fronds of a fern and immediately spread to the secretary. In the end, Greeves skipped off (taking the used cup and saucer along with him) as happy as a young boy on the last day of… well, you know what I mean.

"I'm sorry," Grandfather called after him. "There was one more thing I meant to ask you. You said that you didn't leave your desk all morning, but that's not true, is it?" Greeves didn't turn around but froze a few feet away from us. "You said that you'd spotted Christopher 'running into the school.' In actual fact, he crawled and, from the angle where you sit, you would not have been able to see him."

When he finally turned back to us, every muscle in his face was twitching. He was like an emotional bandalore, going up and down and back and forth, then all over the place. "I… well, I didn't mean to lie to you. I simply didn't want Mr Hardcastle to find out that I'd left my desk. You see, he told me expressly to stay where I was before he went upstairs, and I didn't want it getting back to him that I'd ignored his instructions."

"The man was dead, man!" It was Grandfather's turn to snap.

The secretary's mouse-like nerves jittered one last time. "I'd seen no proof of that and didn't want to get into any trouble." Clearly not eager to hear more accusations, he turned and cantered off.

"Another unexpected development," I said, as it's the kind of vague comment Doctor Watson might make in order for Holmes to look very clever in comparison.

"Hardly unexpected." Grandfather finally stood up from our shaded spot, using his silver cane to support him as he went. "The man's been as jumpy as a ferret since we first saw him this morning, he clearly knew more than he was letting on."

"I mean the missing money. Who do you think could have taken it?"

He half-turned then studied my face for a moment before repeating the question back to me. "Who do *you* think could have taken it?"

"Well, it's quite the conundrum." I tried to do some working out in my head, but – like history, chemistry and Latin – mathematics has never been my strongest subject. "Greeves could be involved. Perhaps he only told us about the money to distance himself from the crime."

"Yes?" He wasn't making it easy for me.

"And perhaps this is connected to whatever the Crabb sisters have been up to. It would be more their style than murder."

"Jolly good." Though there was a surface sheen of positivity to the words, he clearly wanted something more and maintained his expectant gaze as I failed to think up another name.

"And... And, well it's quite the conundrum."

He deflated a little and shook his head. "Hardcastle, Christopher. Hardcastle himself could have stolen the money. Why else would his attitude have changed so dramatically when Greeves spoke to him? It's a real possibility that Hardcastle was defrauding the school and, when his secretary discovered the discrepancy, he offered to be the man to look into the matter."

"How clever!" I let this new theory bounce around my brain for a minute. "But how is any of this related to his murder?"

He finally looked pleased with me. "That, my dear boy, is the question we must answer."

# CHAPTER NINETEEN

"One way or another, there is a sophisticated conspiracy at play here." Grandfather muttered to himself as we began our journey to... I wasn't exactly certain where. "What's not clear, as yet, is whether the various threads of criminality that have been running for some time at Oakton are connected or coincidental."

I really wanted to say something clever then to help solve this mystery. My mother has often told me that I am a pleaser. I can't help wanting to put people at ease. Awkward silences are an anathema to me, but knowing that I had nothing sensible to say, I resisted my ingrained urge to blather and kept my lips locked.

"Could a man like Tobias Hardcastle be ensnared in one of Connie and Dorie Crabb's schemes?" He paused to suggest his incredulity. "Who would have thought that such an esteemed school as this one would become a hotbed for sin and immorality? For theft, fraud and now even murder?"

I had a number of questions of my own I might well have put to him, but that wasn't my style anymore. I was so nonchalant and aloof, as we strolled in the English sunshine, that I really wasn't the slightest bit concerned over where Jonathan Greeves had been when he wasn't in his cubbyhole, the reason Mr Hardcastle had been stealing money, how the killer had planned to get away from the scene of the crime or what Dominic Rake was doing in the school.

"Each new question leads to another." He had apparently failed to notice how resolutely quiet I had remained – there's clearly no impressing some people. "But at least we have Greeves figured out a little better."

*Have we?* The old Christopher would have said, but instead I smiled and nodded.

He looked at me side on as we passed the gymnasium. "Oh, so you've worked out where he was, have you?"

Abominations! He clearly expected an answer. It would have to be vague, of course, so I went with, "Yes, I thought it was quite obvious."

He was astonished then. "Really? I was genuinely surprised. I'd never expected a fragile creature like Greeves to be involved with the

Crabbs. But I suppose it goes to show just what a manipulative pair they can be."

"Wait!" I'm afraid to say that my nonchalance deserted me. "So you're suggesting that the school secretary is in collusion with Matron and Doreen?"

"It certainly looks that way. Greeves was in a cupboard with Doreen when you entered the school." He sounded puzzled once more. "But I thought you already knew that?"

I mumbled some abstract sounds and was saved from my humiliation by Inspector Blunt, who came storming towards us with a growl in his throat and a scowl on his lips.

"Now, listen here, Edgington. I've had enough of this." His finger was pointed like a pistol, straight at my grandfather. He'd set a course to intercept us. "Every witness I come across, you've already spoken to. Every piece of evidence I find, it turns out you got there before me. I'm telling you, it ain't on."

A mask of anger passed across Grandfather's face. "If you're too slow to pick up the scent, that's got nothing to do with me."

Blunt was only feet away now and wouldn't back down. "Typical toff arrogance. I don't know what else I could have expected from a man like you."

"And I don't know why you're bothering to investigate when you already think you've got the killer."

Blunt spat on the ground to clear his throat and it landed mere inches from my grandfather's spat-top boots. I might have warned him not to spit on grandfather's spats, but the moment passed.

"Oh, and you thought I'd fall for that, did you?" Blunt tried to put his face up close to his old boss's but was far too short and ended up craning his neck. "You don't think I noticed that you barely said a word in the chemistry teacher's defence? I know your game, Edgington. You wanted me tied up with Herbert Mayfield all day, so that you'd be free to find the real killer."

"You let him go?" To say that I was surprised would be an understatement.

"Course I did. We got nothing but circumstantial evidence on 'im." Blunt's snub-nosed finger was dangerously close to the old man's chest. "Now stop changing the subject."

"I'm not changing the subject. I've done nothing wrong and, today of all days, you can't forbid me from talking to members of staff at my grandson's school."

"Stop you?" Blunt's voice rose as though he were terribly offended. "Why would I stop you? I'm saying that I want you to report to me. I'm tired of getting nowhere whenever you're around, so you might as well keep me informed of your progress." A great smile spread across the grubby officer's face and the wider it became, the more dejected my grandfather looked.

"You're suggesting that I (former Superintendent, Marquess of Edgington, Lord of Cranley Hall)…" He didn't say these last words, but I know he was thinking them. "…would report to you? As my superior officer on a murder investigation? The very idea is unthinkable." He was quaking with disbelief.

"Fine. Then why don't I clear out the school and send you packing?"

The quake subsided and Grandfather peered up at the few soft clouds above the quad. "Oh… very well. I'll tell you anything we find out, in exchange for whatever help we require."

Blunt looked less certain all of a sudden. "Um, yes. I suppose that can be arranged. What sort of *help* do you *require*?"

Taking a step back so that he no longer had to smell the man's breath, Grandfather was ready with a list. "You'll have to call my old colleague Simpkin at the Yard and tell him I need as much information as he can drag up on our various suspects. Start with Herbert Mayfield – as we should never be too hasty in ruling out a suspect – then Hardcastle himself, Mrs Hardcastle of course, Dr Steadfast, Greeves the secretary and, though I probably wrote most of their criminal file myself, he might as well take a look at Crabb and Crabb while he's at it. Very good researcher, Simpkin. He can always be relied upon."

"No doubt, your Lordship." I'd never heard a formal address used so disparagingly. "It's a pity he died six years ago, though."

"Oh, that's terrible. I'll have to send his widow some flowers." Grandfather clicked his fingers irritably but did not let his rival's arrogance dissuade him from his course. "So call his son, young Simpkin. Another good man, and he'll get to the truth if anyone can."

Blunt stood staring into space, looking more than a little stunned by the conversation.

"Come along, man." Grandfather clapped his hands twice, as though he were talking to an inefficient waiter. "Look lively. There's a murder to solve."

The old man turned and shot off in the other direction before Blunt could utter a reply. We were already thirty feet away by the time he found his words.

"I don't think you grasped what I meant when I said you'd be reporting to me."

My own superior officer emitted a quiet laugh once we were out of earshot. "Well, that perked me up again. I can tell you. Do you understand now why I didn't do anything to stop him taking your teacher away?" He was all smiles once more.

I considered lying, but my father always said that lying is a sin and sinners will be punished in the eternal fires of hell. And besides, I'd already got caught once that day. I daren't have risked it again. "No. No, I have no idea why you didn't stick up for poor Herbie. I've been wondering about it ever since it happened and could hardly bring myself to forgive you."

If anything, this made him more gleeful. "I thought as much. You really must learn to hide your feelings better, Chrissy. I can read you like a single word on a piece of plain paper."

This did nothing to improve my mood. "Are you at least going to explain?"

"I did it to protect him. I knew that if I raged and shouted in an attempt to make Blunt see sense, he'd become more convinced that Mr Mayfield was to blame. Our only hope was to do nothing, and I have to say that it worked better than I had predicted. With young Simpkin of the Yard looking into our suspects, we might just as well go back to the picnic and have one of cook's pork pies."

This made me feel a great deal better. "Is that where we're going then?"

His smile vanished. "No, of course not. There is someone I need to speak to who I didn't feel we could inconvenience without Blunt's approval."

I racked my brains for who this might be. "My games teacher, Mr Bath?"

"No, Christopher. Not Mr Bath. Think again."

114

# CHAPTER TWENTY

The Hardcastles' cottage was only accessible through a wooded path behind the games hut. Delilah spotted her master from the picnic and ran to join us. She leapt after butterflies and darted in and out of the trees on our way to the clearing where the house sat. It was quite the most picturesque area in the school grounds and far more comfortable than the run of terraced cottages which the other teachers occupied on the far side of the field.

The building itself was as pretty as any gingerbread house, with a barley twist chimney, flowers creeping up the walls and a pair of blue (or possibly coal, great or crested) tits cheerfully hopping about the garden. A neat yellow fence divided the property from common land and the whole place was bordered by trees, as though they had sprouted up there in reverence.

A police officer was on duty and nodded to us cordially as we arrived. There was no bell to ring, so Grandfather walked straight through the gate and along the stepping-stone path to the front door. He paused before knocking and we caught the sound of tears from inside.

"Come in," was the weak response when it arrived, and my companion turned the handle to discover that the door was unlocked.

We entered through a narrow hallway, where long rows of muddy boots and pretty heeled sandals were lined up. There was a selection of men's shoes too, and I realised how sad a task it must be for a widow to have to sort through her husband's possessions. Tasteful watercolours hung on the walls, and there was a bouquet of campanula in a vase on the side table to put the perfect finish on that hospitable space.

"I'm sorry to interrupt you, madam," my grandfather called out cautiously. "I'm afraid that I must speak to you about your husband."

When we reached the doorway to the sitting room, the two of us peeped inside with some hesitation. Celia Hardcastle was lying upon a cream-coloured sofa, her head on a cushion and her eyes as red as the flowers in her garden. I thought she might not even sit up to greet us, but, slowly and drowsily, she finally did.

"Come in," she said once more, as though she couldn't remember having uttered the words. "I'd offer you some tea..." She looked around the room then and I assumed her grief prevented her from carrying out even the simplest tasks.

There were tears pouring out of her, and she was the picture of despair. I don't remember too much about my grandmother's death, though I know the impact it had on my grandfather. He locked himself away from the world for a decade to mourn her passing. Sadly, this was just the beginning of Mama's own bereavement.

"You're not to worry, madam. We have recently partaken of some refreshments."

We sat down in the armchairs opposite her, and I examined the room. It was by far the smallest residence I'd ever been in. Most of my parents' friends lived in manors and abbeys, which made the Hardcastles' cottage look like a doll's house in comparison. And yet, I would have given up the grandeur of Cranley Hall, and the comforts of my own house at Kilston Down, to dwell in that perfectly welcoming environment.

The room we occupied was as elegant as its lady owner. It was much like being in a meadow, with the flowers from the garden stretching over onto the floral curtains, wallpaper, and neatly displayed crockery. I could smell them too. The whole place was filled with notes of the summertime; roses, lavender and a definite scent of freshly cut lemons. The furniture was practical, yet somehow chic, and the place was spotless.

I noticed framed photos on a dresser in the corner, with pictures of the formerly happy couple together. There was one of Hardcastle and Mama on their wedding day, in which he already looked several decades older than her. Another frame held a photo of them during the war, working together in whatever civilian role they had fulfilled. There was a snapshot of Mama on her own in front of a university and, the picture that really caught my attention, Tobias Hardcastle in army uniform from the turn of the century. It made me wonder why he hadn't been drafted to the a service battalion when the time came.

"As I said, Madam," my grandfather began in a sensitive tone. "I would not wish to disturb you at this time, but there is no one else at the school who can offer me sufficient insight, not just into your husband, but the world in which he lived."

Though she made no sound, two steady streams of tears were

flowing from her, and I wasn't convinced she'd have the strength to answer his questions.

"Perhaps you could start by telling us how you met?" he prompted.

This seemed to jog some happy memory in poor Celia as she lurched up to standing and went to seize a clutch of the photographs. "It was during the war." There was a jauntiness to her voice that I hadn't been expecting, though it came with the promise of more tears. "Tobias was my boss on a factory line." She laughed dejectedly. "Well, that's what we tell people, but I was no canary. I'd studied at Oxford, you see, and was afforded a job in a nice cosy office. Despite the horrors that so many girls went through in the munition factories, and all that suffering on the continent, it was rather a jolly time for us."

She poked the photo of a factory under our noses and stood waiting to move onto the next stage in her life.

"You worked at Royal Arsenal?" Grandfather enquired.

"That's right. It was a buzz of activity. Lots of young girls out on their own for the first time in their lives. The feeling was unique." Her smile was like a flickering candle that looked as though it might extinguish in any passing breeze. Even through this burst of cheer, her eyes never dried. "Tobias rather swept me off my feet. He was not a young man and had lost his first wife before the war, but he was simply charming. I think the other girls were rather jealous that the boss had taken a shine to me."

"Did you study chemistry at university too?"

She shook her head. "Gosh no. Toby was the chemist. I studied ancient languages."

"What was Mr Hardcastle's job during the war?" I asked, as though I knew what the point of this conversation was.

"Tobias oversaw experimental research. He had a team of girls and the odd non-conscript, but we were mainly dealing with paperwork rather than anything dangerous. He'd studied chemistry at university and so he was needed here more than at the front. I believe he was quite the whiz." With a proud look on her face, she slotted the next photograph into my hand. "We were married before the war was over."

"You look so pretty," I said and immediately wished I wasn't an idiot as she burst out crying and had to sit back down. "I'm sorry, Ma... I'm sorry, Mrs Hardcastle. I didn't mean to upset you."

She raised one hand to wave away the apology, and then Grandfather had a more sensible response for her.

"This must be very trying for you, madam. But I'm afraid we must know more about your poor husband. When did you come here to Oakton? Who did he get on with?"

She took a whole minute before replying, staring down at the swirls on the burgundy carpet, with her hand to her mouth to compose herself. "We arrived here in 1921. The old headmaster had reached eighty and the parents gave him the boot. Tobias had been a deputy headmaster in a school in London until then, and this suited us better. We had hoped to have children of our own and that living in the countryside would have been…"

It was another sentence she couldn't finish and so she shook her head, tutted to herself and moved on to Grandfather's next question. "My husband had a strong character, but I believe the rest of the staff admired him. Mr Arthurs and Mr Balustrade in particular enjoyed his company. The three of them took tea together after lessons and seemed to have a similar outlook on life." I couldn't disagree with her on this point. All three of them were hard-hearted disciplinarians. I didn't feel she needed to hear this though.

"For him to be murdered in such a fashion, things at Oakton can't have been perfect." Grandfather sounded as though he were pleading with her for some vital clue.

She looked out despondently through the leaded windows. "No. Life is never perfect. Tobias had all sorts of confrontations with the boys, as you both know. And there was the odd parent who- Well, I'm sure you're aware how demanding parents can be of their children." She stopped for a moment. "And we had our own problems to deal with. I admit that Toby and I argued sometimes, but I loved him with every ounce of my being. No matter what petty issue we fought over, we never went long without putting things right."

Her emotion came in waves. One moment she found some joyful memory to concentrate on and the next her face was disfigured with sorrow. But she cried throughout, her bloodshot eyes sending two constant streams to splash down over her cheeks.

I could see that Grandfather was becoming impatient with her cautious manner. I was rather worried his temper would catch alight, so I spoke on his behalf.

"Then what of Herbie?" My words seemed to hang in the very air.

The question had surprised her, though, when she answered, she was calm. "He's a sad case, but I don't think he would have harmed my Toby."

"Did he ever confess his feelings to you?" Grandfather showed both his palms as though to reassure her.

She attempted a conflicted smile. "Not in so many words, but his intentions were clear. You see, when Mr Mayfield arrived, I made the mistake of being a little too welcoming. He was quite the loneliest young man I'd met, and I felt it was my duty to take him under my wing. Tobias encouraged it even, but I should have drawn a firmer line."

"He told us as much." Grandfather took pity on her then. "But we can little control the whims of God and men. You must not take such blame upon yourself."

The comfortable room fell silent, and I caught the sound of blackbirds chirping away in the garden. Well, they might have been something far more interesting – perhaps a fieldfare or ring ouzel, of the type I'd seen in my book – though they were probably just blackbirds.

When it was clear that Celia Hardcastle would offer nothing more, Grandfather set off on another line of exploration. "There is something that has been puzzling me, and I'm eager to know whether you were aware of it." Much like a blackbird in fact, his head twitched curiously as he spoke. "I have detected an unusual plague of lawlessness at this school, which I would never have expected at such an institution."

Mama clenched her knees together and dried the corner of her eyes with the back of one hand. "Really? I've always found boys' schools to be absolute dens of iniquity."

His tone hardened once more. "I'm not talking about the pupils, madam."

"Neither am I. In the last school where Tobias worked, the headmaster had to be rescued by their head boy when he got into a fight in a tavern. The matron was having an affair with the caretaker behind her husband the rector's back and the cook in the school canteen was eventually arrested for trying to poison the matron who was engaged to the caretaker. As long as the parents knew nothing about it though, no one seemed particularly worried. It was another reason that Tobias wished to find a school in the country. He'd hoped it would be a more innocent environment for us to start a family."

"That's fascinating!" Grandfather exclaimed, and Mrs Hardcastle looked pleased to be of assistance.

"Oh, yes. Teachers today are prone to lascivious existences – just as actors possessed such fame in centuries past." I noticed that sophisticated tone to her voice once more and considered that her role as headmaster's wife would have offered few opportunities to make use of her education and abilities.

"Truly fascinating," the old man repeated. "And what of Oakton, then? What of the staff here? Even if Tobias wasn't involved in any way, there might still be a connection to his death."

She had rediscovered some of the composure she'd been lacking, though her cheeks still glistened in the light. "Oh, I shouldn't think so. Everything I've heard about the place has been fairly low key compared to many schools. I very much doubt that a few drunken staff parties or the odd disagreement would have led to murder."

*Drunken staff parties*; her words reminded me of the rumours that had gone around school. I was about to point this out when Grandfather begged her to continue.

"Please, madam," he spoke slowly and softly, his eyes never leaving our witness. "Anything you can think of might turn out to be useful."

She paused, her lip trembling as she answered. "No. I'm sorry, but I'm not the person to talk to about such things. I lived quite the sheltered existence here. I was happy in our cottage, and Tobias rarely mixed socially with the other staff. There are people here who can tell you everything that went on, but I simply don't know the details."

Grandfather shook his head, and I had to wonder what ideas were coursing through it. I imagined that fabled space to be something like a storm of regular brilliant flashes and big booming noises. With suspicions firing off every few seconds, and the odd accusation shooting out of it, his mind was a place to marvel at, but not to visit.

He angled his head again to talk to her and it occurred to me that he was playing the part of the kindly old man. He had hunched his shoulders and sat a little lower in his chair than he usually did. A smile crossed my lips as I realised why.

"Then I'll move on to the final topic on my list. Theft." He pronounced this last word crisply, but Mama did not seem intimidated and repeated it back to him.

"Theft? Why, who's been stealing?"

Grandfather examined her expression. He moved forward a little, as though his eyes were weak and he needed to refocus. "I have reason to believe that your husband was taking money from the school coffers."

I don't know what he inferred from the hesitant reply she provided, but it seemed genuine to me. She didn't try to deny the accusation, or make an issue of her ignorance. She gave a direct answer. "That... That doesn't sound right. Tobias was no thief, and he loved this school. Whoever gave you your information must have his own motives."

There was a hint of anger in her voice. My mother once explained that women aren't commonly allowed to show their feelings – that men would prefer them to remain mild and meek and speak when spoken to. Personally, I think it was only right that Mrs Hardcastle should show her distaste at the insinuations being flung about over her dead husband's honesty.

"Then tell me who would lie about him and why?" The edge in his voice matched her own. "Tell me who wanted to kill him."

There was no reply. She could only lock her muscles – her bare feet crossed over at the ankles, her fingers curled into balls – and wait for Grandfather's next demand.

"Please, madam. Politeness and prevarication will not help me find the man who murdered your husband. You must tell me what you know."

This time, the emotion flowed out of her in deep, trembling sobs. She attempted to dry her eyes with her handkerchief, but this made the tears come faster.

"How can I? You must know that I wish justice for Tobias more than anything else on earth, but how can I incriminate his friends? The people we've lived among for the last four years?"

Grandfather glanced at me then. I wondered if he was checking whether I was able to follow what was happening. I can't honestly say that I could, but it was awfully entertaining nonetheless.

His eyes were like magnets and clicked back onto her. "Because I think there's something you know which could help find the killer, and I think you're afraid to tell me."

I could see that she longed to look away – to extricate herself from his gaze – but it was no good. "I don't know who killed my husband. If I did, I would say. If I did, I would be shouting it to the heavens. All I know is that there are people at this school who've done things that they're not proud of, but I won't be the one to get them into trouble."

# CHAPTER TWENTY-ONE

"You mustn't be too hard on her, Grandfather. You more than anyone should know what she's endured today. She's lost her husband in the most horrific manner imaginable."

We were marching back through the woods with Delilah bounding along at our side. The noise of the picnic travelled over to us as beams of sunlight broke the foliage like arrows through a murder hole.

"It's not a question of sympathy. I can sympathise with her and still find her behaviour idiotic." My Grandfather was not a man to mince his words. "And you more than anyone should know that!"

Delilah could tell from the tone of her master's voice that he was in a bad mood and rubbed up against me to commiserate. She was an awfully loyal and perceptive dog, and I was glad to have her with me when things weren't going Grandfather's way.

I offered no response and he eventually spoke again. "I'm sorry, my boy. I really am. It's just that I can see that Celia Hardcastle is protecting someone, but I don't know who or why and couldn't find the key to getting it out of her."

I stopped walking and felt rather wonderful to have picked up on a detail that he had overlooked. "Actually, Grandfather, I might have an inkling of what she knows."

He turned back and his face was illuminated by a beam of sunlight which had found a route through the dense foliage. "Go on."

"The parties, Grandfather. It's not just Mrs Hardcastle who's heard of them. There were rumours you see. Derek McGeorge was told by Evelyn Peters who swears that George Tapsfield-"

"Yes, yes, Christopher," he interrupted. "Perhaps you could get to the point."

Even this didn't put me off, and I raced to explain. "The point is that Prasad Makwana – the nice Indian chap who started at Oakton last September – is certain that he heard music and singing coming from the dining hall one night when he sneaked outside."

He didn't move for several seconds, but held me in his vision. "This is very interesting."

"I know it is," I replied, a little too confidently. "Makwana says that there was a band playing and that it sounded like a whole crowd of people were there. He would have gone to investigate, but the caretaker was prowling the quad and so he whizzed back inside."

The old man let out an exhausted sigh and clicked his fingers through the air to express his frustration. "It could still be nothing, but I should have picked up on it. I'm really not myself today. I think it's being back in this place."

"You mean, it's not the murder that's unsettled you?" I asked, perhaps a little too naively.

We arrived at the field and he came to a grinding halt. Delilah sat down in front of us to listen to what he had to say – or perhaps she was hoping he'd throw a stick for her.

"Yes, that too, of course." He ran one nervous hand back through his silver-grey, shoulder-length hair. "You know, I've seen the evil that humans are capable of a thousand times over in my life and I still can't fathom what could drive a man to kill. Spite, selfishness, stupidity, they're all explanations, but not true reasons." His words faded out and he stood there in his long coat, as though unaware of the soaring temperature.

I didn't break his concentration but watched as he studied the scene in front of him. My Grandfather always had quick eyes that darted about as though infinitely searching for something. His whole existence had been an exercise in trying to understand human avarice, and yet he still hadn't reached a conclusion.

"Perhaps I'm a fool to try. Perhaps some irate parent slipped in when Greeves was off helping Doreen and we'll never know why Hardcastle was murdered. Perhaps the killer is out there sipping champagne cocktails with his family and I haven't a hope of finding him."

His tone was so despondent that I had to try something to cheer him up. I did the only thing I could think of to distract him at such a moment; I asked a silly question.

"I've been wondering about that. How could Greeves have seen me coming into the school if he was with Doreen in the cupboard?"

It gave him the perfect opportunity to send one of his knowing looks in my direction. His left eyebrow had risen to meet his hairline, and the right-hand side of his mouth curled down. "Honestly, Christopher, you do say the most ridiculous things. Greeves evidently poked his head out of the cupboard to see you." He let out a quiet tut and then, in a much softer voice, added, "But I appreciate your companionship, nonetheless."

I'd put a smile back on his face and he'd put one on mine. Delilah practically always appeared to be smiling, so she let out a woof to make sure we knew how happy she was. It was time to make our next move when Blunt's voice came through the Marconi speaker system. "Dominic Rake, Herbert Mayfield, Dr Steadfast and Doreen…" He'd clearly forgotten her surname. "…the dinner lady, should report to the school immediately." There was a screeching noise as he knocked the microphone and then fussed about trying to make it right. "Infernal thing, why can't technology be simple?" With one last crackle, the channel went dead.

"What's the man up to now?" Grandfather was about to set off to find out, when we were joined by a small procession.

Mother arrived first. "I thought this was supposed to be our day together as a family? I've hardly seen the pair of you."

Her father paused to deliver words of comfort. "My apologies, Violet. We've been rather busy."

"I have no doubt. But I'm not Delilah!" Our dog looked a little put out by Mother's comment. "I'm tired of waiting around, so I'm coming to investigate with you."

"Oh, that sounds like quite the lark," Horatio Adelaide exclaimed as he stumbled over. "Count me in."

Grandfather wasn't amused. "Ridiculous. The art of detection is a serious business, not a casual pastime. This is not a scavenger hunt and, besides… I work alone." There was a caveat to this statement. "With my grandson." Delilah let out an indignant woof. "And my trusty canine companion."

He turned on his heel just as Marmalade arrived to coerce Horatio back to the blanket. "How about a spot more lunch, eh, Father? To tamp down all that champagne?"

The tipsy chap's anger ignited. "Don't talk to me like I'm a child, boy. I don't need to eat anything." His eyes were swimming about in their sockets, and it was clear that he was approximately twenty-three sheets to the wind. Heads were beginning to turn, and even Grandfather had stopped to observe him. "Look at them, staring like

I'm on the stage. They're happy enough to take my money when they come begging."

This caught the old man's attention. "How do you mean?"

Adelaide's hazy gaze just about managed to pick out the speaker. "Oh, hello, Lord Edgington. What a lovely surprise to see you here." The thickset character, who I had found utterly terrifying on our first encounter, looked really rather silly then. He was swaying on the balls of his feet as though he were about to start dancing.

"The money, Horatio," Grandfather moved closer to urge him. "Tell me about the money you donated to the school."

A bored expression passed across his face. "Oh, that. It was old Hardcastle. He telephoned to beg me for some change. I gave him two thousand pounds for a new building they've planned. There was mention of them naming it after me, but I'm not one for showing off."

"When was this?"

His head wobbled on its axis and his son rushed in to prevent him from falling over. "Yesterday, I think. But then I'm uncertain what day today is. So…" He shrugged and gave up on this thought altogether.

"Thank you, Adelaide." This revelation had given Grandfather a burst of positivity. "You've been most insightful."

Marmalade wordlessly tugged his father back towards the lake. As they got closer to the other families, Horatio had one last pronouncement to make. "My money was good enough for you then, wasn't it? And you call me a scoundrel!"

To cover the scene, Mr Bath – who appeared to be the last member of staff not implicated in a murder investigation or dead – called the lower school choir on to the stage. They began singing 'Jerusalem'. They weren't particularly good, but they were particularly loud, and made up in volume what they lacked in musicality. The three Williams were supposed to be performing Desdemona's death scene from 'Othello', though perhaps, given the circumstances, such blood-thirsty theatrics would be postponed.

Grandfather hadn't moved a muscle and stood with his eyes fixed on the ground, working through some complicated theorem.

"I'm beginning to see a pattern!" He finally turned to leave and Mother, Delilah and I chased after him like good little puppies.

Dressed in her usual elegant manner – in a pale-yellow dress with a neat lace trim – Mother did not look like an archetypical detective. But then, who am I to comment? I was still wearing the shorts and jersey from my running kit, which I now noticed had several stains on. I think I must have spilt Cook's minestrone soup without realising.

"Is this all to do with money?" My astute mother enquired. "Was the headmaster murdered to access school funds?"

We'd caught up with the ex-superintendent by now, but his eyes stayed dead ahead. "It's becoming a genuine possibility. We know there were discrepancies in the accounts and that Hardcastle was alerted to this the day before he died. We also know that he almost murdered Marmaduke and young Christopher as a result of his bad mood."

My mother was horrified. "What do you mean he almost murdered them? Chrissy, are you all right?"

I winced, remembering what we'd been through the night before, but Grandfather had a less sensitive reply for her. "Why worry about an unrealised crime, when we have a real one to solve? The boys were fine, but it speaks to the man's temperament that he would have threatened two children in his care with a cricket bat."

"A cricket bat!" My poor mother. Her voice went so high that I doubted a man of Grandfather's age would have the capacity to hear it.

He certainly made no sign that he had. "What I must discover is why Hardcastle would have needed so much money in the first place. Why rob a school when it was already providing him with a good living?"

This problem appeared to occupy him all the way back to the school. I took advantage of this brief silence, to inform my mother of everything we'd discovered up until then. She made the appropriate horrified responses, but mainly seemed grateful that nobody had bludgeoned her little boy with a piece of sporting apparatus.

We found Inspector Blunt inside the school assembly hall with only two of the suspects.

"What's going on here, Blunt?" There seemed to be an unspoken agreement between my grandfather and his rival to begin every conversation with a disgruntled question. "You're disrupting my investigation."

"Eh!" the officer replied, standing on the stage in front of Mr Hardcastle's lectern. "This is my investigation and you'd do well to remember that."

That abandoned pup Jonathan Greeves was positioned alongside him. I had to wonder whether the man had latched onto the inspector to make up for the loss of his old master. Doreen was sitting in the front row where we boys would normally have been. Her pinafore was covered in grubby handprints and the scent of her kitchen wafted over to us.

"I called everybody here to get something straight." Blunt stepped to the front of the stage and paraded back and forth like an unkempt soldier.

"Well, you haven't done a very good job of it. Half your suspects are missing." My grandfather was the king of the dry retort and his caustic tone instantly fired Blunt up.

"You watch your mouth, Edgington, or I'll have a mind to-"

"I'm sorry I'm late, Inspector Blunt," my chemistry teacher came hurrying into the hall to interrupt. "I was sorting through my possessions in my house and got trapped behind a wall of boxes. I came as quickly as I could."

"Not to worry. You're here now." I suppose this is what passed for charm coming from Blunt, but he shook his head disapprovingly. "Has anyone seen Steadfast? And that boy, what's his name? Rake? I've been trying to talk to him since I got here and he's always wherever I'm not."

Grandfather let out a huff of laughter. "Imagine someone not wanting to talk to you, Isambard. The very idea is absurd."

"I said, watch it, Edgy!"

Grandfather looked horrified that someone would condescend to shorten the historic name of the house of Edgington.

Luckily, my mother was on hand to cool hot heads. "Gentlemen, this is getting us nowhere. Inspector Blunt, you called us here for a reason."

"Thank you, madam. And, may I say, that it is always a pleasure to be in your presence." I think I preferred it when he was being rude. "You speak more sense than the rest of us combined. I did indeed call the suspects here to explain something."

He paused then and looked around the incomplete group. Doreen Crabb was finally paying attention and peered up at the stage as she attempted to pull a long black hair from her chin. Herbie looked rather nervous again, perhaps worried that the inspector had changed his mind and would be locking him up for murder after all. This was nothing compared to Greeves though, who was unable to stand still anymore and was vibrating like a doorbell.

"What I called you here to say was that all evidence suggests that one of you is the killer." He'd evidently spotted my grandfather raising his hand in correction and rushed to follow this statement up with, "Only I can't 'cos two of our suspects have failed to turn up."

I was surprised to see that Doreen was the first to react. "I've never killed nobody in my life. Threatened 'em from time to time, and I broke my fella's thumb a while back when he were saucy with me, but I've never killed nobody. It's more hassle than it's worth."

"I'm not sure that your argument would do much to persuade a judge, Dorie," Grandfather chipped in.

Doreen suddenly became more polite as she replied to him. "Oh, hello, Lord Edgington, sir. Awfully nice to see you and I'm so glad you're still alive (at your age)." Not being the most tactful human on earth, she actually said these last three words.

"Can we have a bit of decorum, please?" With his tetchy manner and quick evasive gaze, Blunt was not the man to hold a crowd's attention. "The point is…"

"Oh, I was hoping you'd come to that eventually." Grandfather was positively juvenile as he grinned across at his former colleague.

"The point is…"

It was Jonathan Greeves's turn to react. He collapsed into a chair and put his head in his hands to breathe out long, heavy breaths. "This can't be happening, this can't be happening," he began, then said it once more for luck. "This can't be happening. I'm just the type that juries love to convict. I'm going to hang for this, I know I am, but I didn't do it."

"Pull yourself together, man." This note of reprimand came, somewhat unexpectedly, from Mr Mayfield. "We're all in the same boat and panicking won't get us out of it."

It was at this moment that the hall descended into chaos. The three suspects shouted across at one another as Blunt failed to calm them down. The situation was only exacerbated when Doreen jumped to her gargantuan feet and thudded towards the stage. Grandfather looked on without commenting. He was visibly enjoying the ruckus.

"Would everybody stop acting like children?" The room fell silent and all eyes turned to my mother. She was quite imposing, standing with her hands on her hips and a look upon her face which showed she was not to be trifled with. "That's better." As the various offending parties adopted guilty expressions, Violet Prentiss took to the stage. "This is getting us nowhere. Instead of everyone talking over one another, Inspector Blunt will interview you separately in order to find the murderer of Oakton Academy's beloved headmaster."

It was my turn to laugh inappropriately and my turn to receive a reproachful look. "By which I mean to say, yes, Mother. That's a terribly good idea."

Even Blunt looked repentant, as he addressed the fine lady he was standing beside. "Indeed, madam. Now, does anyone have anything important they'd like to tell me?"

The silence remained.

"No? Nothing?" His eyes rolled up to the ceiling and back down. "Well, there's a surprise."

"I'm sorry to interrupt, Blunt, but this is getting us nowhere." Grandfather strutted across the hall to lay one hand on the dinner lady's filthy sleeve. His fingers barely reached halfway around her impressively muscular arm. "Doreen Crabb, it's time we had a conversation."

# CHAPTER TWENTY-TWO

We huddled together in the lower school art studio. Poorly daubed pictures of dogs and castles papered the walls and there was the distinct smell of turpentine in the air. As we'd entered the room, Grandfather had taken in the exhibition with a triumphant smile on his lips, no doubt considering his own artistic interpretation of a poppy-filled meadow a grand success in comparison.

"Don't know nothing about it." This was the seventh time the dinner lady had used the response.

"You don't know your sister?" He sounded unconvinced. "And what about Mr Hardcastle? Did you know him?"

"Don't know nothing about it."

My mother decided to ask a question. "But you do know that he's dead, don't you?" Doreen seemed to accept this, so she continued. "We only wish to discover the truth. No one's trying to shift the blame." She had a natural tenderness to her that my grandfather had to work hard to achieve.

Doreen cocked her head to one side to size her up. "Is this your daughter, Mr Lord Edgington, sir?" She possessed the same deference towards my grandfather that her sister had shown. "She's like a smaller, prettier version of you."

The famous detective softened his tone. "That's right, Dorie. This is my daughter, Violet. Now, why don't you answer her question?"

Sitting up on the teacher's desk, with her legs swinging over the edge, her grim expression returned. "I don't know nothing about no question. What question?"

My mother's porcelain cheeks rounded before she spoke. "I asked whether you'd heard that the headmaster had died."

"Might have." There was something about her that reminded me of a nine-year-old boy. She was moody, secretive and quite contrary. "But I never had nothing to do with him being poisoned."

"He wasn't poisoned," Grandfather was quick to point out, his tone scalpel sharp. "He was killed with a... He was bludgeoned to death."

Doreen bobbed from side to side quite cheerfully. "There you go then, don't know nothing about it. And, even if I did know, I wasn't

131

doing nothing criminal here. I'm just the dinner lady. Ask little Prentiss, he's eaten plenty of my food."

I had to shudder at the memory of some of her greyer offerings. Her pease porridge, Windsor soup, rolled oats and lamb stew were barely distinguishable.

I supported her story in as honest a manner as possible. "I can confirm that she has produced 'food' during her time working at the school."

This seemed to perk her up. "There you go. I am the Oakton Academy dinner lady and I 'produce food'."

Grandfather was a few feet away from her and now made a point of standing at his full height. "You can trust me, Dorie, you know that-"

"No," was the answer that came back to him, and I thought that would be the end of it. "I want the pretty lady to ask me questions. I like the pretty lady." She shot a dreamy smile towards my mother, who was positioned on a low seat between my grandfather and me.

My dear mummy looked rather vindicated just then. "Of course, Doreen. So why don't you tell us anything that has occurred here at the school which could shed a light on Tobias Hardcastle's death?"

"Yes, Miss. Course, Miss." Doreen cleared her throat. "Oakton is a pit of loose morals and criminality. My time in Holloway Prison was less shocking than the years I've been working here. The teachers are all raging alcoholics, and the kids aren't much better. I've seen wild abandon, drunken brawls and even a mugging – though admittedly, my sister was behind it. Oh, and a few weeks ago, Balustrade the Latin teacher got knocked over the head with a wine bottle."

"And was your sister behind that too?" Mother was quick to enquire.

"No, course not... that was me. But he had it coming. He was always trying it on at the parties they threw."

"Jolly good, Doreen, this is what we need to know." Grandfather poked his thumbs into his waistcoat pockets and looked a little more relaxed.

Mother clearly did not appreciate the interruption. "Did Mr Hardcastle know what the other teachers were getting up to?"

The ex-convict turned dinner lady glanced about before answering. "No, not old Hardy. He thought this place was as pure and innocent as a seminary. He didn't like no one having booze around here. Liked to say he was a good Christian man, but he treated that wife of his no better than chattel and I don't reckon that's very Christian like, is it?"

My mother, who could never resist a good cause, immediately looked concerned. "Do you mean he hit her?"

"Nah, nothing like that. But he made her wait on him hand and foot. Only time I ever saw her was when she were running about the place doing his shopping, or helping clean the school so they didn't have to pay the cleaner."

Our not particularly seasoned, but very capable inquisitor continued. "You mentioned lawlessness. What exactly did you see?"

After another quick check for spies, she ducked her head and whispered, "Gambling, fighting, gambling on fighting, you know the sort of thing. Late nights in The Oakton Canteen are a real knees-up. All sorts of folks come by. Not just the teachers, but locals too. It's rotten good fun." She had veered off track by some margin and sat smiling at the ceiling.

Grandfather looked at me and I knew it was my turn for a question. "Who organised these parties?"

Doreen looked shifty then. Well, shiftier. "I wasn't involved with that side of things. But they didn't have nothing to do with murder or nothing like that. They was just a bit of fun. Nothing wrong with a bit of fun, is there?"

From painting Oakton as one of the seven circles of hell, she had suddenly warmed to the place. My mother determined something that I was too slow to spot.

"But if you weren't involved in organising the parties, and you don't know anything about Mr Hardcastle's death, how can you be certain that the two things aren't connected?"

Doreen's face dropped. She was now a nine-year-old who'd just been caught lying. "Well... I don't think... Them's never the way..." she mumbled without finishing any of her sentences.

"Was your sister responsible?"

The counterfeit dinner lady would no longer make eye contact. "I don't know nothing about my sister and I don't feel comfortable talking about this particular matter, thank you, sir or madam." She reeled this statement off as though someone had made her memorise it.

"That's all right." Mother had a smile that could make orphaned kittens trust her implicitly. This isn't a metaphor; I'd seen her rescue any number of stray animals. "So perhaps we could discuss something you do feel comfortable addressing. Why not tell us what you know about the figures closest to Mr Hardcastle. Dr Steadfast, Mr Mayfield-"

"Yeah!" she interrupted. "They was both at the parties. Steadfast's got a pretty good left hook in fact."

I was more interested in the other name. "Herbie was there drinking and gambling?" It certainly didn't sound like my chemistry teacher.

Doreen spluttered out a laugh. "Oh, yeah. Little Herbie drinks himself into a stupor. I have to carry him home every Friday night."

I could see that this lit a spark in Grandfather's head. He listened intently to what she had to say next.

"Steadfast made more of a scene, of course. Herbie normally cried in the corner while old Steady was up on his feet dancing or causing trouble."

"Were there illicit substances at these parties of yours?" I think we were all taken aback by my grandfather's sudden question.

Doreen took a moment to consider her answer and, clearly unsure of the best response, opted for her stock phrase. "I don't feel comfortable talking about this particular matter, thank you-"

"So that's a yes then," he growled once more.

"Hey, that's not fair. Connie said that, if I answered like she told me, no one would know what I was really thinking. But you always know." A thought pinged in her brain and she looked very pleased. "Are you a witch, your highness, sir?"

Grandfather couldn't resist a smile.

"What about Jonathan Greeves?" my mother continued. "Did he go to these parties?"

"I wouldn't say that exactly. I mean, I might have seen him there, but he was hardly enjoying himself."

"Then what were you doing together this afternoon, around the time that Mr Hardcastle was murdered?" It was another moment for Grandfather to cut through Doreen's bluster and shine a light on the facts of the case.

She looked to my mother for help. "I... He was helping me move something. That's it. Yes, sacks of flour in fact."

Grandfather let out an almighty tut. It was so loud that the parents on the field must have heard it. It might even have awoken Horatio

134

Adelaide from his drunken nap. "You know, I kept an eye on you and your sister when you were in prison. I felt a little guilty that you were given long sentences for such petty crimes and I tried to make sure you didn't suffer too much whilst you were in there."

The gigantic woman crashed her hand down on the desk beside her. "So?"

"So, I know that you won the prison-wide weight-lifting competition for ten out of the twelve years you were in there. You can raise a sack of flour above your head with one hand, whereas Jonathan Greeves can barely lift a loaf of bread."

"Now, perhaps you'll answer the question." Mother rose to her feet to drive her message home. She and Grandfather made an awfully good team. "Why were you and Jonathan Greeves together this afternoon?"

Throughout the interview, Doreen had been dozy and distracted but now gave us her full attention. "I don't even know no Jonathan Greeves. Who's that?"

"You just admitted you saw him at the parties," I said, because I was feeling left out. I must confess, it felt awfully good to be back on the team.

Mother repeated her original question. "What were you doing?"

"Sacks of flour." Doreen faffed and flailed with her hands to distract us.

Grandfather went for the kill. "Did Hardcastle find out about whatever scheme you've been running here? Is that why he died?"

Oakton's dinner lady jumped down from the table and pulled her mangy sleeves up her monstrous arms. "I've not got no time to sit here talking nonsense. Who's going to burn the boys' dinner if I'm not in the kitchen?"

Mother wasn't giving up. "Did your sister tell you to do something to Mr Hardcastle while she was on the field this afternoon? Did she tell you to deal with him?"

Now, Doreen clearly had no great intellect to defend herself, and was already incriminated in a number of ways, but she wasn't about to confess to murder. Looking back and forth between the three of us, she attempted one last response.

"I don't know nothing about no murder and I don't feel comfortable talking about this particular matter. Thank you, sir or madam."

# CHAPTER TWENTY-THREE

As my mother and I discussed our interpretation of the afternoon's events, my grandfather collapsed into a chair to fade out of animation. He sat completely still, and I had to keep an eye on him to check he was breathing.

I presented my theory. "Let's suppose that Matron and her sister were involved in something illegal which my puritanical headmaster found out about. Matron could have used the sports day as a cover and sent Doreen to kill Hardcastle. No one would suspect her if she was standing in front of hundreds of parents at the time."

Mother was not convinced by my logic. "In which case, what has Jonathan Greeves got to do with this?" It didn't take much to unravel my detective work.

"Well… maybe he helped somehow. Maybe he swept up the dining hall after all the drinking and gambling."

She shook her head and focused on more critical elements of the crime. "After what you told me about your interview with Mrs Hardcastle, the question we have to ask ourselves is who she's trying to protect."

I'd been wondering this for some time already, but didn't like to say it out loud. "You don't think we were wrong all along and, just maybe, Herbie isn't quite so-"

"Dominic Rake!" Grandfather returned to life to exclaim. "That's who I'd like to talk to." There was a sparkle in his eyes and he appeared to have rediscovered his confidence. "There's no point asking a Crabb sister what mischief they've been up to. I trust Steadfast about as far as I can kick him. Mr Mayfield may have been drinking at these illicit parties, but there's no reason to believe he was involved in their organisation. Greeves is clearly afraid of the sisters and won't be drawn on the matter. And so, it's young Rake we must interview."

"The prefect?" My mother sounded surprised. "But he's just a boy. What could he possibly know about any of this?"

Grandfather was already on his feet and halfway to the door by the time he spoke. "Do you know how many adolescent boys I arrested when I was working for the police, Violet? Do you know how many ended up in prison or worse for their crimes? I'm sorry to say that youth is no guarantee of innocence. Even our dear Christopher here has it in him to become a savage killer."

Mother's face turned serious before she and her father exploded in a brief fit of laughter. "Oh, Daddy. You're simply too witty sometimes."

I was rather tempted to defend myself. I considered telling them that, with a bit of training, I would make an excellent killer, thank you very much, but the conversation moved on.

"The point still stands," Grandfather said. "I remember what the prefects at this school were like. Unless things have changed since my days, Rake is the head of a spy network and would know exactly what was going on around here."

He was about to step from the room when Blunt appeared in the doorway to deliver some bad news. "We've got another one."

"Another what?" You can always count on me to ask the obvious question.

"Another body, only this one's not dead."

"What on earth are you talking about, man?"

Blunt was only too happy to have piqued my grandfather's interest. A self-satisfied grin unfurled across his lips. "One of my men just found Steadfast in his house. He's been knocked out cold, though it looks as though the killer was hoping for more."

Grandfather shot from the room. "Take me to him this instant."

Blunt clapped his hands together and beckoned for us to follow. After the humiliation he'd suffered in the school hall, he was clearly relishing the opportunity this new development presented. I was appalled by the idea of that pernickety little man solving the murder before my grandfather. And I could only imagine how the great Lord Edgington himself would have felt.

The main block of teachers' houses was behind the kitchen. The whole area smelt of mushy peas and brown soup. Perhaps there are methane-belching lava fields in some far-flung country that offer a more rancid olfactory experience, but I very much doubt it.

The staff cottages were in one long row of terrace houses, broken up into separate accommodation. Each member of staff had a small apartment, and there were the two larger residences at each end which were reserved for the senior teachers. Dr Steadfast's door was the closest to school. It had a rather neat garden in front of it, with love-in-idleness pansies and dark pink stocks arranged in pretty beds. There was not a bird in sight, however, as the place was a hub of activity. Various bluebottle police officers were buzzing about and Steadfast was lying on his back on the ground, grutching.

"I'm fine, I tell you. I'm fine. All I need is for you people to leave me alone and everything will be right with the world."

There was a channel of fresh blood dripping from a gash on his forehead, so nobody took his claim too seriously.

He was half inside the property, half out, with his legs supported by the front step and his head resting on the garden path. Not far from his feet, I noticed a heavy stone about the size of a rugby ball.

The officer who was nominally in charge looked alarmed on the injured man's behalf.

"You could be dead!" Blunt vociferated.

Grandfather stopped at the fence and took a moment to process the scene. "You should be dead, more like. Where did the bullet go?"

I was truly lost at this point and struggled to understand where a bullet came into any of this. Rather like when my maths master Mr Arthurs asked me to solve an algebraic equation, I heard a ticking sound in my head and attempted to isolate the various pieces of information that I would need to unravel the problem.

Surely it was the stone that had hit him on the head, not a bullet. Let's call that X then. So Dr Steadfast walked through the door and X fell onto his head, which, for the purpose of this exercise, we'll call D (for dome! Ha!) X descended onto D, somehow knocking Dr S backwards. So $X+D$ should have equalled minus S; though the stone clearly didn't hit him dead on and he escaped the worst of it. But that still didn't explain what a bullet had to do with anything.

The best I could strike upon was, $(X+D \neq -S) = B$? Which told me... precisely nothing.

Blunt was scratching his head, and I wondered which of us would be the first to break.

"What bullet?" Good old Inspector Blunt!

"The stone in the doorway has a rope tied around it." It came as no surprise that it was my mother who provided the answer we were looking for. "What's more, there's a small hole in the open door. Had

Dr Steadfast collapsed forwards, as the killer would have expected, the bullet would have shot straight through him."

"Excellent work, Violet!" Her father sounded jolly impressed. "As the stone fell to the ground, the rope triggered a gun within the house." He turned his attention to the not-dead man. "You're very lucky to be alive, Dr Steadfast."

He did not seem particularly enthusiastic. "Oh, am I?"

"How ever did you avoid the bullet?" My mother sounded a little awestruck.

Pushing himself up to sitting, despite the protestations of the local bobby, Dr Steadfast mumbled out an answer that was too quiet to interpret.

"I beg your pardon, sir?" It was not every day I had the chance to pull one of my teachers up on his poor diction, so I resolutely jumped at it.

"If you must know, I tripped over." He went from one extreme to the other and bellowed his response. "I heard the stone falling, the twang of a rope, and instinctively pulled backwards. I got a bash on the head and a bruised toe, but it could have been a great deal worse."

Grandfather did not reply. He was already calculating the endless possibilities for what had taken place in that attractive (though somewhat malodorous) garden. He stepped through the gate to examine the glossy red door where the rope was pulled taut. I watched as he poked his finger through the tiny hole at waist height. Steadfast was more than just lucky; the bullet should have cut him in two.

"Has anyone been inside yet?" Grandfather addressed the young bobby who was crouched at Steadfast's side with little more than a handkerchief to offer in way of first aid.

"Yes, sir. The trap has been neutralised if that's what you're worried about."

Lord Edgington nodded his thanks to the man and, somewhat gingerly, pushed the door a little wider. My mother and I followed him into a small entrance parlour. It was surprisingly well appointed, with a pair of leather armchairs beside a dark wooden coffee table. The design of the place was masculine but homely and I would never have imagined my slovenly history teacher occupying such a tasteful property.

140

There was one thing in the room that was not quite so welcoming, however, and it was pointed right at me. I couldn't help myself and jumped out of the line of fire as soon as I spotted it.

"Don't be ridiculous, boy," my grandfather was quick to pull me up on this. "It's a spring-gun; they only hold one shot. We know this one has been fired and that the police have disconnected the trigger."

He was right – not that it made me feel much safer. The rope hung down over the door, then looped around the internal handle and trailed across the floor to where it had previously been attached to the gun. The weapon itself was tied in place atop a small bureau which stood beside the opposing wall.

"A crude enough device," Grandfather began, but it was his daughter who finished the explanation.

"When the stone fell, that should have been enough to do some damage, but the killer didn't want to take any chances." I don't remember the last time I'd seen my mother so full of excitement. Her eyes positively shone as she strode about the room trying to make sense of the scene. "He set the spring-gun, tying the rope to the stone at one end and the hook of the gun at the other. When the door was opened, the stone fell, the rope pulled tight and the gun was triggered. It's a miracle he wasn't killed."

"Oh, yes. Quite the miracle," Blunt popped through the door to declare. "Providence smiled on Oberon Steadfast."

Grandfather was still examining the mechanism that was attached to the bureau. It didn't look like a gun by modern standards. It was merely a tube, a hook and a spring, all fixed together in a macabre fashion to allow a killer to ply his trade without even being present. Crude indeed, but very effective.

"Spring-guns like this one have been banned for a hundred years." Grandfather looked back at the inspector. "Where would one get hold of such a device in the twentieth century?"

Blunt grunted before responding. "I don't suppose it would be so difficult. People collect all sorts of old things these days. My Auntie Imelda likes porcelain teapots in different shapes." He smiled to himself at the thought. "But a friend of mine likes guns. Must have a hundred of the damned things. And you'd be amazed how many he's picked up at scrap yards over the years."

Though normally not one for conversation, this was clearly a topic that the inspector enjoyed. I could only wonder where his own interest in collecting lay. Ceramic pigs? Matchboxes? Human skulls?

"The caretaker," I suggested. "Spring-guns were used for killing animals. They might be illegal now, but estates like this one have all sorts of old equipment that no one ever gets rid of. I dare say we could find any number of similar devices at Cranley Hall if we looked through the gamekeeper's hut."

All three of the adults turned to stare, but it was my grandfather who was the first to congratulate me. "And that, Christopher Aloysius Prentiss, is why your help is invaluable. Every so often, you'll strike upon something I've overlooked. As soon as we finish here, we'll have to seek out your caretaker."

My mother put her hand on my shoulder and there was a moment of cheerful familiarity between the three of us, which Blunt clearly felt excluded from.

"I'll get one of the men to dust for fingerprints, but I doubt it will do much good. Who would go to all this trouble to set a trap and then leave his fingerprints all over it? It's only the really simple-minded criminals who forget to wear gloves these days." He didn't wait for a response but trundled back outside with his usual air of disgruntled impatience.

"The door must have been open," my mother pointed out once he'd gone. "For the stone to have stayed where it was, the door would have been ajar when Dr Steadfast arrived."

Grandfather's eyes were flicking about the place again, as though he were a carpenter measuring up the room for a new bookcase. "That's right. And, unless the killer climbed out through a window, he must have left through the back door."

I was rather fired up by my success and sped from the room, along a narrow corridor and all the way to a cupboard-like kitchen at the back of the house. It contained a miniature gas stove, a sink and, as expected, a back door. There was glass on the floor and the window beside the turn-latch lock was shattered.

Grandfather had arrived and let out a *hmmm*. He pushed past me to step carefully over the glass and make his way around the outside of the building, searching the path as he went. There was not a lot of space between the side of the property and the garden wall, and he soon found what he was looking for.

"There," he said, pointing at a flower with a broken stem.

"Oh, that's terrible. I believe it's an iris. Why can't people be more careful where they walk?"

My previous insightful remark was forgotten. He turned to me with a look of sheer disbelief. "Not the flower, boy, the footprint in the earth alongside it."

"Ah, I see," I blustered. "But it's still a shame for such a pretty flower to be cut down in its prime!" I tried to make it sound as though he was the one not thinking clearly.

Unsurprisingly, he rolled his eyes. "Once the ambulance arrives and the doctors have seen to your history teacher, we'll have to send them on a tour of the garden to attend to any fallen leaves or trampled blades of grass." To say that he employed a sarcastic tone at this moment would be an understatement. "The point is, boy, that, judging by its size, the boot that made this print did not belong to Dr Steadfast."

"Except, of course, we can't be sure that it was made by the killer. Or that it happened today." My mother had appeared from the front garden and was busy raising relevant points again to make me feel dim. It's terribly challenging coming from such an accomplished family. At least my brother Albert is no genius. I don't feel nearly so ignorant when he's around.

"It rained overnight," her father replied with a competitive air. "It hadn't rained for a week but, last night, between three and six in the morning, the hot weather broke and there was something of a downpour. This print, therefore, was left today. The fact that it is under a window suggests that whoever made it was looking to see whether Steadfast was at home."

It was not just pride that caused him to smile then, but his anticipation of what we might devise in response. Unlike in our first investigation, where the weight of sorrow and family responsibility had hung around his neck like the ancient mariner's albatross, Grandfather was finally able to enjoy himself.

"Yes, but that doesn't prove that it belongs to the killer." Mother stepped closer to look for any defining marks in the tread of the imprint. "It's the last day of term, so any young lad could have been here to play a joke on his history master. The postman might have called by with a package, one of the prefects could have been here to deliver a message and-"

"Touché, Violet," he conceded. "You've made your point, don't rub it in. I thought you would have learnt by now that nobody likes a braggart."

I considered pointing out that he is often only too happy to highlight his achievements, though I'm sure he would have landed upon a good excuse.

"Perhaps we should speak to Dr Steadfast again, before he forgets anything," I said, rather more diplomatically.

"Lead the way, my boy." Standing up from his examination, the old man winked at me to show there were no hard feelings. "Time and tide and history teachers wait for no man."

# CHAPTER TWENTY-FOUR

Back in the front garden, someone had fetched Dr Steadfast a chair from his dining room and he was sitting with the ruddy cloth to his head, looking dazed.

"Before you ask, I don't know anything about it," he said, with great disdain in his voice as my family and I approached. "I've already told this lot, I don't know who would have set a trap for me and, no, I don't think one of the boys would have gone to such lengths to exact revenge for poor marks."

All of his chins wobbled indignantly as he addressed me. "What do you say, Christopher? Was this Tom Geoffries getting his own back for yesterday's detention?"

I had little desire to encourage him, but I couldn't lie. "Not likely, sir. There are worse punishments than lines."

"Quite right, Prentiss. Quite right. I have never caned a boy in my career as a teacher." He delivered this speech in the manner of a battle-hardened general. "I do not believe in the slipper, the strap nor the back of my hand in an academic context. No boy in this school either loves me or despises me, which, in my opinion, is just the way it should be."

Grandfather was not won over by his proclamation. "Which doesn't change the fact that someone has gone to great lengths to murder you in your own home. And what's more, he did it in such a way as to make his involvement in the crime nearly undetectable. So, why would anyone be so desperate to do away with you?"

A couple of bluebottles had stopped to listen. Steadfast directed a grimace in their direction and they returned to their work. "My good Lord Edgington, you have uncovered yet another mystery. Who is the killer? Why was dear Tobias Hardcastle taken from us? Why did-"

"You do love the sound of your own voice, don't you?" Grandfather was quick to interrupt. "We know about the drinking club that you've been a part of in the dining hall. We know that there was money going missing from the school, and I can personally attest to the fact that at least two members of staff at this fine establishment have criminal records that date back to the Victorian age. Now, what I'd like to know is how you were involved."

My history teacher was clearly taken aback by how much we'd discovered in one short afternoon. His response, when it came, was marked with puff and rage. "What an accusation! You don't have any authority here. You're nothing more than an amateur, and yet you dare to connect Dr Oberon Steadfast – an educator with over twenty-five years of experience – with common criminals. Shame on you, sir. Shame on you!"

Even more than in our classes, he delivered every word in a theatrical baritone and gestured about the place as though he were summoning up the spirit of Major-General Stanley from 'The Pirates of Penzance'.

It was not enough to sway my grandfather's opinion.

"I wouldn't be so sanctimonious if I were you." He paused to strike fear into the chap with an iron stare. "No matter what else might happen, I can promise you now that this will be your last term working at Oakton Academy."

Steadfast bolted forward in his seat. "What on earth do you mean?"

My mother raised her hand to interject and Lord Edgington nodded his agreement. "My father means that, as soon as the other parents discover you've been fighting and gambling on school premises, you will not be welcome here any longer."

He hesitated before replying, perhaps unsure whether to overstep the rules of polite society entirely. "Then more fool the lot of you. I should be in charge of this place. I'd do a better job than Hardcastle could. Whatever has occurred over the last few years was on his watch."

Mother was not deterred. "Your time here is over, but if you've any hope of receiving a recommendation for another school, it would be in your best interest to tell us what you know."

Steadfast opened his mouth to speak but changed his mind. Instead, he crossed his arms and stared into space as though we were no longer there.

"Very well then." Grandfather gripped the garden gate but did not step through. "You clearly aren't worried about your own neck and so, once the officers have finished searching for prints, I will tell Blunt to relieve them of their duties here."

"What do you mean?" the swollen relic demanded.

Lord Edgington turned to leave but offered one last look over his shoulder. "You don't think that the killer is done with you, do you? I have no doubt he'll be back to finish the job posthaste."

Perhaps it was the loss of blood, but Dr Steadfast suddenly looked rather peaky. "I… Well, wait just one moment. Maybe it would be safer if one of the officers stayed behind, just for a short while."

Grandfather dashed away at his usual confident pace. "Our suspect may not have provided the information we require, but I feel that we gained from the exchange nonetheless." He could not help showing his pleasure at cutting down that tall poppy for the second time in a day.

The four of us followed the path along the kitchen and dining hall and soon came to a small hut on a scrappy piece of ground, out of sight of the main school. We could hear the sound of a large metal object being scraped across the floor and, as we approached the door, the craggy-faced caretaker loomed out.

He looked down at Delilah as though she were a rat or weasel. "There are no beasts allowed on school property."

Grandfather immediately sized the man up and took a step closer. "Well that's clearly not true."

"I won't be to blame if she's accidentally shot dead." He spoke with the casual cruelty he was known for. As much a resident goblin as a member of staff, we boys had learnt not to go anywhere near the chap. Delilah had the same idea and went to sit down in the shade of a broad horse chestnut.

"What's your name?" Grandfather's tone was firm and unyielding.

He spat on the ground before answering. "Scuttlewell."

"I've no doubt." There was a moment's silence, which gave the two men the chance to glare at one another. "We're here for information."

"Oh, ay?" He chewed throughout the conversation, and I could smell his tobacco from several feet away.

Dressed in a torn shirt, with poorly sewn patches and grease stains all over it, Scuttlewell had the look of a vagabond or a navvy. He did not appear intimidated by our presence there and leaned territorially against the doorframe.

"There was a trap set in one of the teachers' cottages. A man almost died and we believe the weapon could have come from here."

"I've got all sorts of tools that could kill a man." Another glob of black leaves shot to the ground. "You'll have to be more specific."

I could tell that my grandfather was taken aback by the man's hostile attitude. He was used to violent characters, and could deal with the arrogance of someone like Dr Steadfast all day long, but the Oakton school caretaker was a different breed. He clearly wasn't troubled by what we thought of him, nor wary of Lord Edgington's questions.

"A spring-gun," I decided to speak up. "A trap was set that triggered an old spring-gun of the sort gamekeepers used to employ. You know the kind. There'd be bait on the end of a hook which would trigger a bullet as soon as an animal touched it."

"I didn't hear any question there, Master Prentiss. What exactly did you want to know?" He was a wily old beast, not much younger than my grandfather in fact. Despite his prickly demeanour, there was intelligence behind his callous gaze, and I struggled to answer.

"Oh, I... Well, I was just wondering whether you possessed any such device here at school."

He looked into the gloomy hut. The structure was made of corrugated iron, which appeared to have been propped up rather than built, and might have fallen down at any given moment.

"Yep, I had one. Never used it, mind. I'm a law-abiding citizen, I am."

"So it's not here anymore?" Mother enquired.

He raised his arm to point at a spot on the wall behind him. For a moment, he reminded me of death itself, extending one bony finger towards our final destination. "It was hanging over there, but it's gone now."

"When did you notice it was missing?" Grandfather demanded with great insistence.

Scuttlewell tugged at his mutton-chop sideburn. "I'd say... Yep, I think I first realised about fifteen seconds ago."

My grandfather had no time for pedants and showed his irritation. "Very well. Then when did you last see that it was there."

He reached into his pocket to extract a small tin which he fished a dirty finger inside to pull out more tobacco. He stuffed his treasure into his cheeks and only answered the question when he was good and ready.

"You know, it's a funny thing. I don't tend to keep a record of when I see what. It was there a year ago when I tidied my shed and it's gone now. But I can't say what happened in between."

148

Grandfather's patience was nearly exhausted. "Perhaps you set the trap yourself."

Scuttlewell had started chewing in earnest and would not be distracted from his task. When his words arrived, there was no sign of fear in them. "I suppose it's possible. But, if you're trying to fit me up for these murders, I couldn't have killed Hardcastle. From what Doreen in the kitchen has been telling me, I reckon I was setting up the hurdles over on the field when someone did for him."

My illustrious grandfather clearly wasn't used to being shown so little respect, even by a suspect. "Oh, really. And can you tell me the exact time at which you left the school?"

"You know what? It's another one of those things which I don't tend to note down. But if you were after an educated guess, I'd say half-past eleven at the latest."

His reply squared with the account that our chauffeur Todd had given. As nice as it would have been to identify such a scurrilous character as our killer, even Grandfather could see that it was a futile venture and gave up.

"You've been most helpful."

Lord Edgington was about to turn away when the caretaker spoke again. "Aren't you going to ask me who I think took it, then?" His jaw hung open to place a question mark on his sentence, and I could see the black goo sloshing about on his tongue.

Grandfather made one last exasperated sigh. "All right, who do you think took it?"

His stained teeth came together, and I could count every last one of them as he smiled his crocodile smile. "What's in it for me?"

# CHAPTER TWENTY-FIVE

"A cat?" I'd rarely seen my grandfather so unnerved. "I ask you! A cat?"

I was glad that Mother was there to calm him down. I would have only said the wrong thing and upset him further. "You mustn't get worked up, Father. He's a rotten little man and there's no dealing with such people."

"Yes, but to suggest I buy him a cat in return for information. He's lucky I didn't hand him over to Blunt for obstructing an investigation." He clipped the end of the word, presumably remembering that he was no longer a serving member of the Metropolitan Police. A retired officer, no matter how many years he's served, is still a civilian by most people's definition.

"You should have given him five pounds and told him to feed up a stray." In actual fact, I'd have paid double that if it meant we could find the killer and head back to the field to watch the entertainment.

"It's not about the money, Christopher. It's the principle." He was stomping back and forth in front of the main entrance to the school, unable to relax. "Back in my day, members of the public were only too eager to assist the police. They didn't expect something in return."

I lost my concentration at this point. It's something which occurs whenever a member of my family uses the expression *in my day*.

Mother stepped in front of us to interrupt the looping conversation and ensure that he didn't mention the cat again. "Let's think rationally. Do you have any idea who he could have been referring to? Who do you think stole the spring-gun?"

"Well, I can narrow it down to approximately four people."

"That's a good start." My mother's expression lightened.

"But then there are only five suspects in the first place and the killer just tried to murder one of them." Unable to find a solution to the newest of our dilemmas, Grandfather sat down on the steps leading up to the building. Delilah took this as a sign that he needed comforting and attempted to nuzzle his face. He resisted at first, then sat there while his loyal companion tickled his beard and whiskers with her nose. I sometimes wondered whether she took him for her master or her son.

Grandfather looked close to giving up, Mother was just as disheartened, and so it was down to me to encourage them. "You're both being far too negative. There's nothing to say that Scuttlewell has got the first clue who took the gun. He's probably just trying to get a free cat. Instead of wasting our time talking in circles, we should start from the beginning and see what we actually know."

I was rather amazed that neither of them told me off for being foolish just then. To be perfectly honest, I'd have enjoyed the interruption, as I hadn't a clue where to begin. Mother, Grandfather and even our golden retriever sat looking up at me expectantly, and so I opened my mouth to see what might fall out.

"There are certain people that we can disregard for at least one of the attacks. My physical education teacher Mr Bath, for example, has been on the field all day and could not be involved in Hardcastle's murder." As no one had ever suggested the possibility of Mr Bath being the murderer, this seemed like safe ground to set off from.

Of course, my grandfather never liked things to be too easy and made his opinion known. "You're jumping ahead of yourself from the beginning, Chrissy. Bath could have been working with an accomplice. He could have set the trap for Dr Steadfast before the school day began, and he might even have paid an assassin to carry out the deeds on his behalf. We simply cannot exclude him for certain. I hoped you'd have learnt that by now." He shot to his feet. "Come along, child. That was a useful start, but I'll take over now."

He helped me down into the space where he'd been sitting and reclaimed his mantle as the expert in our mismatched band of amateur detectives. "With the attack on Dr Steadfast in his home, the possibilities of the case have not narrowed but expanded. It increases the likelihood of a team of killers working together. Or it could be a single operative who had a vendetta against both Hardcastle and the bad doctor. And we must not overlook the very real chance that Steadfast knows something that the killer would do anything to keep a secret."

"I was just about to say that very thing!" I sounded like a crow with its wings tangled.

Grandfather looked down critically. "I'm happy your skills of deduction are improving, Christopher. But nobody likes a braggart." I bit my tongue, and he continued. "Ultimately though, this second attack should not distract us from the facts of the case. Though the trap in Steadfast's cottage could have been set at any time today, there are still only five people who had the opportunity to murder the headmaster. He was alive at ten minutes past twelve but dead some fifteen minutes later when Christopher invaded the staff corridor."

This was the most significant detail for my mother. "You did what, Christopher?" She lovingly slapped me round the back of the head. "I can't quite believe that a son of mine would do anything so imprudent. Wait until your father hears about this."

I let out a feeble laugh and wished that Grandfather would get back to dissecting the evidence.

"Whilst we know that Jonathan Greeves was away from his desk and, in theory, anyone could have walked in, it's also true that Christopher was spotted as he climbed the stairs and that Dr Steadfast himself left the building shortly before. What we don't know is why Greeves and Doreen Crabb were together, and whether they could have sneaked upstairs to Mr Hardcastle's office. Nor can we say what Mr Herbert Mayfield was doing between the time he was called back to the school and my arrival there just before one o'clock."

"But you've acted from the beginning as though the idea of his involvement was implausible," Mother pointed out, and I had to feel bad for poor Herbie that we were even considering that lovely chap as a suspect.

Grandfather had come to a stop but, with this puzzle presented to him, took the opportunity to resume his slow pacing. "That is correct. Though we cannot rule him out entirely, my instinct tells me that the man would be quite insane to implicate himself in the murder in such a manner. It's one thing to plant evidence in order to confuse the crime scene, but the bubbling mixture of chemicals was practically a visual confession. So what does that tell us?"

I put my hand up, as I'd forgotten that this wasn't a lesson.

It wasn't a problem, as my grandfather had forgotten he wasn't a teacher. "Yes, Christopher?"

"It tells us that someone was trying to frame Mr Mayfield as the obvious culprit."

He pointed first to me and then to his impressive snout. "Quite right, my boy. Quite right and we now have more evidence that would reinforce this idea." He moved on to his next pupil. "Violet, why do you think that the killer chose to carry out the murder today of all days?"

Mother thought for a moment before replying. "Perhaps because there are so many people around. If he had waited until tomorrow, there would have been fewer possible suspects and a higher probability of getting caught."

"Indeed, but there's something else which I didn't consider at first. Something which I only discovered when we spoke to Mr Mayfield in his laboratory. Christopher..." My turn again! "... would you like to hazard a guess as to exactly what that might be?"

I racked my brains. I tried really hard to think of something that would answer his question, but my mind was a complete blank. "No."

"No, you wouldn't like to hazard a guess?"

I think I might have blushed a little then. "No, I have no idea what- Wait!" A thought popped into my brain and started jumping up and down with its arm waving in the air like an overeager boy in the front row of Latin class (*id est* my friend William). "The ingredients which were used to make the substance that was placed on top of Mr Hardcastle's body came from Herbie's cupboard, which in turn suggests that..." This was as far as I got. "Ummm... Actually, I'll return to my original answer; no."

"Very well, I'll put you out of your misery." He pulled at his collar, perhaps finally feeling the heat that was thick in the air around us. "The fact that the killer went through with the crime today implies a number of key facts. First of all, I believe that he chose parents' day because tomorrow Mr Herbert Mayfield will no longer be an employee of Oakton Academy."

I was a little annoyed at myself for failing to work this out and muttered a troubled, "Ohhhhhh!" in which my mother accompanied me.

Grandfather wasn't to be distracted. "Furthermore, though it may be vain of me to make such a statement, I don't believe that the crime would have been planned for this particular date if the killer had known I would be in attendance." This was another exceedingly good point that I had overlooked. I could see where this might lead and, on cue, Grandfather had a question for me. "Chrissy, did you tell anyone that I would be coming here today?"

I didn't need to think long to answer. "Yes. My three best friends

William, Billy and Will."

"And?"

"And Mr Mayfield."

"Precisely." He clapped his hands together and I could see his energy and confidence replenishing. "Your friend Herbie told me how excited he was at the thought of our meeting."

I wasn't the only one who was impressed by my septuagenarian grandfather's recall. Mother had a clap of her own. "That's right! He couldn't stop talking about all your old cases. And he knew everything that happened at Cranley during the spring ball."

"Indeed. Would a man who had followed my career so intently plan a murder knowing that I would be on hand to solve it?" Having perfected a humble tone mere moments earlier, the old man now acknowledged his genius.

"Of course he wouldn't." I admit that I am often my grandfather's biggest fan. Just as some people follow cricket players or film stars, I couldn't help admiring the legendary policeman for his detective work. They'd both had a clap, and I felt it was my turn.

He immediately raised one hand to silence my applause. "Too soon, boy. Far too soon." He grew serious again and took a few steps without speaking. "The fact is, that coming close to ruling out one single suspect is not enough. There are four more still in the running and we're presented with a scenario so taxing that, while I may have my theories, I am still unable to prove one for certain. Time and time again, I return to the same exact question. Why was Tobias Hardcastle murdered?"

None of us made a sound. Even Delilah was as quiet as a chinchilla and slumped down onto the warm stone step a little resignedly. It was my mother who finally offered a ray of hope.

"It may not lead us to the killer, but the least we can do is explore the various criminal activities that have been taking place."

Her father nodded. "I agree."

I also agreed, but he'd already said that. So, instead, I murmured, "Even if the stolen money and wild parties aren't the reason that Hardcastle was murdered, by investigating them, we'll be able to see the case more clearly."

"Absolutely."

I was spurred on by his encouragement and kept talking. "The

155

question now is where to begin? The Crabbs aren't going to admit to anything. Jonathan Greeves is scared witless, Steadfast apparently isn't afraid of you." I should probably have found a more delicate manner in which to phrase this. "We know that Mr Hardcastle stopped his wife from socialising and we've hardly seen a trace of Dominic Rake all day which only leaves-" I was about to say *Herbert Mayfield* but, before I could get the words out, my chemistry teacher had appeared at the door behind me with a smile.

"May I be of assistance?"

# CHAPTER TWENTY-SIX

Herbie wasn't the only fortunate arrival just then. Cook turned up with another hamper for us.

"I thought you might like some afternoon tea, milord?"

My grandfather's manner brightened. He always adopted his gentlest possible attitude with his favourite domestic. "How terribly kind of you, Henrietta. Now tell me, have you eaten anything yourself?"

"Oh, don't worry about me, Lord Edgington. I'll make do with whatever I can find in the kitchen. Some of Doreen's offerings look... like food."

"Nonsense. You will join us in the rose garden. It's not every day we go on an outing together. I'll call Todd along too." He was already walking off – a common trait of the man, which in most people would be considered rude. He clearly knew that we couldn't resist his will though, and all four of us (plus our furry companion) happily trailed after him.

In the end, our chauffeur refused to leave his post and so we left him some provisions and cut back through school to the rose garden. Herbie looked a little perplexed by this rather unusual break in the middle of my grandfather's investigation. I knew more than anyone, however, that my family's motto should be, "Everything stops for tea."

Cook had packed all we would need into the large wicker basket she carried. There were flasks of hot and cold drinks, a number of rather complicated-looking dishes – which told me she was back to her usual level of experimentation – and, rather usefully, even a picnic blanket, though she herself opted to eat on a bench at a discreet distance.

"Lovely tomato soup," my chemistry teacher declared, shouting over to her. "What are these unusual morsels within it? They provide a truly distinct flavour."

"That'll be raw ginger, sir. Oh and chunks of swede."

Grandfather hadn't said a word until this point as he prepared, cooled and consumed his serving of tea. He let out a satisfied *ahhhh* once the cup was drained and got to work with his interview.

"Now, tell me, Herbert," the men were already on first-name terms. "What goes on at these parties that are held in the dining hall?"

"They aren't just parties. From Wednesday to Saturday each week, The Oakton Canteen is a nightclub. It's known throughout Surrey as the only spot worth drinking in. Gosh, people come all the way from London to see what the fuss is about. There are cocktails of every kind, professional dancers and a live jazz band. It's a sparkling microcosm of our golden decade, transplanted into this stuffy old institution." He sounded quiet poetic as he relived those lost nights.

"How on earth did Mr Hardcastle not find out about them?" Mother asked, inspiring a short burst of laughter from the teacher.

"Luckily for everyone, his house was far away, and he was a heavy sleeper. But there were lookouts posted just in case." His optimism abandoned him, and he shook his head. "I must admit that I was a fool to get involved. When wishing to drown one's sorrows, alcohol is a vital ingredient. As Tobias didn't allow any on the premises outside of the ancient tradition of parents' day, the club was the only way for me to quench my thirst."

Lord Edgington sucked his cheeks in a little irritably. "No one is blaming you, Herbert. We merely want to know what goes on there. I've heard gambling mentioned, what else occurs?"

"It's quite a circus, I can tell you. There's boxing once a week, card games every night and a stage show on a Saturday. Customers slip in through a hole in the fence, and all sorts of people turn up, from robbers to barons."

"Is there anything else illegal going on? Drugs, for example?"

Herbie nodded. "Yes, I believe so. But I'm not interested in such things and wasn't at my most observant at the best of times. I'm sorry to say that I sailed away every Friday night on a boat named drunkenness."

My mother turned her head sympathetically to comfort the poor soul, as her father moved on to his next question. "Do you know who organises these shindigs at least? Who's behind them?"

With his legs folded beneath him, Herbie sat up a little straighter. "I can't tell you for certain. There are no posters printed advertising the debauchery, if that's what you mean. But I can tell you the figures who attend most often. Steadfast makes a regular appearance, and he's a main attraction. He boxed at some point in his youth and will take on any challengers. Mr Balustrade usually has a pop once he's got some grog inside him. He invariably hits the mat within a round or two though."

158

My grandfather's eyes narrowed. Despite the idyllic setting, I could tell that he might just as well have been in a gloomy London police station. "Who else?"

"Matron and the dinner lady are in charge of drinks and were particularly instrumental in turfing out the stragglers at the end of the night, though I don't think they're the brains behind the operation. Greeves is often there, looking nervous. I've never seen a drop of alcohol pass his lips and don't really know why he goes. Mr Bath shows up with his wife from time to time. They order drinks, have a quick argument then she heads home again."

"What about Mrs Hardcastle?" I thought I should check, which made Herbie smile.

"Celia? Not likely. Tobias never allowed her to enjoy herself. A little pruning here in the rose garden and a weekly trip to the shops were the extent of her social life. I think that's why I fell for her. I've always wanted to play the white knight." He looked wistfully at the colourful flowers that were in bloom all around us. They scaled the old walls of the garden like prisoners trying to break free. "She wasn't so much his wife as a live-in dogsbody."

"Maybe that's why he was killed," Mother put forward. "Perhaps you weren't the only one who adored her from afar. Perhaps the killer decided it was time to liberate Celia from her domestic servitude."

The thought offered Herbert no respite from his suffering, but he pulled a gasp of air deep down into his lungs and searched for a silver lining. "I can't say she's not better off now. Though I wish a man hadn't had to die to achieve it."

"And that still wouldn't explain the trap left for Steadfast." As Grandfather spoke these words, I could tell that he was waiting for Mr Mayfield's reaction.

The teacher ruffled the short hair at the back of his head as he tried to make sense of this news. "Someone tried to kill Oberon?" He stuck his neck out in surprise. "How would he fit into any of this?"

No one else had an answer to this question, so I gave it my best shot. "We don't know for certain, though he's been extremely economical with the truth each time we've spoken to him and Grandfather thinks he must be keeping vital information from us."

The old man did not look happy that I'd given so much away to another suspect and raised a hand to return us to the main topic. "What about the boys? Were there any Oakton pupils at the nightclub?"

Herbie hesitated once more. "Well, yes, actually. There were." He swallowed down whatever guilt he was feeling and managed to get his words out. "Dominic Rake and his prefects took the drink orders. They ran about the place like waiters."

"Edgington." A voice suddenly carried across the garden. At first, I thought it was coming from the loudspeakers. "Edgington, I've been looking all over for you." Blunt rushed through the gate with a note of paper in his hand. "We got the information you were after."

Grandfather was up on his feet in two shakes of Delilah's tail. "What did you find out? Is it that brute Steadfast?"

Blunt wore an expression that suggested it was his own unrivalled police work that had led to the discovery. "No. We didn't turn up much on him. It's the secretary, the pale-faced boy Greeves who jumped out at me. Turns out that he's Hardcastle's nephew. And that's not all." The lips on one side of his face ticked upwards. "Jonathan Greeves has a background in chemistry. He worked with his uncle developing gas bombs during the war."

We all needed time to process this revelation, and I watched first Mr Mayfield and then my grandfather as they attempted to recalibrate their understanding of exactly what had taken place that day. Oddly, I was the first to come to a conclusion.

"Perhaps that's who Mama was protecting. She might well be the only person who knew that Greeves and Hardcastle were related, but she didn't tell us because she didn't want him getting into trouble," I suggested, but my grandfather was focused on a greater concern.

"Where's Greeves now?"

"He wasn't in his office when I went past. Could be over in the teachers' cottages, I suppose, but I didn't see any sign of him before I left Steadfast."

There was another pause, another slight adjustment in Grandfather's thinking as the map of evidence in his head expanded. "Jolly good work, Blunt."

I'm not sure I'd ever seen the inspector smile with anything but gloating pleasure before, and he seemed quite humbled by his old boss's words. "Thank you very much, sir." The cheer on his lips soon disappeared as he remembered that he was supposed to be in charge. "Or rather; yes, I know."

Lord Edgington had no time for the man's vanity and snapped out some new commands. "Leave Dr Steadfast to his own devices. The man has made it perfectly clear that he doesn't need any protection. But station an extra officer in Mrs Hardcastle's cottage. Though it would be convenient to link the murder to the litany of crimes that have taken place at this school, it's still possible that there is a family element I had not previously envisioned."

I could tell that Blunt would have liked to take issue with these orders, but even he could see that my grandfather was speaking sense. He let out a huff of breath and retreated from the garden without another word.

"Do you really believe that Celia is in danger?" Herbie asked. "I'll go this minute to be with her if you think that's best?"

"No." Grandfather's voice had flattened down and could barely be heard over the birds chirping in the bushes (serins, if I'm not mistaken, though I probably am). "No, you'd better stay clean away from her for the moment. There's a killer on the loose and it's still not entirely clear what he hopes to achieve."

"I have every faith in you, milord." Throughout this conversation, Cook had been watching like a spectator at a variety show. She was awfully excited to be part of the action.

Lord Edgington looked over to her with some amusement. "Thank you, Henrietta. You should probably go back to the kitchen to pack away your equipment. I believe that our day out at Oakton Academy is drawing to its natural conclusion."

"What about us, Grandfather?" I asked him. "What should we do next?"

He thought for a moment, studying the serene garden as though he had noticed his surroundings for the first time. "There's still one suspect I haven't had the opportunity to talk to."

# CHAPTER TWENTY-SEVEN

I felt rather like a tennis ball that day. I'd been knocked about from school to field and back so many times that I was becoming quite dizzy. I hadn't eaten nearly enough either and was sorely upset to leave Mother and Herbie to their repast when Grandfather suggested we head to the end-of-year prize-giving.

Up on the stage, Mr Bath looked terribly overwrought. He was stuttering through the ceremony, trying to make sense of the notes which were Mr Hardcastle's legacy to him.

"Now if David Pratsmouth could come up... No, sorry, that's David Portsmouth. If you could come up, we have your prize for achievement in lower school geology... geography!" He waited with a nervous expression plastered across his face and, when no one approached the stage, consulted his notes once more. "Perhaps I've misunderstood something, or..." With our host desperately flicking through the pad of paper in search of answers, Grandfather pointed to a free space on one of the benches and sat down to watch.

There was a row of empty seats on the stage where the Hardcastles and other senior members of staff would normally have been sitting. As the games teacher's confusion increased, the audience became more restless.

"How difficult can it be to hand out a few cups and medals?" one unquiet mother heckled.

"Get on with it, man!" my grandfather joined in with mischievous delight.

Mr Bath's eyes jumped about the scene as he desperately hoped that someone would come to his rescue. "I'm terribly sorry, ladies and gentlemen. You see, I wasn't supposed to be leading the ceremony today and I can't quite make sense of Mr Hardcastle's handwriting-"

"Stop making excuses!" another parent complained. "A bad workman blames his tools."

I wasn't entirely sure that this comment was relevant in the situation, but it stirred Mr Bath into action. "I'll tell you what. We'll forget about the original prizes and I'll decide them based on my own knowledge of the boys. How about that?"

He really wasn't cut out for formal events and should have stuck to sporting matters. This new declaration sparked a wave of boos from the audience.

One little boy immediately burst into tears, forcing his father to say, "My son's painting of Saint Paul's Cathedral was chosen as the second finest work of art in the whole of the lower-school. I demand that he get the recognition he deserves." This led to some *hear-hears* and a few whistles.

I thought that my games teacher might end his suffering by jumping head first from the stage, but an unlikely figure came to his rescue.

"I'm terribly sorry, Ladies and Gentlemen. I would like to have been here from the start of the ceremony but was otherwise engaged."

As he clambered up onto the stage, Steadfast was in an awful state. His clothes were stained with blood and what looked like chocolate cake. He wore a long piece of muslin wrapped several times around the wound on his head and I'm quite certain he'd been drinking.

"Now, let's start afresh with the lower school certificates, shall we?" He seized the pad of notes from Mr Bath and pushed the man out of the way. Despite his shambolic appearance, I have to admit that he did a good job with the prize-giving. He made sense of Hardcastle's handwriting and soon calmed the rebellious crowd.

"Elvin Appleton, third place in the school pottery competition." The aforementioned pupil took to the stage, looking both shy and proud in equal measure. "Wonderful work, Appleton." Steadfast was the perfect master of ceremonies and tapped the scroll he was presenting on the young boy's shoulders, as though he were the king knighting a lord. This led to an appreciative titter from the crowd, and the next boy was called forth.

"Adam Fenchurch, outstanding achievement in mathematics. Up you come, Fenchurch."

By the end of the ceremony, Steadfast had the parents cheering for more, and even we boys were laughing away at his quips. It was a marked improvement on Mr Hardcastle's stern, nervous routine. Had I not seen the bile and anger the man had spewed forth earlier in the day, I might well have chosen him as our replacement headmaster. Inevitably, this warm impression did not last long.

"And that brings us to the close of this year's ceremony, the end

164

of our parents' day entertainment, and almost certainly concludes my time at Oakton Academy for young rogues and reprobates." This announcement was met with a mixture of laughter at his joke, disappointment at his departure and confusion at the bitter tone he'd used. "That's right, my devoted public. I am leaving these hallowed grounds behind me, but I would like to deliver one final appraisal of your sons before I go."

Grandfather sat perfectly stiff, bracing for what was to come. Seeing him like that reminded me of the years he'd spent shut away in his suite of rooms, looking out across the Cranley estate. I felt grateful once more that he was there with me, there to see Steadfast's disgraceful display.

"I've been working at this school longer than I care to remember and I'd hate to go without informing you all what a bunch of toffee-nosed, mud-eating, backstabbing future criminals you have sired." I thought that *criminal* was rich coming from him. "I've never seen such ugly creatures in my entire existence and can only assume that it comes down to inbreeding in the upper classes."

Mr Bath had been recovering from his ordeal, but now sat up straighter in his chair and looked about the audience, perhaps searching for some clue as to how to deal with his colleague's outburst.

"And let's not forget the boys' intelligence – as our good Lord sadly did when he was making them." Steadfast raised one hand to list our pertinent qualities. "Ill-informed, empty-headed, dim-witted twits would be one way to describe them. Though I think the term *ignoramus* would suffice."

Practically every parent's jaw lay abandoned on the ground. Most of the boys, meanwhile, adored the history teacher's routine and cheered every new insult he delivered.

"You taught us so well, sir!" Marmalade shouted, which led to another burst of giggles.

"Ahh, a case in point." Steadfast extended his arm in my new friend's direction. "No child has entered my class with such commitment and enthusiasm for getting every question wrong, Master Adelaide. My life will not be the same when you are a distant memory. It will not be any worse, but it will certainly not be the same."

Marmalade roared out his approval and put his hands in the air to clap. His father was probably the only parent there who failed to boo. As the others threw sandwich crusts and orange peel, Horatio Adelaide was having a nice lie down on the picnic blanket.

Steadfast had one last critique left in him. "Let me finish by saying that my time at Oakton Academy has been memorable… Much like the smell of Peter Kingston in the third form. So thank you all, parents and students alike, for being such a worthless-"

This was as much as Mr Bath could take. He finally conquered his indecision and rugby tackled the man to the floor. The disgraced presenter slid from the stage to land in a heap in the front row. Appalled parents were already fleeing the scene. Boys from the lower school were in tears as the throb of the crowd ripped their mothers away from them.

Grandfather showed no great surprise at what had just occurred. He watched as Steadfast picked himself up from the ground to brush off his tatty clothes. He did not appear to be hurt, but walked in a swaying fashion, straight past our stand. A cloud of alcoholic fumes followed along behind.

"Shouldn't we speak to him, Grandfather?" I suggested, but he was not concerned with the teacher after all.

It was fascinating to stay right where we were and see the people running in every direction, as though my shamed history teacher would transmit some exotic disease. I swear I saw one boy jump into the lake and swim to safety!

We were in the eye of the storm, and Grandfather was happy to observe the destruction. "There they are," he finally uttered, once half of the crowd had dispersed back towards school.

Lord Edgington had his eyes fixed on a group of students dressed in black blazers who were doing their best to calm panicked parents. He waited until the prefects had filed past us, then prodded me down off the spectators' stand. After everything they'd just witnessed, I don't suppose Dominic Rake or his subordinates paid much attention to an old man, his plump grandson and our charming dog. We had to hurry to keep up with them, but could hear every word they said.

"What if he tells our parents the whole story, Dom?" Rake's deputy asked in a beseeching voice.

"Why would he say anything?"

"Why would he get up on the stage and tell everyone what he really thinks of them? He's drunk, his job here is over and the headmaster has been murdered. Do you really think he'll protect us now?"

Dominic Rake – his face as gaunt and harried as ever, his fine eyelashes batting like butterflies' wings – had no answer to these questions and pressed on a little faster. It was clear that his gang of licensed bullies were waiting on him to reassure them, but he was the one who needed it most. As we fell into step alongside him, he had the terrified look of a rabbit on a chopping block. He knew he was in trouble and there was nothing he could do about it.

Over by the gate which gave access to the main school grounds, there was a human traffic jam forming.

"You heard the Sergeant's announcement earlier this afternoon," the young bobby was telling everyone. No parents or students are allowed within the school while we carry out-" this was as much as he managed to say before the disgruntled parents surged forward and pushed him out of the way.

The crowd streamed through the opening and, as soon as we were inside, my grandfather reached his long arm out and nabbed the head prefect by the shoulder.

"I'd like a word with you, Master Rake. I believe you've been avoiding me."

# CHAPTER TWENTY-EIGHT

Rake took a deep breath and his skin turned a shade whiter as he took in the elderly detective. He was either unwilling or unable to speak. Instead, he silently nodded his consent and my grandfather extracted him from the throng of frightened-looking minions.

We walked away from the school, following the high fence from which the Marconi loudspeakers were suspended at regular intervals. When we made it to the dining hall, Rake held the door open for the two of us like the good boy that he pretended to be.

The dining room was empty, but we could hear regular noises from the kitchen like the clanging of some immense, inhuman machine. It was actually just Doreen and Cook cleaning up, but there was something ominous about the rhythmic banging of metal on metal.

Grandfather led the way to a table in the centre of the vast room, the floorboards creaking beneath his feet. I almost thought I could hear Dominic's heart beating from the pressure, but it was probably just my imagination playing tricks on me – and my affection for Edgar Allan Poe putting ideas in my head.

He waited for the stately old gentleman to sit down before taking a seat in front of him. My grandfather tossed the tails of his morning coat out extravagantly, and I wondered what sense of dread he hoped to inspire with such a flamboyant gesture.

I stood alongside them, happy to watch the scene unfold. While such positioning may seem excessively passive, I assure you that's not the case. If I'd been sitting at the table, I would have fallen under the great Lord Edgington's spell. His sonorous voice and magnetic gaze would have left me stunned. Standing back as I did gave me a fuller understanding of his mastery. Little by little, I was coming to learn the art of the detective, and it was fascinating.

"Back at the scene of the crime." He smiled deferentially as he delivered his opening line. "Back at The Oakton Canteen. Home to unlicensed boxing matches, all-night drinking and illicit drugs."

Rake breathed in sharply. "I don't know what you're referring to, sir. I can assure you that Oakton is-"

"Enough!" The command echoed about the deserted space.

There was something eerie about being there without any other students. I half wondered whether one of the countless school ghosts – who any number of boys had witnessed, though no one could prove their existence – might emerge from the shadows to steal our souls. Even the bright sunlight which was streaming in through two walls of high windows couldn't make up for the feeling of ice tingling down my spine.

Grandfather breathed in and back out again, taking his time as he prepared his first question. "What was it like, being here at night with all those adults? Did it give you a vicarious thrill? Is that why you went along with the Crabb sisters' plans?"

This was a rare misstep from Grandfather. He'd rolled the dice and lost.

Dominic smiled as he realised that we didn't know everything after all. "You mean Doreen and Matron? They weren't behind all this. They were little more than barmaids."

"So who then?" A note of anger infused the words.

"Isn't it your job to find out such things?"

Grandfather linked his hands together behind his head. "It could be my job to tell your parents about the situation in which you now find yourself." His face creased a little in reflection. "Where were you hoping to study next year? Cambridge? Or Oxford perhaps? I happen to be rather close with some influential men at both institutions. I'm certain they would be fascinated by the story of the Oakton Academy nightclub. They'd be quick to tell their administrations not to let a single prefect from this school attend their universities, of course, but they'd enjoy the tale while it lasted."

Rake no longer looked so sure of himself. "I didn't help out because of any thrill. There was no other choice."

"You'd be surprised how many times I've heard that excuse from criminals. It's rarely accurate of course, but I've heard it a lot."

I'd noticed that my grandfather barely blinked when interviewing suspects. His eyes were fixed onto the young man in front of him as firmly as any padlock.

"It's true. I swear."

"A young mother stealing bread for her starving baby? Fair enough. A boy brought up into a life of crime whose only defence against his father's brutality is to go along with whatever he's told? That I can accept. But you?"

"I didn't have a choice." The sudden high pitch to Rake's voice betrayed his nerves.

"You were born rich. You go to one of the most prestigious schools in the country and – if you're the son of Baron Carlson Rake, which judging by your anaemic appearance you certainly are – then your parents own most of Sussex. No matter what pressure someone put upon you, you could still have told Mr Hardcastle or your parents. You could have got out of it if you'd tried."

Rake glanced down at the black table that had been scratched over with initials and crude drawings. "You don't understand." It was the kind of declaration that my brother Albert enjoyed making which, in my family, was normally greeted with cynicism.

"Then tell me what happened." My grandfather gave the boy a moment to find his words. The silence seemed to build up around us like a rising tower.

"When I became head prefect, I was determined to do a good job for all the boys. I couldn't have imagined what a poisoned chalice I had accepted."

For a moment, I thought Lord Edgington might interrupt to correct Rake's false assertions, but he held his tongue and the testimony continued.

"Even before they started the nights here, my role was a dubious one. I was expected to be a spymaster, reporting back to the teachers on any number of petty crimes which my fellow schoolmates committed. There's a reason that none of them like us prefects and it's got nothing to do with drinking or gambling."

"So when did all this start?" Grandfather spread his hands out to gesture to the room around us.

"Only this year. And it was innocent enough at first, just a few of the teachers and their wives getting together to let their hair down. A couple of the other boys and I came on board to serve drinks, and it was a lot of fun. We felt grown up and made a little money at the same time."

"So it was the teachers who organised the club?"

He gave a slow, solemn nod. "That's right, and it's probably why things got out of control so quickly. Bath invited all his friends from the local rugby club, and that's when the fighting started. It's amazing that Hardcastle never found out about it."

Grandfather looked off in the direction of the school and muttered under his breath. "As far as we know. I've been wondering if that's what got him killed in the first place." He took a moment to let the possibility rattle around his brain and then turned back to our suspect. "Carry on, Rake."

"The fighting led to gambling and an influx of new clientele. The gambling showed everybody involved that there was money to be made and that's when things got serious. Dr Steadfast had me rope more boys into the plan. We opened the club up to the locals and Scuttlewell cut a hole in the fence on the far side of school so that no one would get caught – he was in charge of security as everyone is terrified of him."

Rake seemed less jumpy than before and settled into his story. "You have to understand that, out here in the country, there's very little excitement. We've all read about the buzz and sparkle of clubs in the city, and people would come from villages all around to experience it for themselves. The teachers thought they were American gangsters and that this was a prohibition saloon. It was exciting for a while, but soon grew tiresome.

"I couldn't concentrate on my classes whenever I'd been working the night before. Even when I was at school, everyone wanted something from me. My maths teacher, Mr Arthurs, would take me out of class to send messages to the other teachers. I had to drive into London on Friday afternoons to pick up great shipments of drink, which we could only bring in once the headmaster had closed his watchful eye for the night. And Matron…" He never finished that thought, so I took the opportunity to make an observation of my own.

"You came to Steadfast's class yesterday afternoon, didn't you?" It finally clicked who'd been knocking on the history teacher's door when I was writing out lines.

He looked at me as though he'd forgotten I was there. "That's right. I was a regular messenger pigeon. I got the other boys to do it sometimes, but the teachers preferred me to keep their secrets for them. They ended up fixing a box to the wall in the prefects' office where I could pick up their notes each day." He let out a troubled sigh, and I realised that, if this were all just an act, I'd fallen for it completely.

My Grandfather still needed winning over. "What sort of messages were they?"

"I never opened them, but they were mainly from the teachers who were involved in the club. I imagine it was safer than meeting in person all the time to discuss it."

He served a fresh question straight back. "Did Mr Mayfield write any?"

"Not to my knowledge."

"And what about Mrs Hardcastle? Did she ever go to the club?"

"Is that a serious question?" Rake's face extended in disbelief. "She was lucky if her husband let her take tea with Mrs Bath."

"So, no notes either?"

He thought for a moment. "If you're asking whether she sent any, then I never saw her handwriting. But I used to deliver to her."

"Who from?"

"I told you, I didn't open any of the messages." There was a note of hesitation in his voice, which he soon explained. "The funny thing is, though, that the handwriting looked like her husband's spidery scrawl."

Grandfather had no response to this minor revelation and Rake kept talking.

"I suppose it's a waiter's curse, but practically everybody who came to the club confided some secret in me. Mrs Bath was in love with Herbie, who we all knew was in love with Mama as he spent his whole time talking about her. Mr Bath gambled every night and lost money every night and ended up in debt to just about every regular who came to the club – including several of the prefects. Steadfast and Balustrade had a competition going to see how many local girls they could charm – with both of them reaching the grand score of none.

"Things quickly got out of hand, of course. We had locals fighting in the road after hours. People kept getting robbed whenever they'd had too much to drink, and they always had too much to drink. It was complete bedlam most nights, but the teachers were enjoying themselves and making such quantities of money that the other boys and I were stuck. When one of us tried to leave, Steadfast would threaten to send letters home to our parents."

Grandfather tapped his finger on the table in front of him, but gave nothing away in the stony look he wore. "How did Jonathan Greeves fit in with all that chaos? He doesn't seem the type to get involved."

Rake looked as though he didn't want to answer. He ran his finger over the bright yellow letter P on his breast pocket, but eventually coughed the words out. "He was trapped like me."

"But what was his role?"

There was another moment's hesitation before he spoke. "I don't know exactly what he did. I wondered if he was in charge of the money. Whatever it was, he did not seem happy to be here and normally sat in the corner looking miserable."

Grandfather was silent for a minute. I could see his brain working, his mind fitting together the different bricks that Dominic Rake had provided for us to build a resilient case.

"You said that you were specifically chosen as head prefect, but Hardcastle knew nothing of the club, so how can that be?"

Dominic smiled rather sadly then. "Mr Hardcastle didn't choose me. It's the head of the sixth form who picks the prefects. He laid on all the charm to win me over. He said that he'd seen something in me which would make me the ideal candidate for head prefect. What he really wanted was for me to recruit a team of lackeys who would report to him alone. If anyone's to blame for what goes on around here, it's Steadfast."

# CHAPTER TWENTY-NINE

I was in the unusual position of feeling sorry for Dominic Rake.

He was nothing like the Marshall Brothers, but he'd still used his position to intimidate his schoolmates. He'd bullied and berated us, confiscated property he had no right to take and got innocent boys into trouble with the teachers. I could see how scared he was, but had to wonder whether his own suffering could compensate for the harm he'd caused.

The concepts of punishment and forgiveness had been on my mind a lot over the last month. My Grandfather had introduced me to the idea of sympathetic criminals and corrupt policemen. He had blurred the lines of my understanding, so that my once clearly defined moral outlook had become hazy. It made it harder to know what I really thought.

Rake had broken no great laws himself, but he'd acted like a petty Napoleon; ordering younger boys about, commandeering whatever took his fancy and enjoying the power he could wield. He claimed that, at the time of Mr Hardcastle's death, he'd only been in the building to fetch equipment for Mr Bath and knew nothing of the murder until the sergeant's announcement. We had no evidence to contradict him, and yet I remembered the troubled look he'd worn as he ran from the school and felt sure there were more secrets to be revealed.

Grandfather continued questioning him for some time, but he offered no further insight into the wave of immorality that had swept the school. The very idea of an American-style *speakeasy* in Oakton would have shocked me just days before, but after a murder and a man trap, it now seemed positively innocent.

"Thank you, Dominic," the ex-policeman said when the interview was over. I could see the compassion he possessed for the boy, even if my own feelings were less clear.

Rake looked back at him as though he didn't believe he was really free to go. He stood up from the table nonetheless and escaped the dining hall as swiftly as his good manners allowed.

When we were alone, Grandfather sat in one of his contemplative trances. I considered going back to the afternoon tea that Cook had prepared in the rose garden, but he finally snapped out of it.

"What a perplexing case," he announced, without turning to look at me.

"But does any of it explain why Hardcastle was murdered?" I considered this an open enough question not to make me sound like a total imbecile.

"I don't know yet. I really don't. But we're beginning to fill in the gaps in our story and that's something." His words faded out, then he shot to his feet in his usual urgent manner. "And what's more, I know who we need to speak to next."

Before I could stand up, he had sped off along the aisle between the long rows of tables where children dined in the daytime and adults revelled at night. He disappeared through the swinging door to the white-tiled kitchen, and I tried to keep up. The heat and that indescribable school dinner smell had got to me, and I was feeling rather sleepy.

He was already wagging his finger at Doreen the giant when I arrived. "You didn't tell me the whole story and I'm disappointed in you." He had adopted the easy-going tone that Herbie used with us when we were messing around in class. Whereas most teachers screamed and yelled, Herbie could make us feel like real rotters just by speaking softly. I could see that my grandfather's words had a similar effect.

"Yes, sir, Lord Superintendent Edgington. Sorry, sir."

"So you'll come clean, won't you?"

She nodded enthusiastically. "Oh, yes, sir. Of course, sir."

I went to stand next to my grandfather, and we waited for her to continue. Eventually the old man tapped her on the arm to get her started, but then she burst into life once more.

"It was the teachers what organised everything. We was only helping out and never really did nothing wrong."

"So you and your sister mixed drinks and made sure no one got out of hand?"

"Something like that, yeah. It was fun to play at being a barmaid." Her childlike nature emerged, and I could see that so much of what she did was just a game to Doreen. "I tell you what; I was good at mixing drinks. Manhattans, Sidecars, even Blue Blazers – I could do them all. I wouldn't mind getting a job in one of them fancy cocktail bars up in London. I could work at the Savoy."

176

Grandfather was running out of patience with her rambling and interrupted with a dry comment. "It may be time you changed your career. Now, Doreen, will you please tell me what either of you gained from your participation in the club? I can't imagine you gave up sleeping four nights a week for the sake of the company."

She shifted her weight from side to side. "Well, I certainly never picked no one's pocket, no matter what you might've heard."

"Did Connie?"

"Ummm..." She tried to recall her stock refrain but struggled to get the words in order. "You don't know nothing about being comfortable and my sister can't talk about this particular matter, thank you, madam..." Her eyes flicked about the kitchen and landed on Cook, who was busy cleaning the surfaces and pretending not to listen.

Grandfather emitted a long, weary breath. "Very well. Why don't I tell you what I believe happened and you can correct me if I'm wrong?"

She thought about this for a moment and seemed happy with the arrangement. "I don't think Connie would have a problem with that."

"Wonderful." Grandfather straightened his back and put forward his theory. "It seems to me that, after you finished working at the bar, it was your job to make sure the revellers left poorer than when they'd arrived."

My grandfather's diplomatic tone and clever way with words cheered Doreen up again. "Ooh, yeah, I like the way you put it. That's right. I was just making people a bit poorer. Nothing illegal about that, is there?"

Grandfather shook his head in bemusement, but soon took up his thread. "Did any of the teachers know what you were doing?"

She let out a noisy laugh. "Course not. They didn't even know what day it was by the end of most nights. We robbed them- I mean, we made them poorer, just like everyone else."

"And that was the only way you benefitted from The Oakton Canteen?"

"Yes," she said, whilst shaking her head.

"So you were involved with the gambling too?"

"No." A big nod. "I never fought nobody, and I certainly didn't knock the captain of the local rugby team out twice a week."

"Where did all the money go that you earned?"

"I don't know nothing about no money. But I can tell you that we all enjoyed a bonus in our salaries at the end of each month. I've never had much of a head for numbers, so I left all that to Connie."

Grandfather frowned, trying to make sense of our unreliable witness's constant shifting between truth, lies and obstruction of the facts. You can imagine how amazed I was when something rather clever occurred to me.

"But you two were working here for years before the club started. What were you doing all that time?"

She looked uncomfortable again, and I was worried she might give her standard response another whirl. Instead, she hunched her shoulders, put her head down and said, "I miss the pretty lady. Where did your daughter go, Lord Mr Edgington? I want her to ask the questions."

"Never mind my daughter." Grandfather's voice was a weapon. "Answer the boy's question."

"We were on the straight and narrow, weren't we!" Even Doreen sounded like she doubted this. "We were practically law-abiding members of society."

"Practically?"

She puffed and moaned and flustered, then finally provided an answer. "Well, it would have been boring if we'd become goody two-shoes overnight. Girls need hobbies you know."

"And that's why you recruited Dominic Rake?" Grandfather was several hundred miles ahead of my own thinking and I've no idea how he'd worked this out.

"What do you know about Rake?" Doreen sounded just as surprised as I was.

He didn't hesitate in his response, even if it wasn't true. "He told us everything."

The counterfeit dinner lady's jaw rocked from side to side. She was nothing but a gnat in my grandfather's web. Whatever she did, he'd get the truth out of her in the end.

"Well, we couldn't get away with robbing the boys, so we got someone else to do it for us."

"Rake, and the other prefects before him, confiscated whatever they could from the boys and you sold it on to your contacts. Is that how it happened?"

She nodded, and this time she really meant it. "But we weren't stupid. We'd wait till the end of every term before cashing in. That way, if a parent asked for an antique pocket watch or crocodile-skin purse back, we could hand it over. They never did, of course. The families at this school have more money than friends."

I was tempted to tell her that she'd mangled the expression, but I didn't want her to mangle me.

"Final question, Doreen." At his full height, Grandfather was still an inch shorter than the muscular behemoth in front of us. This didn't stop him from towering over her though. "Why were you inside the school building when Mr Hardcastle was murdered?"

The dinner lady's cheeks turned red. "Oh. Ummm... whoops, you got me."

# CHAPTER THIRTY

"Pure and simple robbery!" As we exeunted the empty dining hall, my grandfather looked supremely contented. "With the Crabb sisters, you can guarantee it will never be anything more complicated."

I had approximately seventeen and a half thousand questions I wanted to put to him and the one I absolutely couldn't resist was, "How in heavens did you know what they were up to?"

The great, famous and legendary – not to mention much-admired – former superintendent was very close to looking smug just then. He curtailed the expression that was blooming on his face and adopted a stern look.

"It was quite simple, Christopher. Dominic Rake became nervous whenever I mentioned the Crabb sisters. Though he provided plenty of information regarding the exploits of your teachers, when we mentioned your dinner lady and matron, he swiftly changed the topic. And they were the same when I spoke of your head prefect. Rake didn't do anything so damning at the club and so it only made sense that he was ashamed of whatever task the Crabbs had set him."

"Still-" I began, but he hadn't finished setting out his brilliant discovery.

"Add that to the fact that Rake has been avoiding me for much of the day and it stood to reason that he was either involved in killing your headmaster – any evidence for which we have failed to discover – or had committed a lesser offense which he did not want me to investigate. Knowing the Crabb sisters as I do, it did not take an uncomfortable stretch of the imagination to realise what that crime might be."

His explanation had left me reeling. It was jolly hard to keep up with his logic, and I considered asking him to speak more slowly.

"But it's you I should congratulate, Christopher. I wouldn't have known any of that if you hadn't first observed the discrepancy in Doreen Crabb's story. She and her sister did not take up employment at Oakton Academy in order to boil stew and make beds. They saw their roles here as a one-way ticket to easy riches. The club and the gambling and all that went on at The Oakton Canteen was a distraction from the simple facts of the case."

"So it's got nothing to do with why Mr Hardcastle died?"

He smiled once more and his twin moustaches curled up too. It was as though he had three mouths instead of one. "That, my dear boy, remains to be seen."

It struck me, yet again, just how much he had worked out that I had failed to. "You think you know who the murderer is, don't you?"

His three mouths smiled more widely. "The issue is not what I think, it's what I know." He let out a reflective *hmmm*. "The case is building nicely. I believe we are almost at its end."

"And I believe you sound a little smug," I countered.

We were approaching the school, and he stopped to cast a critical eye over me. "It is not smugness, boy. I am merely taking pride in my work," he replied... smugly. "If I didn't have confidence in my abilities, I wouldn't be able to achieve such results."

"Ahh, I see." I was amazed at how insolent I was being to a man who I had lived half of my life in mortal fear of. "I stand corrected, Grandfather. Your abilities are most impressive and we must all bow before them."

"Hmmm," he murmured once more, then followed it up with, "I also have the ability to detect when you're being sarcastic." He clapped me affectionately around the back of the head and we walked into the school.

The bobby from St Mary Under-Twine was sitting in Jonathan Greeves's cubbyhole.

"P.C. Evans," Grandfather said, enunciating each sound clearly – I had to wonder how he knew everyone's name all the time. "What developments have there been in our absence? Has Greeves turned up? Is Mrs Hardcastle safe at home?"

The young man didn't know whether to stand to attention, salute, or stay right where he was. Instead, he sat up very high in his chair, which I thought a fair compromise. "I've had no reports on either matter, sir. Inspector Blunt has set two men to watch over the headmaster's cottage as you instructed."

"Jolly good." It was Lord Edgington's turn to appear uncertain. Perhaps he had done all the investigating he required and it was time for another tea break. "And what about-"

He would not finish that sentence as, right at that moment, there was an almighty bang at the other end of the hallway. We could make out two figures pressed up against the frosted glass of the far exit. It was all very exciting, and I thought P.C. Evans would go running over to break up the fight, but then the door swung open and Jonathan Greeves crashed through it. Following closely behind him was one of the most daring young gentlemen I'd ever had the good fortune of knowing.

"I caught this creature trying to get away, milord." Our chauffeur Todd strutted down the corridor with all the presence and personality of an American film star. "He was acting strangely as he dumped a suitcase in his car and wound the engine. I thought I'd better bring him in to you."

"I haven't done anything wrong," Greeves complained, whilst crawling along the floor away from his pursuer as though he feared for his life. "I've got every right to leave the school."

Grandfather was quick off the mark and strode down the corridor towards our previously missing suspect. "We're in the middle of a police investigation and there are a number of questions I'd like to put to you. You haven't got the right to go anywhere."

Greeves was mewling on the floor and I was rather surprised when my grandfather walked straight past him and began opening doors just beyond the stairs. "Christopher, which side of the corridor did you hear Doreen's voice coming from this morning?"

I walked a little way closer and pointed to the right-hand side.

"Ahh," he replied, in that warm tone he sometimes used when he wished to pretend that everything was fine and free of suspicion. "So not this door where extra rations of food are kept? That's interesting." He crossed the corridor and ended up at the door to a small room which Dominic Rake used as his office. "Would this be the one?"

I nodded, attempting to make sense of his behaviour.

"Very interesting indeed." With his urge satisfied, he walked back down the corridor, picking up Jonathan Greeves on the way and steering him into the assembly hall.

I scampered along after him and realised that we'd left Delilah behind somewhere. I wasn't certain where, though I was sure she'd be enjoying herself. Perhaps she'd found a squirrel to chase.

Todd graciously allowed me to enter the hall in front of him. I was immediately reminded of my night-time visit, back when Mr

Hardcastle was still alive. Childish pictures of teachers having their bottoms kicked looked quite naïve after everything that had happened since. I had to wonder if Marmaduke Adelaide and even the Marshall brothers were the marauding barbarians I'd taken them to be. Perhaps they were mere boys, just like me.

My grandfather had taken to the stage. The scene rather contrasted with Inspector Blunt's attempt at drama earlier that afternoon. "If things had turned out differently, Mr Tobias Hardcastle would be up here in my place. Around now, he would be giving out reports to the boys and saying a few words about the academic achievements of this year's upper sixth form as they set their sights on pastures new. But instead, he is dead."

Greeves didn't know where to look. He stood in front of the stage, his head twitching back and forth. "I told you, Lord Edgington. I haven't done anything wrong. I was-"

"I know what you were doing, man, and I'm not impressed." If he hadn't been born into wealth and luxury – and then given that up to join the police, before having to fulfil his responsibilities as Lord Edgington of Cranley Hall when his brother died – my grandfather would have made a wonderful headmaster.

His voice was full and strong, and it dominated the large hall. The wooden boards at the back of the room, which bore long lists of past sporting champions, vibrated as his words bounced off them. The blue curtains on either side ruffled slightly whenever he spoke. He was a force of nature; his very own weather system.

"My first question is this, did your uncle give you your job knowing that he could control you as he wished? Did he make you turn a blind eye to his theft from the school?"

Greeves was already stuttering before he'd made a single sound. "I... Rather... He... I never said he was the one taking the money."

Grandfather pulled his long coat beneath him and sat down on the side of the stage. "So then who took it? Was it you?"

I imagine that looking into my grandfather's hypnotic stare at such a moment is like gazing into the eyes of a python. Greeves was helpless before him and pulled at his tightly knotted tie. "No, of course it wasn't. I've never stolen a penny in my life."

"But you told me yourself that it was Hardcastle's job to keep an eye on the school's income. So who are you suggesting is responsible for all that money going missing? It was thousands of pounds, wasn't it?"

His reply, when it came, was like the shriek of a hunted bird. "I lied." He was back to the old habit of his expression failing to match up with his mood. He smiled gaily then looked distraught, before settling on a melancholy grimace. "I was the one who looked after the school accounts. It was my job, I just didn't want you thinking I was a thief."

"You may not be a thief, Greeves, but you are still something of a scoundrel."

The curious chap laughed when he should have been crying. "I've done nothing wrong."

"We'll see about that." Grandfather leaned back on his elbows, as though he were enjoying the sunshine in the rose garden. "It's true, is it not, that you assisted in the running of an illegal gambling ring and unlicensed drinking establishment right here on school property?"

"Yes, but I never wanted any part in it. I-"

"I suppose you had no choice?" This was my grandfather's fifth and final eye roll of the day. It was his best yet.

The pressure was affecting the school secretary, and tiny beads of sweat had amassed on his temples. "I didn't. They made me do it, the other teachers forced me into it. They said they'd get me into trouble if I didn't go along with their plans. They said I'd lose my job."

The old man eased up a little on our witness just then. He could see how much Greeves was suffering and slowed the pace of his questions. "As the school bursar, you could feed the money that the club was making back through the books to make it look as though the teachers had high salaries, but everything was legitimate."

"That's right, how did you…?" He didn't finish his question, but I knew the answer. I suddenly understood Doreen Crabb's comment about her monthly bonus.

Lord Edgington pressed on. "But then money started going missing from the school and you had to tell your uncle. Or did you make that up to throw me off the scent?"

He cleared his throat exaggeratedly, buying time before he had to deliver the answer. "I wasn't lying. The money went missing from the accounts, both here at the school and at the bank. The quantities didn't add up. Even if you discounted the money we made at the club, the school should have been accruing a healthy sum each month, but all of a sudden it was running at a loss."

"And you told your uncle because you didn't want someone blaming you." It was high time for me to declare something out of the blue, so that everyone would turn to look at me and I could immediately wish I'd kept my mouth shut.

Grandfather didn't seem to mind and jerked his head in my direction to prompt Greeves to answer.

"Yes, that's exactly it. I was scared that someone was trying to make it appear as though I was the one defrauding the school."

"And it didn't cross your mind that it could have been Tobias himself who was stealing the money?"

"No. No, it didn't. My uncle and I... Well, we weren't close. He terrified me in fact, but I've always believed he was an honest man. He saved me from the front line by giving me a job during the war, and then he called for me when he came to work here. He never acknowledged me publicly as his kin. But, in his way, he treated me fairly."

Grandfather was yet again astonished by the behaviour of one of our suspects. "And you didn't think it would be a good idea to make a clean breast of everything after he was killed?" He paused, perhaps hoping for a sensible answer. When it didn't come, he offered a suggestion of his own. "You might have tried something along the lines of, 'Hello, Lord Edgington. I'm the dead man's nephew. That's right, I was in charge of the accounts for the school and informed my uncle of a discrepancy just before he was murdered. Oh, and by the way, I have rather a lot of experience working with chemicals!'"

When his words faded out, the silence was audible. The secretary's gaze had fallen to the oak steps in front of him and my grandfather was looking at the man in disbelief. Standing by the door in his neat green livery, Todd adjusted his position a little and his black boots squeaked on the shiny wooden floor. This faint sound was enough to stir my grandfather, and he continued his interrogation.

"That last fact is interesting, don't you think? Your uncle was murdered; a flask of bubbling chemicals was placed at the scene for no apparent reason other than to throw suspicion on an innocent member of staff. Then, later on, I discovered that you had assisted your uncle with his investigations into chemical weapons during the

186

war. Something of a coincidence, don't you agree?"

"I had nothing to do with his death."

Lord Edgington descended the steps from the stage. "So perhaps your uncle set the scene himself then? His attacker struck him about the head with… an ornament, and, using his last reserve of strength, Tobias reached out for a handful of bicarbonate of soda and a few other ingredients, then placed them all together to balance on his nose like a seal in a circus. He even managed to light a firework to add a little more flair to the spectacle before swiftly dying for my grandson to find him."

Grandfather stood inches away from our suspect for five ticks of the old school clock. When it was clear that the secretary would not be intimidated, Lord Edgington walked over to the windows that overlooked the quad.

"Don't mock me," Greeves finally screeched.

"Huh," my grandfather scoffed, putting his hand to the frame in front of him, presumably to ensure they really were nailed shut. "I'm not mocking you, man. In actual fact, I don't believe you're nearly as stupid as you've been acting. I think you've probably got quite the brain up in that skull of yours. But like so many people I have known in this world, you are a victim of the forces that whirl around you. You are a tiny fish tossed and beaten by the waves, hunted and harassed by your larger compatriots. Your uncle, the Crabb sisters and so many others have bullied and abused you in order to achieve their goals."

I felt quite sorry for the poor man. I can't say I'd ever been particularly keen on the fellow myself, but there was no need to go overboard with the insults. I also thought that Grandfather had devised superior metaphors in the past and should make more of an effort.

"That is exactly it." Far from being downhearted by his interviewer's words, Greeves was suddenly invigorated. "I have been used by every last person at this school. I am everybody's fool."

"Is that why your uncle is dead?"

Again, my grandfather's harsh words failed to have the effect he had intended, and Greeves seemed quite satisfied with the change in the conversation. "No, not at all. But it is the reason that, at around the time he was murdered, Doreen the dinner lady had forced me into a cupboard and was threatening to hurt me in a number of unpleasant ways if I told anyone that I'd caught her robbing the students."

I was a little confused about what was happening. From what I could tell, the more miserable the topic, the lighter his tone became. "And I'd only found out about it because I'd bumped into the monstrous woman while she was picking up a sack of her ill-gotten gains from the prefects' room. I've no idea where Dominic Rake was though. Have you considered that he could have been upstairs killing poor Uncle Tobias?"

Grandfather looked less than impressed by the question. "Yes, thank you. The possibility had occurred to me. Rake entered the school to let Doreen into the prefects' room. And have you considered that he was able to leave without being seen after you abandoned your desk?"

Greeves's self-pity had apparently filled him with confidence, and he met my grandfather's gaze once more. "I, sir, am a victim of fate." He was quite Shakespearean in his delivery. "I am no killer and I am no thief, and yet I have been surrounded by such people since I set foot on Oakton Academy's grounds. I beseech you to believe me, sir. I was mistreated first by my uncle, who was happy to pay me less than any other worker, then by Dr Steadfast when he forced me into his schemes." He'd moved on from the bard and now sounded like some grim eighteenth-century novel of confessions and hardships. He was a modern-day 'Pamela'.

"Wait. You're saying it was Steadfast who forced you to hide the club's earnings?"

This was another chance for Greeves to detail his woes. "Yes, I would have to stay up all night just to write a few numbers in the books whilst my uncle was asleep. We put any large amounts down as donations from generous parents."

Grandfather rushed forward, his face alive with excitement. "You're missing the point entirely. You're telling me that it was Oberon Steadfast who convinced you to take part in their illegal activities?"

Greeves let out his high, fragile laugh one last time. "Yes, of course. The man's a monster. He was the one who threatened me with scandal and suffering if I didn't do as he required. The reason I never imagined Tobias stealing the money was because I was so sure that Steadfast was behind it. I had no doubt that he'd blame it all on me, which is why I told my uncle."

He had reached the peak of his pity, and everything that followed was a mere recapitulation. "But it was Steadfast who organised the club and started the gambling. He brought the alcohol and whatever else was needed into the school and he was the thug who coerced me into his plans."

My grandfather seized the man's shoulders and looked him dead in the eye. "I have one final question for you."

Greeves had grown nervous again and began to whimper. "I never meant for anything bad to happen. I had no-"

"Calm yourself, man. This isn't about you anymore." The Marquess of Edgington fell silent for a moment. "Did you tell Dr Steadfast that there was money missing from the school?"

"Yes... Yes, I did."

# CHAPTER THIRTY-ONE

The quiet hall exploded into life as my grandfather issued his various orders.

"Christopher, collect Mr Mayfield from the rose garden. Todd, fetch Inspector Blunt while I find the other suspects. If anyone sees Dr Steadfast, he's to be arrested on sight for the murder of Tobias Hardcastle. We'll meet at the headmaster's cottage."

"Yes, milord," Todd answered and slipped from the room to fulfil his task.

Grandfather was soon after him, off in search of the Crabb sisters and Dominic Rake. Which meant that I was left behind with Jonathan Greeves, whose tears had finally arrived.

"I'm just so relieved," he wailed. "I was sure as soon as you found the body that I'd be the one blamed for it."

"Oh, ummm, congratulations." I'd clearly chosen the wrong response. It caused his cries to ring out louder.

"I've never been a lucky person. I've spent my whole life being kicked around and mistreated. My father never-"

I could see this would end up being a lengthy explanation, so I decided to interrupt. "Perhaps you should come with me." I turned to leave the assembly hall, with the sobbing chap at my heels.

"Father didn't love me. He was a cold-blooded sort, though I can't really blame him as he never knew his own parents..." The story went on like this for some minutes and I was soon au fait with a large part of the Greeves-Hardcastle family history. I really did feel sorry for the fellow, though I was glad when we arrived at the rose garden and I no longer had to listen to his sniffling.

Mother and Mr Mayfield had evidently enjoyed a pleasant afternoon together as we'd been interrogating suspects and identifying murderers. Delilah was lying on the blanket beside them, taking up half the space. I should have known that she'd stay where the food was.

"Oh, Chrissy," Mother said, her voice as warm as that summer's day as we approached. "How nice to have you back with us. There are still some pork pies left if you'd like to join us."

"There's a drop of tea too," Herbie added, picking up the flask and shaking the contents. "Can I tempt you, Jonathan?"

"I would absolutely love a cup of tea," Greeves said in a mousey whisper. "That would be just the ticket for my frayed-"

"Sorry. No time for that." I felt I should inject some urgency into the proceedings. "Grandfather has identified our culprit and we're assembling the suspects over at the Hardcastles' cottage."

"Astonishing!" Herbie said. "Who's the killer?"

It didn't feel nearly dramatic enough to just blurt it out like that and I dithered, which meant that Greeves gave the game away on my behalf.

"It was Dr Steadfast." His mouth formed a suspenseful O and he found another way to feel sorry for himself. "I've never told you this, but Tobias was my uncle and I'm terribly upset about it."

I was happy that mother left Herbie and me to pack away the picnic hamper so that she could comfort the school secretary. I like to think of myself as a sympathetic person, but my patience had run out. I'd never met such a lachrymose fellow before. He was as wet as a dishcloth.

Herbie helped things along by striding out of the rose garden rather masterfully. I fell in step with him as the others trailed behind, and then Todd and Inspector Blunt soon joined us. I felt very purposeful, marching along as a gang, off to solve a crime. As we reached the field, a terrifying feminine scream rang out in the woods and, half a minute later, one of the constables appeared.

"Inspector," he called from the path. "You'd better come quickly, we've arrested a man. He came into the cottage with a knife."

"Very good, Wilkins!" Blunt replied, quickening his step to a canter. "Lucky you were there."

I failed to see how luck came into it when my grandfather had predicted this very outcome and set men at the cottage to prevent any further loss of life. I didn't say anything though. I had no doubt that the superlative Lord Edgington would be along at any moment to reveal just how clever he'd been.

Even Mother and Jonathan Greeves were animated by this new development and the whole lot of us ran into the woods to discover the fate of the various players. Delilah got there first, of course. She seemed disappointed when we arrived at the cottage and, rather than a third picnic of the day, we found a large history teacher being held on the sitting room floor by two police constables. Mrs Hardcastle was passed out on the sofa and, while the rest of us thrilled in the excitement of the scene, Delilah looked positively miffed.

"Is the lady all right?" Blunt asked, and Herbie immediately rushed to her side.

"Celia?" He put the back of his hand to her forehead, though I doubted that her shock could bring on a fever. Either way, the gesture seemed to rouse her, and she made a faint murmur.

P.C. Wilkins peered around the side of his detainee. "She collapsed when we caught the chap, sir. We spied him coming and hid either side of the door. He didn't put up a fight, but we got the knife off him." He gave Steadfast a shake, and the disgraced teacher looked away indifferently.

"That's sterling work, boys." Blunt was ecstatic. "Really top notch policemanship."

Mama was wide awake by this point, and Herbert helped her to sit up. "I'm so sorry," she said to the room, but she might well have been talking to her admirer alone. "I don't know what came over me. I saw the knife and just…" She didn't manage to finish that sentence and, for a moment, I thought she might faint again.

My chemistry teacher turned to address the culprit. "You swine, Steadfast. How could you murder another man in cold blood? I might have had my differences with Tobias, but I would never resort to such wickedness."

My beloathed (yes, I'm aware it's not a word) history teacher actually smiled then as he turned back to face his accuser. He took pleasure in the pain he had caused and opened his mouth to insult the good man further. "No, of course not, Herbert. In fact, you're nauseatingly saintly."

I have to say, that of all the things I'd discovered that day, Mr Mayfield's innocence was the most rewarding. If Grandfather had turned up at that moment and revealed that the kind, softly spoken chap was the true killer… well, I'm not certain whether I could have trusted another person for as long as I lived.

Grandfather turned up at that moment, and I had a minor heart attack. "Excellent work, Thompson, Wilkins," he said, addressing the officers who stood either side of their prisoner.

"I was just saying the very same thing," Blunt added, as though this in itself was an achievement. "Excellent policemanship." This was not a word I was previously familiar with, though apparently the inspector was keen to make as much use of it as possible. He stepped closer to Steadfast and peered up into his arrogant face. "You're going to prison for a long time for what you did, matey."

"Is that right?" the murderer asked. "So would you like to explain what I'm accused of?"

It was Blunt's turn to run short of words. "Well... you've... you know, murder and the like. I don't know the exact details, but you're clearly guilty. I knew it from the moment I saw you." He looked over at my grandfather for help.

As Doreen, Matron and Dominic Rake now entered the room, our party had swollen to fourteen people. It was lucky that Delilah was outside playing with the gnomes in the garden, as there was standing room only in the small sitting room. Grandfather would have answered the plea, but had to navigate past his chauffeur, daughter and the school secretary before he could get a clear view of Steadfast.

"He's guilty of... Actually, this is ridiculous. Perhaps it would be better if we all went outside where there's more space. I can barely breathe in here, let alone think."

A brief murmur of agreement led to an awful lot of shuffling as this plan was enacted. Thanks to Doreen and Matron blocking the doorway, no one could leave until a short dance had taken place to clear the bottleneck. Finally though, we made it outside.

Even the garden wasn't big enough for the lot of us, so we spaced out around the clearing, like pagan monks in some ancient ritual. It was most exciting, and I couldn't wait to hear how Grandfather had arrived at the truth.

Once everyone was quiet, and all eyes were pointed his way, Lord Edgington began. "I could list the crimes of the man who stands before you and explain exactly how I came to discover his guilt, but I rather think that I should ask one of my assistants to tell us what happened."

My grandfather could flit between proud and magnanimous depending on his mood. He extended his arm, as though he were allowing me through a door in front of him, and everyone there waited to hear what I had to say.

"This is your moment, Christopher," he pronounced rather dramatically.

I really wish he hadn't.

# CHAPTER THIRTY-TWO.

"Right, yes..." I thought this was a good strong start to my imminent detailing of every last scrap of evidence and red herring that we'd come across. "Dr Steadfast... Dr Oberon Steadfast – named, one assumes, after the king of the fairies in 'A Midsummer Night's Dream' by William Shakespeare (1564 to 1616)."

Despite my waffling, and the fact that I was supposed to be laying out the case against him, Dr Steadfast seemed rather happy that I'd remembered these dates correctly.

"But my history teacher was born neither king, nor magical creature. He is very much mortal and prone to human sin."

Grandfather clearly wanted to be home in time for dinner and hurried me along. "Yes, thank you, Christopher. But perhaps you could ease off on the melodrama."

I cleared my throat and started again, still trying to summon up what I knew for certain about the case. "Much like in a Shakespearean tragedy, we had two opposing forces crash up against one another. Julius Caesar and the Roman senate, Macbeth and his own ambition, Cleopatra and the asp. And sadly for Tobias Hardcastle, he would be cast in the role of the fallen king."

The dead man's wife let out a stifled cry and grandfather made a brief shake of the head to remind me to choose my words more carefully. I had hoped to be clear and concise, but, alas and alack, everything I said had turned into a lecture on Elizabethan drama.

"I found Mr Hardcastle murdered in his office this morning, not fifteen minutes after he'd been called to school because of a note left on the secretary's desk. A note in Mr Hardcastle's own handwriting." I realised I'd already missed out an important fact. "And, ten minutes earlier, my chemistry teacher Mr Mayfield had also been called to the school through the Marconi public address system, which had recently been installed at great expense."

I won't lie. I was really struggling to get to the point. I was happy to focus on the slightest detail in the hope that some great revelation would soon come to me and I could construct a case against Dr Steadfast. Though the cool of the evening was beginning to set in, my whole body was clammy with sweat and I wished that someone would speak up to end my humiliation.

I paused, looking around the faces of foes and loved ones alike. "We know that there were five people in the school building at the time that Mr Hardcastle was murdered. But, when I arrived there some minutes later, both Dominic Rake and Dr Steadfast had fled the scene. Meanwhile, Doreen Crabb – ex-convict and inferior dinner lady – was in the prefects' room on the ground floor."

Doreen snarled across at me. I kept talking, despite the fear that she and her sister both inspired. "I heard her as I climbed the stairs towards the staff corridor. She was talking to someone, though it was only this evening that we discovered it was the school secretary, Jonathan Greeves. There is one thing we never found out though. Mr Greeves, where exactly were you off to when you spotted Doreen in the prefects' room?"

I thought this must be very relevant and that we'd been terribly stupid not to have asked it before. The truth didn't quite live up to my imagination.

"Well, if you must know..." He'd stopped crying by now, but looked as nervous as ever. "I was on my way back from the lavatory. I knew that Mr Hardcastle would be furious if he caught me away from my desk, but I simply couldn't wait any longer."

My face turned as red as the carnations in the Hardcastles' garden. "Right, yes... thank you for your honesty." I quickly changed the topic. "So, anyway, I was in the school, climbing the stairs to visit the-"

I had just built up a head of steam when Dr Steadfast interrupted. "What were you doing poking about where you weren't supposed to be? Why weren't you running in the quarter-marathon?"

I thought it rather rich that a murderer would attempt to impart moral lessons. His superior tone could still cut through me though. "Oh, ummm sorry, sir. It was nothing really, just end of term larks. You see there was a pigeon that smiled at me... or rather, Marmaduke Adelaide saved me from-"

"Christopher!" It was Grandfather's turn to tell me off. "Can we please stick to the facts of the case?"

"Ah, righto. So up in the staff corridor, I tiptoed towards Mr Hardcastle's office and, when I was about to enter, there was a colossal

196

bang. Pushing the door open, I discovered my headmaster propped up dead beside his flogging block. There was blood pouring from his skull and his head had been tipped back for the killer to place a beaker of bubbling green liquid on top of him."

I realised that the details of Hardcastle's death would only serve to upset his wife more. Luckily, she had my mother to support her, who managed to dampen down her cries.

"My first fear was that my chemistry teacher would be involved but even the police could see that the chemicals and the explosion were nothing but red herrings."

"Hey," Blunt intervened. "What do you mean, 'even the police'?" It seemed that I'd offended just about everyone by this point.

I kept my eyes ahead and pressed on. "When I returned to the scene of the crime with my brilliant Grandfather in tow, he was confident that Mr Mayfield would not have taken the risk of implicating himself so directly in a crime, even as a ruse. He also noticed a number of important elements in the headmaster's office. There was a long scorch mark on the floor and the remnants of an exploded firework. There was paper wrapped around the bubbling flask as well and, perhaps most importantly, we found the murder weapon; an ornamental monkey carved from a coconut which had previously sat on the dead man's bookshelf."

This caused a murmur of laughter from Todd and the Crabb sisters, as they were yet to hear the whole story. I found it very off-putting, but luckily my Grandfather was there to move things along.

"Perhaps you can tell everyone the reason that such a long fuse was used on the firework and why there was a piece of paper secured to the chemical flask?"

It was very good of him to help me out like that, even if I didn't have a clue what the answer was. "Well, that's obvious, isn't it?" I said to cover my ignorance.

"Of course!" My mother was still standing with Mrs Hardcastle, but had been following the story far better than I had been telling it. "The killer – or rather, Dr Steadfast – made sure that the firework would explode sometime after he'd left the building. And the paper was most likely wetted so that, whatever substance was placed on top of it would eventually leak through, thus delaying the chemical reaction which you witnessed when you found the body."

"Exactly," I said, realising that Grandfather had explained this fact hours before, and it had completely escaped me. "Using a mixture of bicarbonate of soda, green food colouring and other common ingredients, Steadfast made it look as though the reaction had only just taken place when the explosion went off. He also tied the murder to Mr Mayfield who was known to be in love-"

It occurred to me that it would be indiscreet to finish that sentence. Mrs Hardcastle was standing right there in front of everyone, and it would have been uncomfortable for her to have to listen to the rest of it.

I pretended to sneeze, and started again. "Mr Mayfield was known to be in love... with chemistry." I thought I'd done rather well to get away with this, but Herbie spoke up nonetheless.

"It's all right, Christopher. I don't mind admitting it." He sounded very noble and regarded the Mama of Oakton Academy as he spoke. "I have been in love with Celia Hardcastle since the day I met her. I should have expected that anyone with a grudge against her husband would tie the murder to me. But I am no killer." He directed a look of disdain at the real murderer.

It's funny how, when I'd heard my grandfather summing up cases, everyone fell silent and listened as though King George had popped by with an important message. On the scant occasions I'd tried to copy him, it felt more like a debate than a presentation, with everyone eager to contribute. He was smiling at me then, urging me to continue, and so I did what I could.

"We spoke to Mr Mayfield before the police arrived. He had been called back to the school, just like Mr Hardcastle, but, when he went to his classroom, there was no one there – which left him without a shred of an alibi. Aside from this and the fact that various items were missing from his laboratory, we discovered nothing more which would suggest he was involved in the crime."

Grandfather let out one of his soft, hmmms, so I turned to look at him. "Sorry, I didn't mean to interrupt. It's just... Well, Herbert Mayfield did come running back from the teachers' cottages shortly before we learnt of Dr Steadfast's injury. And perhaps you didn't notice that his story differed in some key respects from Mrs Hardcastle's when-" He hesitated then and finally cut the explanation short. "No, no. I'm sorry. It's not relevant. Please carry on."

I really wished at that moment that I had taken the time to get changed. As if all the interruptions weren't embarrassing enough, I was still wearing my running kit. I decided that, if there was one more interruption, I would hand over to my mother, as she was clearly far better at this detecting business than I was.

"So... where was I?" I raced to answer my own question before someone else could jump in. "Yes, we interviewed various suspects, slowly coming to the truth and exposing any number of dark secrets along the way. Just for example, it turns out that Doreen the dinner lady and Matron are sisters!"

I'd hoped for a big reaction to this, but everyone stayed mum. To be honest, now that I could see the two of them standing next to one another, I had to marvel that I had failed to notice the similarities between them. They were practically identical, right down to the hunched backs and goitres. And, though I'd never actually seen them in the same place until then, I felt terribly dim not to have made the connection.

"Not only that, but they are convicted felons who were known to my grandfather from his days on the force. Though they attempted to deny it, we could tell that the two of them came to work here with a nefarious goal in mind. You see the Crabb sisters' speciality is petty theft. Doreen does the heavy lifting and Constance is the mastermind. They pressured the head prefect into confiscating as much valuable property from the other boys as possible, which they could then sell on."

Matron did not appear grateful that I had detailed her crimes in public, but at least she kept quiet.

"This was just the beginning. We soon discovered that they were involved in a gambling den and nightclub which was being operated out of Oakton's dining hall. A gambling den which Dr Steadfast himself was instrumental in establishing."

There was still no reaction. I suppose it's harder to impress a crowd with tales of drunken revelry and betting when there's already been a murder.

I walked into the centre of the circle to better address my attentive audience. "Dr Steadfast wasn't the only one to break the law, though. Someone was stealing money from the school's coffers and..." I looked to my mother for help, but she was no use. "And..." I turned to my grandfather, who was willing me on, but that didn't tell me what to say next. "And that's as much as I know."

I felt like a total failure. Delilah looked terribly sympathetic, Herbie gave me an encouraging wink and even Inspector Blunt crumpled his face a little tighter – which I was willing to interpret as a supportive gesture.

"I'm sorry, Grandfather. I wanted to live up to your expectations, but there are some parts of the story which I've really struggled to make sense of."

Swishing his grey coat through the air, he joined me in the centre of the clearing. The cheerful look on his face already made me feel better.

"There's nothing to be sorry for, boy. You've done a truly remarkable job." He gave my shoulder an affectionate squeeze, then spun on the spot like a ringmaster. "Christopher has displayed his skills of observation and reasoning quite admirably today, but, if you don't mind, I'll take over from here."

# CHAPTER THIRTY-THREE

The falling sun cast long shadows across the clearing. Standing in the middle of his audience, Grandfather's silhouette stretched across the ground to turn him into a giant.

"Practically everything that young Christopher has told you is true. A man was murdered in an elaborate fashion, a seam of criminality has been found to run through the school, and several of you present have been complicit in a number of crimes."

Having been at her master's side throughout, Delilah decided that this would be a good moment to go for a walk around the inside of the circle. It was hard to know whether she was sizing up the suspects or merely saying hello to everyone.

"The initial crime scene suggested many things, but I refused to be taken in by the picture that the killer had painted. I considered why he had relied on a weapon found within the office, instead of bringing a club or knife. I noted the chemicals used. Bicarbonate of soda, citric acid and cornflour are easily purchased in a chemist's or grocer's, though the killer helped himself from Mr Mayfield's laboratory to further link him to the crime. This combination of substances would ensure a dramatic reaction. The delayed trigger of the wet paper atop the flask would work to suggest that our culprit was still close by."

He stopped and glanced at the guilty party. "Of course, I didn't fall for such obvious manipulation. The concoction was decidedly amateurish in its conception; the sort of experiment you might find in a beginner's chemistry book, available in any school library." Steadfast snorted at this. It would be hard to imagine any greater insult to the haughty chap than being described as an amateur. "In fact, with a little careful persuasion on my part, not even the police would make that mistake."

Blunt didn't complain this time, but crossed his arms and looked back towards the field.

My Grandfather continued, unconcerned by any offence caused. "What I did notice was the timing of the murder. The fact that it was committed on the very last day of school – the very last day of Mr Mayfield's employment – was hugely significant. You see, the more obvious option would have been to wait until tomorrow. There would have been fewer people around to get in the way and less chance of being caught in the act. But tomorrow, Mr Mayfield would not have been present to take the blame. I also found it interesting that the killer went through with his plan despite the fact I was on the premises to witness the prelude and aftermath of the crime.

"These two facts revealed just how essential it was for the killing to take place today and further cemented the idea in my mind that Mr Herbert Mayfield was not the killer. With the police interrogating the obvious suspect, I moved on to consider who else could be guilty. I quickly ruled out the majority of Oakton pupils, for the simple reason that it is the last day of term, the holiday is about to begin and, were they to be caught, they would miss out on those carefree days of summer. Even the head prefect Dominic Rake, who had been spotted in the school shortly before the murder took place, would have been unlikely to take such a risk on his very last day as an Oaktonian."

He looked over at Rake, who appeared ashamed at his part in all that had occurred. He cast his gaze down and would barely glance up again until Grandfather's speech was over.

"The presence of two convicted criminals on school grounds might normally have swayed my suspicions in their direction, but I happen to know Doreen and Constance Crabb rather well. They are immoral, light-fingered and selfish but, based on our lengthy acquaintance, far from violent creatures."

Having seen what the dinner lady could do with a ladle, I was not so convinced by my Grandfather's argument. I wasn't going to be the one to contradict him though.

"Ahhhh, fank you, Mr superintendent Lord Edgington," Doreen cooed. She was clearly moved by his words.

"Awfully nice of you, Your Highness," her sister echoed.

"I could not rule them out so quickly, of course. As I have learnt many times in my career, past behaviour is not always an indicator of current probity. And if anything, their employment at Oakton made me question what scheme they had in mind. True to form, theft and opportunism were the magnitude of their crimes, but they were helpful enough to point me towards a key part of the mystery."

"You're very welcome, Your Majesty," Matron gabbed once more.

"Such a lovely fella," Doreen whispered to her sister.

"Lovely!" Matron agreed. "It's always been a pleasure to be arrested by Mr Superintendent Cranley Lord Edgington Hall."

They continued muttering like this for some time as Grandfather got on with his explanation.

"What surprised me was that the larger crime ring in operation at Oakton was not directed by my hapless former acquaintances, but the teachers themselves. What started out as a social club for staff to let their hair down without the puritanical headmaster finding out, soon degenerated into a society of sin. Excessive drinking, fighting, gambling and illicit substances converted the Oakton pupils' dining hall into a popular nightclub. Locals came from all over the region to experience The Oakton Canteen. An American-style *speakeasy* in the heart of old Surrey." He pronounced this neologism as though it was a scandal just to utter it.

"But with illegality, comes the need for respectability. Something had to be done with all of the money that was flowing through the pockets of the club's founders and some bright spark had the idea to coerce the school secretary into the operation. Jonathan Greeves is a callow, weak-willed young man who has suffered much abuse in his life at the hands of those around him."

Greeves said nothing, though he appeared to agree with the assessment. He shook his head sadly throughout, but looked a little cheered by the pity he was receiving.

"By hiding the money within the school's accounts, the teachers could increase the wages of all those who were involved in the scheme. Not least of course, the ringleader and effective *rumrunner* of the gang, Dr Oberon Steadfast. The only problem that was likely to arise was if Mr Hardcastle himself were to investigate the Oakton academy accounts. But what chance was there of that? Hardcastle had the moral education of his pupils to deal with and had little time for such worldly concerns. And besides, he had placed his nephew in the role of school secretary. Jonathan Greeves was terrified of his uncle, and Tobias could trust that his own kin would not go against his wishes."

This drew a gasp of surprise from several in attendance. Evidently the Hardcastle family likeness was less noticeable than that of the Crabb sisters.

"As our immortal bard wrote, 'If money go before, all ways do lie open' and the trail of money led once more to Dr Steadfast's door. But Jonathan was not the only young man to be caught up in these transgressions. As head of the sixth form, Dr Steadfast chose school prefects that he could easily manipulate and then roped them into the running of the nightclub. Though he had been hired to impart knowledge and high principles to his students, his desire for money trumped all other concerns. He was no better than Fagin; a kidsman who cares nothing for the children he has corrupted."

My grandfather approached the odious fellow and looked at him severely. His tone and the abundant quotes he laced his speech with told me that he was playing Steadfast at his own pompous game.

"A history teacher, of all people, should have learnt that, 'The love of money is the root of all evil'. But perhaps more importantly that, 'A fool and his money are soon parted'. Through some unlucky twist, Tobias Hardcastle did indeed discover the wealth pouring through the school and decided to keep some for himself. Greeves realised that money was missing and, not suspecting that his upright uncle would have been involved, told Dr Steadfast of the situation. Steadfast didn't like the outcome and plotted to kill his boss. And that, as they say, is the end of the story."

My grandfather clapped his hands together, as though he were dusting them off after a long day's work. No one spoke. It was not because we were so bowled over by his skills of deduction, but the fact it had concluded so rapidly.

I dared put a question to him. "Is that really *it*? Have you got nothing more to add?"

He looked rather put out. "There are plenty more details, but that's the thrust of the case. Steadfast is a greedy, querulous man who killed for money. What more does anyone need to know?"

I wasn't the only one who felt a touch swindled by the experience, and a rumble of conversation spread around the group.

"But what about the trap in Steadfast's house?" Blunt was quick to ask.

"And why did he intend to attack Celia?" Herbie was most distressed over this matter.

"Where's your evidence for any of it?" Steadfast himself

demanded, his wobbling chins protruding indignantly.

Grandfather looked quite aggrieved at the response and emitted a tired sigh. "Is that really what you want?"

"Yes!" half the assembled witnesses shouted at once.

"And you can't fill in the gaps for yourself?"

"No!"

"Oh, very well then."

# CHAPTER THIRTY-FOUR

He gave me a wink, which I found nigh on impossible to interpret. Was he saying, *Good job, Christopher, you laid the groundwork nicely*? Or, perhaps he meant, *Watch me go, this is the good bit!* Either way, he proudly strutted out into the ring, just as a pair of collared doves came to land in the elm trees nearby. Incidentally, they were definitely collared doves. Such birds are unmistakable and I am absolutely ninety per cent certain that's what they were.

"Tobias was murdered for the money he had taken from his own school, which had come from the Oakton nightclub disguised as parental donations. He must have been surprised to discover such a glut of funds and filtered the money off for his own ends. Unluckily for him, his nephew spotted the discrepancy and, to avoid being accused of the crime himself, told his uncle about it. Hardcastle, in turn, became nervous and did what he could to cover the shortfall. He rang the one parent at this school who he was sure he could flatter into handing over enough money; the notorious Horatio Adelaide – former criminal, turned well-to-do landowner.

"We can ascertain from his excessively violent treatment of two of his students for their end-of-term hijinks that Tobias was shaken by the position he found himself in. Lamentably, however, the damage was done. The donation he had obtained from Adelaide would not arrive in time to prevent Dr Steadfast exacting his revenge."

Delilah had finished her tour and came to sit beside her master. He stroked her long, silky ears absentmindedly as he got to a key point in his explanation. "This brings me to one of the first pieces of evidence which led me to identifying our culprit. Dr Steadfast, as he revealed to me this morning when discussing my grandson's academic progress, considers himself something of a *graphologist*. In layman's terms, a *graphologist* is an expert in handwriting and the good doctor (of history) went into great gushing detail about the elegance of Christopher's written script.

"Now, I don't know about you, but I very much doubt there would be more than one *graphologist* on Oakton's staff. Which led me to wonder, who would be better placed to falsify a note from Tobias

Hardcastle than a *graphologist*?" He stressed the word each time he said it in order to underline the very basic message he was conveying. "I have no doubt it would have been incredibly simple for a man of Dr Steadfast's talents to produce the note, not least because he already had some experience copying Tobias's hand." He didn't explain this point just then but rushed on to the next clue.

"Add this to the fact that his sleeves had traces of white powder this morning, which was too coarse to be chalk dust, and that he is also one of the most pompous and self-involved beasts I've ever had the misfortune of meeting, and I was on my guard with him from the very first moment."

This stinging critique led to some cheering, with which, I must admit, I felt compelled to participate.

"Ha!" Matron bellowed. "He's got you there, Steady."

"You deserve everything that's coming to you." Herbie sounded quite furious for once.

"It serves you right for giving me two hundred lines!" I'm aware that the man had committed far greater crimes, but, for yours truly, this was the one that cut deepest.

Grandfather raised one hand and closed his eyes to wait for silence.

"Of course, no one had been murdered when I met him, but Steadfast was the first name that came to mind when I inspected the headmaster's body. The circumstances of the death pointed to a killer who thought he was cleverer than everyone around him – so far, so Steadfast. The killer had done everything he could to distance himself from the murder – forging the note in Hardcastle's writing, not bringing a murder weapon to the scene but relying on whatever he happened to find there, lazily attempting to frame an innocent man for the crime – and together, these elements formed a pattern. It was hard to believe in the superficial evidence when I already knew so much of it was staged for the benefit of the police. Which is why I've held onto the belief that the man now standing beside P.C. Wilkins is a murderer.

"As for the trap that was set at his own front door, the supremely intelligent Dr Steadfast had once more struck upon a stratagem so fiendish that no one would possibly see through it. Except, of course, that I did. Knowing that I suspected his involvement in the murder, he left our interview determined to obfuscate the investigation. Having stopped at the caretaker's hut to steal the equipment he needed, he broke in through the rear of his cottage to set the spring-gun trap and waited until an officer was in earshot before setting it off.

"The stone only grazed him, as he knew to fall backwards, away from the bullet, which would get nowhere near him. It was a risky enterprise but not without merit. Had a less experienced investigator been in charge, we might have crossed him off our list of suspects for good."

Blunt clearly wasn't happy with my grandfather's choice of words, but was growing used to such minor slights. Taking advantage of this pause in the proceedings to stretch his legs, Grandfather began to pace around the inside of the circle, much as his dog had minutes earlier.

"With this in mind, all I needed was a better understanding of the killer's motives. I learnt about the club and Dr Steadfast's success as a pugilist, but, in truth, money is not the root of anything. It is what money enables men to do that drives them to greed, wickedness and murder. I knew from Dominic Rake that, despite his newfound wealth and boxing prowess, the unmarried Dr Steadfast had little luck in finding love at the nightclub he had established.

"And so he turned his thoughts to other quarters. Forging the headmaster's handwriting to avoid detection, he wrote notes to Celia Hardcastle in which he confessed his love for her. When we interviewed this upstanding lady, it was evident that she was protecting someone's dignity. I believe Dr Steadfast pursued her, perhaps visiting her in the rose garden where she spent her afternoons tending to the flowers. I have no doubt that he attempted to win her over with sweet words and boasts of his burgeoning riches."

I expected another cry from Mama, but she was out of tears and stood as still as the lions in Trafalgar square. In fact, no one made a sound. We were processing the deeds of a truly despicable man as Grandfather guided us along to the conclusion of his tale.

"Steadfast killed out of lust. He lusted after everything he lacked, from money and respect to another man's wife. As we saw at his quite spectacular prize-giving ceremony this afternoon, he believed that he should have been made headmaster and, in his mind, by killing his rival, his problems would be erased. He would ascend to the headship, obtain the woman he desired and retain the money he felt he had earned."

Steadfast had been robbed of his arrogance. The sneering look he so often wore had disappeared, and he stood with a vacant expression on his face, saying nothing.

"I can only imagine what he would have turned the school into if he'd been in charge. He had already succeeded in transforming this ancient academy into a den of iniquity and who knows-"

I have to admit, my grandfather was the one sounding rather pompous at this point, so it wasn't entirely unwelcome when Steadfast slipped his arm free from P.C. Wilkins, threw a punch at P.C. Thompson and, with a beastly grunt, ran as fast as he could into the woods.

Blunt was apoplectic and could hardly form the words he needed as he stumbled after the freshly escaped prisoner and barrelled straight into Wilkins. Herbie and Todd were on the far side of the clearing, Rake looked drained of energy, the ladies were wearing skirts and uncomfortable shoes and my grandfather was an old man. There was only one thing for it.

"Get him Christopher!" Todd shouted after me as, for approximately the nineteenth time that week, I started running.

Delilah immediately joined us, apparently thinking this was the most wonderful game. She bounded alongside me as I attempted to motor my arms and legs in the fashion which Mr Bath was constantly telling me I must. I did not achieve any great velocity but would not let the blighter get away.

I could see Steadfast up ahead, darting through the trees. He might have been as strong as an ox and capable of killing a man with nothing but a coconut monkey, but he was no sprinter and I was slowly gaining on him – slowly being the operative word. I'd seen hedgehogs run faster.

Delilah yelped with excitement and it drove me onwards. I was suddenly happy that I still had my ugly red and white running kit on, as it made things much easier than my target was finding the experience. In another ten exhausting steps, I'd be on him.

I leaped athletically – well, that's not quite the word for it, but certainly not unathletically – over a fallen branch and somehow didn't stop there. For the briefest of moments, I wondered whether I had achieved the necessary speed to counteract gravity as, instead of landing as I'd intended, I continued on through the air to lay my hands upon him. My weight on his back sent the man sprawling forwards, and I knew that the race was run.

I heard a cheer go up from the crowd that had bunched together not so very far behind us. I couldn't respond because I was breathing too heavily and had laid out to recover on the large man's back.

My mother and grandfather strolled over, and I found the energy to smile at them.

"You were incredible, Christopher," my favourite person declared, though her father did not sound so enthusiastic.

"Yes, you outdid yourself. That was even slower than you ran this afternoon."

# CHAPTER THIRTY-FIVE

The two constables seized the murderer to make sure he wouldn't get away this time. Dr Steadfast had ended up with quite the bruise from his fall and, after all that running, looked appreciative of their support. I knew just how he felt.

There was discussion over what would happen to the minor criminals who had played a part in the case, but Grandfather pleaded in their favour.

"A criminal is a criminal!" Blunt complained, eager to get the wriggling Steadfast to a cell.

"Fine, do what you like with the teachers, but don't punish their pupils for what went on at the club." I was surprised by the compassion that my grandfather showed.

Blunt waved a disinterested hand through the balmy evening air and began to move away. "What will happen, will happen, and everyone will get what they deserve. That's the way of the law, God bless it!"

Summoning more sprightliness than I had when pursuing my errant history teacher, Grandfather sped in front of his old rival. "I'm afraid I'll have to disagree there, Inspector." His use of the man's rank made Blunt stop and take notice. "The fifteen years that Doreen and Constance Crabb have already served for their petty crimes were draconian enough. They do not need to return behind bars."

Blunt looked terribly hot and bothered and let out a channel of air up towards his hairless dome. "They're career criminals. If we don't arrest them, they'll run the same con again elsewhere."

"They won't!" Grandfather sounded sure of himself, but I didn't think much of his argument. "They've been denied the opportunities that most people take for granted their whole lives. If you'd just give them a chance."

Blunt let out his cynical laugh. He sounded like a woodpecker. "Oh yeah? What are you going to do? Keep an eye on them yourself?"

Lord Edgington's moustache performed a miniature wave. "That's exactly what I'll do. If you keep them out of your reports, I'll find them employment at Cranley Hall. I can see it now, Dorie can join

Cook in the kitchen and Connie can help to look after the servants' children. They'll learn the skills they should have acquired to do their jobs in the first place." He looked genuinely inspired by the idea.

Blunt was no idealist and remained unconvinced. "It's your house, matey. I wouldn't want them anywhere near my silverware."

Grandfather's positivity would not be diminished, and he hopped off to explain his grand idea to the Crabb sisters. There was someone I was almost as eager to talk to.

"I'm glad you're not a murderer, sir," I said a little weakly, as Herbie stopped to talk to me in front of the charming cottage.

"So am I." He smiled in a way that was very him and I realised that, despite the Steadfasts and Balustrades, the bullies and overbearing prefects, I would always have happy memories of Oakton. Teachers like Mr Mayfield made all the rest of it worthwhile.

"Sir, don't you think you could keep working here now?"

His grin became a… What's bigger than a grin?

"Well, that depends on matters out of my control."

The very fact that his answer wasn't an outright *no* filled me with hope. I looked over his shoulder to where P.C. Evans was having a last word with Mrs Hardcastle. "I understand."

He put his hand out for me to shake, and I happily took it.

"I bet you do, Prentiss."

Like Orpheus leaving the underworld, he allowed himself one last glance towards the little house and then ran off to catch up with Todd. Most of the others were floating back through the woods already, chatting over the developments as they went. Once the constable had finished his interview, Mother stayed behind to check on Mama. It was odd to see them together like that. My real mother and my school mother. Odd and rather heartwarming.

Todd had to ring Cranley to have an extra car sent, as there was no space in the Rolls Royce with all my luggage. While we waited, Mother went into the cottage to make a pot of tea. The three of us returned to the comfortable sitting room, which felt much bigger without a platoon of people crammed inside. I noticed once more what a pretty dwelling it was and caught the wonderful floral smell which seemed to emanate from every surface. Stepping into the house was like entering a meadow and I felt such sympathy for its sole remaining

214

inhabitant, who would now have to move on elsewhere. I half hoped she'd be offered a job at the school, fall in love with Herbie and... Well, perhaps I was getting ahead of myself there.

Celia Hardcastle still looked out of sorts, as my mother and I attempted a cheery conversation around her. Perhaps the first signs of her optimism were returning, but receiving guests soon after your husband has been murdered is hardly the ideal situation. When Grandfather returned, he entertained us with tales of his days at Scotland Yard. I'm quite certain he could have talked for a decade without running out of stories.

He eventually interrupted himself with a request. "I'm terribly sorry to bother you, Celia. But you wouldn't happen to have some lemon for my tea?"

Mother couldn't help laughing at this. "Father, I have never once known you to take lemon. Will you never stop surprising me?"

Celia attempted a smile. "Of course. I'll fetch one."

While she went to the kitchen, Grandfather rose from his armchair to look at a small bookshelf beside the window. "Quite a collection of classic texts you have here," he said when she returned. "Are they yours?"

"That's right." Mama seemed happy to talk about something far from the world of Oakton. "I was a voracious reader when I was younger."

Grandfather was scanning the spines and read off each name. "Middleton, Spencer, Barrett Browning, even Shakespeare. It was chemistry you studied though, wasn't it?" He turned back to look at her as she cut the bright yellow fruit on a saucer and the room filled with the scent.

"No, that was Tobias. I studied Latin and Ancient Greek."

"Ah, yes." He beamed benignly. "An admirable choice. You know, I've been thinking recently that it might be time I went to university myself."

"There you go, Father." My mother took a sip of tea to keep us in suspense. "Another surprise."

"Is it really so shocking that I should want to expand my mind, Violet?" No one answered his question, so he continued. "I joined the police as soon as I left Oakton and never had the chance to dedicate myself to one subject in earnest. Of course, were I to start now, I think I'd choose literature. I've no head for languages and science always seems rather clinical for my liking."

The three of us still seated on the sofas exchanged a polite glance as the old man continued to ramble.

"I would love to know more about the plays and novels I have adored for so much of my life." Spotting an interesting title, he pulled it from the shelf and brought the battered volume over with him. "Othello is a case in point. As a policeman, I've often wondered whether Iago's manipulation, which brings about the tragic death of Desdemona and, indeed, her husband Othello, would have led to his arrest. He lays no hands upon them, and yet, they both die."

My mother's breezy tone had abandoned her. "Father, must we discuss such topics?"

For the first time that day, he paid his daughter no heed. "Celia. What do you think?"

Mrs Hardcastle had her eyes fixed on the door and would not look at him as she spoke. "I'm afraid I don't know the play very well. I've always preferred comedy to tragedy."

"Ahh, I see." He put the book down on the cushion next to him. "Well it's a moot point anyway as Iago goes on to murder two people himself, but I've always wondered what punishment would be handed down for speaking poison in another man's ear." He watched our host as he said this, but she had turned to stone.

The atmosphere in the room had changed. My mother and I could only watch in horror as Grandfather's intentions became clear.

"I had assumed that your friend Dr Steadfast would have peached on you as his accomplice, and I've no doubt that he still will when the case goes to trial. Oh yes, as soon as he realises the evidence that's stacked against him, he'll confess to the crime, there'll be no stopping him from talking then."

He sat forward in his seat and refocused his gaze. "Is that why you set the trap for him, Celia? Could you not trust him to keep your secret? I must say that you did awfully well to engineer the deaths of two men whilst you were far away, with plenty of witnesses around you. In a way, it was that ingenuity which opened my mind to your involvement. Or rather, it was young Marmaduke Adelaide's subterfuge which mirrored yours."

Though my grandfather peppered his speech with questions, it was clear that this would be a monologue, and he was happy to chatter on without reply. "Marmaduke realised that the fact he was running a quarter marathon on the field was the perfect alibi. He could send his accomplice to do his bidding and no one would suspect him. It was not so different from your husband being murdered on the busiest day of the school calendar. The very impossibility of your involvement put the idea in my head that there could be more than one killer. The second attack proved it.

"Steadfast came to woo you, but, instead, you fooled him. You convinced that gullible blowhard that it was your husband who was stealing the money from the nightclub and that the only solution to his problems was to eliminate Tobias. What other incentives did you promise? The headmaster's job? Your undying love, perhaps? I'm sure it was quite simple to flatter the odious character and bend him to your will. You knew you wouldn't be able to trust him once the deed was done. Which is why you set the trap in his house before parents' day began."

My grandfather took a slice of lemon from the coffee table and crushed it above his tea cup.

"Since ten minutes past twelve, when your husband left the field, until this very moment, you've had someone with you to act as a witness. You ruled yourself out as a suspect, by setting everything in motion before you took up your very public spot in front of the crowds. Like Iago, you killed without lifting a hand in anger. You might even have got away with it if it hadn't rained last night. I saw a slender print under the window of Steadfast's cottage. And there are soiled boots by the door to your house which I have no doubt will match."

My mother gasped behind her hand. This was the moment of no return; the moment that proved Celia Hardcastle was not the innocent we had taken her to be.

My grandfather continued, undisturbed. "When we found Steadfast largely unharmed, it presented two possibilities. Either he had set the trap himself, as I've already outlined, or, on finding the door ajar, he was wary of what his accomplice had planned for him and entered cautiously. He desired you, he did as you asked of him, but he was wise enough not to trust you entirely."

He took his time then, selecting a small spoon from the tray and slowly stirring the tea.

"You see, physical evidence of a crime is often discovered after a detective's suspicions are aroused. When we spoke to you here this afternoon, you refused to name a likely culprit. You hinted that there was someone you were protecting, and set us on the track of The Oakton Canteen and Steadfast's role within it. But you had a positive mania not to cast aspersions on anyone directly. It surprised me that a woman who had just lost her husband would do everything she could to avoid helping me find the killer. The truth was that you didn't want to be seen to be shifting the blame. You were faultless in the eyes of so many at this school and couldn't risk your reputation.

"But there was one person who became aware of your misdeeds. Tobias must have known that you were the only other person apart from his nephew who had access to the school's accounts. You were the one who went into the village to do his shopping and presumably had permission to deposit or withdraw money from the bank. Perhaps the saddest thing of all is that he didn't tell anyone of your crime; he did all he could to cover the shortfall in the school funds. He rang Horatio Adelaide to beg for a donation and avoid the scandal reflecting back upon you."

Mrs Hardcastle finally erupted. "You should be thanking me after what he almost did to those boys last night. He would have killed them if I hadn't intervened." Her voice was like a siren and rebounded off the walls of the small room.

"Oh, yes?" her interrogator was quick to bite back. "And what were you doing in the school at that time of night?"

"I... I noticed he was out of bed and went to see what was wrong."

"Or perhaps you went to the caretaker's hut to look for the spring-gun."

"No, it wasn't like that." She pressed on with her defence. "When I saw what he wanted to do to poor Marmaduke, I decided I couldn't live with him any longer. He would never have given me a divorce and-"

"You're lying, Miss," I heard myself say. "There's no way you could have planned two such complicated murders overnight. You must have been working on this for weeks."

218

Grandfather didn't take his eyes off her. "Exactly. You took your time to convince Steadfast. He told you about the illicit thrills of the nightclub he'd established and the wealth it was bringing him, and you saw your opportunity. You started stealing the money to stash away for your escape, knowing that your husband would be blamed after his death. You got greedier and greedier until Greeves noticed how much you'd taken, and everything came to a head on the very day that Herbert Mayfield was leaving the school."

She continued as though she hadn't heard a word my grandfather had spoken. "Tobias Hardcastle controlled me from the day we were married. When we met at Royal Arsenal, my life had promise and joy, but he locked me away in this school and thought my only function was to iron his clothes and make his dinner. I cleaned this house every day, but I hated him for it." Her face had turned scarlet with the rage that surged through her. "I hated him and I'm glad he's dead."

Her eyes were wild like a cornered cat's and I saw her lunge for the knife she'd used to cut the lemon.

"Now," Grandfather shouted at the top of his voice and, in three short seconds, Doreen had come storming into the house to rip the weapon from Celia's grasp.

"Did I do well, Lord Edgington, sir?" the immense woman asked. Her sister appeared shortly after with P.C. Evans in tow.

"Very well, Doreen. You're already learning." Still sitting comfortably on the pretty floral sofa, Grandfather took a sip from his teacup and let out an appreciative, *ahhhh.*

# CHAPTER THIRTY-SIX

I'd given up on not asking questions by this point and decided to accept the fact that I would occasionally sound stupid.

"Why did you ask her for a lemon?" was my first query once Blunt had made his second arrest and we were walking over to the cars to head back to Cranley.

"Ahh, that was one thing I didn't get a chance to explain in all the excitement. When I broke the news of her husband's death on the field, she did not cry. Shock can do strange things to people and I didn't think anything of it. But, this afternoon when we visited her, there was a distinct smell of lemons in the cottage and her eyes were so red that it made me wonder whether she had sprayed something in them to fake her tears."

I was rather impressed. "Oh, so it wasn't anything to do with the citric acid in the beaker in Mr Hardcastle's office then?"

I thought he might frown at me or tell me off for being ignorant, but he actually laughed. "Clever thinking, but no. Citric acid is odourless for one thing, and it would have been in powdered form to avoid starting the reaction with the bicarbonate too soon."

"Oh, I see," I replied, as though I had managed to follow anything he'd just said.

It was my mother's turn for a question. "So the bubbling flask really was just a red herring? Neither Oberon Steadfast nor Celia Hardcastle had any specialist scientific knowledge."

Her father nodded proudly. "That's exactly right. If they had, it wouldn't have been a very good red herring now, would it? As I said all along, it was a simple experiment that you could find in any children's science book. Even Chrissy could have managed it."

We all laughed at this, as it was perfectly true. I'd never been much cop at chemistry.

"It's amazing that she came so close to avoiding detection," my mother continued. "You did exceptionally well to get the better of her."

"And you did exceptionally well to assist me, my dear." They exchanged loving glances, and I have to say I felt a little left out. My mother was clearly a far better Watson than I'd ever be. It only made sense that he would take her along on any future adventures instead of me.

There was still one thing which I wasn't quite clear on. "But what will she be charged with? Isn't it just like Iago in Othello? She persuaded a man to kill for her but was barely involved in the crime itself."

Grandfather adopted a sterner tone. "This is not sixteenth-century Italy, my boy. Times have changed since then. All the police must prove is that she 'aided, abetted, counselled or procured the commission of the murder', and she will be punished just the same as the man who wielded..."

"An ornamental monkey?"

He couldn't resist a smile. "That's right. And besides, Celia set the trap that would have killed her accomplice so she's doubly guilty. Of course, that led to Steadfast trying to kill her in revenge, so they're evenly matched." He looked as though he was calculating something in his head, before giving up with a shrug. "As our dear Inspector Blunt declared, 'everyone will get what they deserve'. More often than not, that is the way of the law."

"God bless it, indeed." With a laugh, my mother threaded her arm through ours and we walked along as a happy trio.

When we reached the school, Delilah dashed off to get the best seat in the Silver Ghost. Our footman Halfpenny had brought the Aston Martin and looked windblown and nervous after his drive in the elegant, grey sports car. Cook had packed up her supplies, Todd had fetched my travelling chest, and there was nothing left to do but wave goodbye to Oakton for another year.

I looked up at the school with a mix of fondness and searing agony. I could only imagine what my final year would be like, but I would surely miss the place over the summer, even after all that had gone on. Mr Mayfield was talking to the police by the far entrance, and I hoped he would take the bad news well. Of course, what I really wanted was for him to return the following term as the new headmaster of Oakton Academy, though the chances were slim.

As I climbed into the back of the vast tourer, I noticed that the only other car still there belonged to the Adelaides. It seemed that Horatio was sleeping off his overindulgence in the driver's seat, while his son flicked through a book on the grass nearby.

"Did you catch the killer?" Marmalade shouted over.

"We certainly did. Two of them in fact." I was rather excited to reveal what we'd discovered.

"Jolly good, Chrissy. See you in September." He didn't seem too interested and went back to his book.

The servants had already climbed aboard the Rolls and Grandfather was pulling on his driving gloves. "Oh no you don't, Christopher. You're coming with me."

With the trepidation I felt whenever I heard those words, I alighted from the Silver Ghost to go across to him. Delilah immediately followed and hopped into the passenger seat alongside me.

"You're welcome to join us, Violet." He shouted over the noise of the engine as he secured his goggles in place.

"No, thank you," my mother sensibly declined. "I'll stick with the professional driver, if you don't mind."

We waved the other car off, and I knew that my speed-demon grandfather would soon be overtaking them. He did not pull away immediately, but regarded me with an inquisitive look.

"What's the matter now?" I suppose it was not just my fear of his driving that he read on my face at that moment.

"Nothing," I replied with as much sullenness as I could muster.

"Come along, Christopher. We're not going anywhere until you tell me why you look as though someone just showed your parents your school report."

I held my words in for a few more moments. "I … Well, I don't understand why you won't simply have Mother by your side in future. She's much better at this whole detective business than I am."

"And why do you think that is?"

I hesitated to answer. "Because she's so much cleverer than me, I suppose."

"Nonsense," he replied, and eased off the handbrake. "Your mother is only competent at observation, extrapolation and deduction because, when she was your age, she begged me to tell her every last detail of my cases and even convinced me to take her along on several of them. She's done nothing today that you yourself aren't capable of… with a bit more training and experience."

"I see." We looped around the front of school, and I tried to look grumpy, but it was awfully difficult. "There is one thing I've already learnt."

"Oh yes?" He raised one eyebrow, and it wasn't clear whether he believed me.

"Yes. Well, I'm clearly a terrible judge of character and always trust the wrong people. So, next time, I'm going to suspect the happiest, sweetest, kindest person right from the beginning."

His moustache bristled cheerfully. "Oh, so you do plan on there being a next time?"

I was grinning from ear to ear by now. "Well, if you don't mind."

"Fabulous!" The warmth in his voice filled me with excitement – though his apparent disinterest in the road in front of us was less inspiring. "I have quite the plan for us this summer. You just wait. There are eight weeks of holiday and we're going to make the most of them. We've old friends to visit, whole swathes of Britain to explore and new experiences to enjoy."

"As long as we get to stay on the ground," I replied. I was still having nightmares about the time he'd convinced me to jump to the earth from a hydrogen balloon.

"Well, we'll see about that."

We zoomed away from the school grounds, and the hot evening wind caressed my hair. I was both looking forward to the summer of adventure that lay ahead of us, and terrified for whatever scheme he would think up next.

"You're going a tad too fast, Grandfather," I told him, as we shot past Todd with a hoot of the horn.

"Don't be ridiculous, boy," he shouted over the noise of the engine and pressed down more firmly on the accelerator. "Though it might be a good idea for you to hold on to something."

# The End (For Now...)

Get another

# LORD EDGINGTON'S ADVENTURE

absolutely **free**…

Download your free novella at
**www.benedictbrown.net**

# "LORD EDGINGTON INVESTIGATES..."

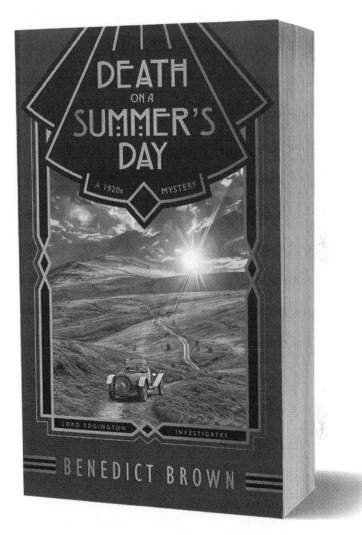

The third full-length mystery will be available in **July** at amazon.

Sign up on my website to the readers' club to know when it goes on sale.

# ABOUT THIS BOOK

I'm honestly not exaggerating when I say that 80% of the people I know are teachers. My mother taught for over fifty years and retired aged seventy-six. Of her four sisters, all but one trained to be a teacher (Auntie Mari, you black sheep!) some of their kids are teachers, both my brothers have worked in schools and I taught English in Spain for fourteen years, until Covid hit and I became a full-time writer. I have known hundreds of teachers and the vast majority are wonderful. I want this book to be a tribute to them, not the minority of Balustrades, Hardcastles and Steadfasts who, thankfully, are a lot rarer these days than in the past.

The good and bad teachers in the book are inevitably inspired by my own experiences. I went to the school where my mother taught and there was a particular teacher there who bullied not just the pupils but the other teachers. He chose one pupil to pick on and humiliate in his class every year, and my incredible mum was one of the few people to stand up to him. He was lazy, vain and cruel and the teaching world is far better off without his sort.

I did not attend a private school like Oakton Academy but my brothers went to two ancient, highly respected schools which they both hated. The story of the P.E. teacher telling Chrissy that he shouldn't have gone to Oakton if he didn't want to play rugby really happened to my brainy, bespectacled brother Dominic. Of course, Dom only told Mum about this once the teacher had left the school, as he knew she would have sped down there in a rage to tell the teacher off. If you haven't worked it out yet, our mother is something of a character.

In a happier story of teachers who've left strong impressions, I can still remember every teacher who taught me at school and university and so, if any of them happen to be reading, I'd like to thank you all. As important as families are for planting the seed of a child's interest in learning, it's often teachers who help it to grow. From my years as a child watching Mum go without sleep for days on end when she had reports to write or an inspection looming, I know you are overworked and underappreciated – but not by everyone.

228

I based the layout of the school on old Billy Bunter novels which my dad adored and I enjoyed re-reading to prepare for this book. It's surprising how fiction from the twenties and thirties can remain so relevant and entertaining. The Edgington books are dedicated to my dad and I know he'd have loved the combination of a classic boarding school novel with a whodunnit. I also got a little piece of his life story into his book as he briefly worked at a bursar at a very posh private school in London where money was being fraudulently concealed. They asked him to continue the practice, he said no and they fired him. It was one of the three jobs he lost for being too honest.

There was one final influence which I must acknowledge; my friend Gemma's children Lennox and Delilah. These two brilliant eight-year-olds were so excited by the idea of their mother's friend writing mysteries that they came up with the idea for a murdered headmaster in a boarding school, a dinner lady suspect and students fleeing the scene. It was really my obligation to fill in the gaps. There's already a Delilah in the series and a Lennox will have to turn up before long.

If you loved the story and have the time, please write a review on Amazon. Most books get one review per thousand readers so I would be infinitely appreciative if you could help me out.

# THE MOST INTERESTING THINGS I DISCOVERED DURING MY RESEARCH FOR THIS BOOK...

Research can be fascinating and tiresome – often in equal measure – but I have discovered any number of things I hadn't known before. Here are some of the most interesting...

Until the Sex Disqualification Removal Act was passed in Britain in 1919, no married women were allowed to work as teachers. And even after this, schools introduced "marriage bars" to get rid of female teachers. This led to women getting married in secret and living apart from their husbands in order to maintain their jobs. The practice continued until it was outlawed in 1944! Crazy!

But not as crazy as the fact that some girls' schools in the interwar periods were so prim and prudish that they made girls take baths under canvas tents so that they wouldn't be able to see their own bodies. As for the cane, the slipper and the strap, corporal punishment was only abolished in state schools in 1987 (the year I started school!) It continued in private schools until 1999 in England and 2003 in Northern Ireland. I'm glad to say I never experienced it first-hand but my mother worked in schools where certain teachers were slap happy.

In her 1894 book 'Fancy Ices' the cookery writer Agnes Marshall – whose books Mrs Beeton's publishers apparently bought the rights to, in order to make the world forget her – suggested using liquid nitrogen to make ice cream. She was about a hundred years ahead of her time though, and it was only in the last twenty years that this method has become popular.

People have very strange collections! Sometimes, even for passing references in a book, I have to do a lot of research into entirely unrelated topics. There's a reference to the kind of things people collect as a hobby at some point and I really enjoyed looking into outlandish collections. I still have my father's antique matchboxes and stamps from all over the world, but, thanks to the internet, I found examples of people who collect belly button fluff, old train tickets and antique nails. Oh, and Johnny Depp collects Barbies – that weirdo! I, on the other hand, collect Christmas-themed Lego – which is totally normal for a grown man, thank you very much.

(Incidentally, when my friend Bridget read that paragraph, she phoned to tell me that her father had a collection of 100,000 train tickets and eventually sold them for £10,000. Apparently, there is a big train ticket collecting community and people meet to swap and sell the rarest ones.)

I also had to read quite a lot about the first world war. The more I learn of that terrible period, the easier it is to understand why it became known as "the war to end all wars". The use of chemical weaponry was abhorrent on both sides. As one nurse said at the time, "I wish those people who talk about going on with this war whatever it costs could see the soldiers suffering from mustard gas poisoning. Great mustard-coloured blisters, blind eyes, all sticky and stuck together, always fighting for breath, with voices a mere whisper…"

We still have the tendency to glorify war but I very much doubt that any soldier who served in the First World War could have come back with that need. It was a terrible period in human history and its lingering effects were felt throughout the 1920s and, of course, led into the Second World War. If the famous Christmas Day truce and football match between English and German troops on the front line in 1914 isn't a sign of the futility of that conflict, I don't know what is.

To protect the British and French troops from gas attacks, The Daily Mail newspaper encouraged women to manufacture cotton pads, for gas masks and respirators. The response was enormous and a million gas masks were produced in a single day. They weren't actually very useful against gas, but it was still an amazing achievement and makes me think of all the people over this past year doing their bit to create extra PPE during the pandemic.

History is fascinating. Many thanks to my mother for helping me realise this fact and all the wonderful history teachers who taught me at school (especially Margaret Long, Sandra Hale and Adrian Grant).

# ACKNOWLEDGEMENTS

I may be at risk of banging on about them, but I'm going to say one last sorry and thank you to all the teachers who end up reading this book. I'm sorry to lump you in with some of the nastier characters and incredibly grateful for the influence you've had on my love of history, fiction and the world in general. I'll single a few out who got me here. Thank you to the brilliant writer Jem Poster who ran my creative writing masters and has always encouraged me. And thanks to Mrs Long, Miss Maslin and Mr Roberts from the Beacon for being wonderful, inspirational people – sorry I messed up my A-levels!

Thank you as always to my wife and daughter for being inspirationally wonderful, to my family for reading my books and my crack team of experts – the Hoggs, the Martins, Esther Lamin and Lori Willis (**fiction**), Paul Bickley (**policing**), Karen Baugh Menuhin (**marketing**) and Mar Pérez (**forensic pathology**) for knowing lots of stuff when I don't. Thanks to my fellow writers who are always there for me, especially Pete, Suzanne and Lucy.

Thank you many times over to all the readers in my ARC team who have combed the book for errors. I wouldn't be able to produce these books so quickly or successfully without you so please stick with me, Izzy and Lord Edgington to see what happens next…

Rebecca Brooks, Ferne Miller, Craig Jones, Melinda Kimlinger, Deborah McNeill, Emma James, Mindy Denkin, Namoi Lamont, Linda Kelso, Katharine Reibig, Pam, Sarah Dalziel, Linsey Neale, Sarah Brown, Karen Davis, Taylor Rain, Brenda, Christine Folks McGraw, Terri Roller, Margaret Liddle, Tracy Humphries, Anja Peerdeman, Liz Batton, Allie Copland, Susan Kline, Kate Newnham, Marion Davis, Tina Laws, Sarah Turner, Linda Brain, Stephanie Keller, Linda Locke, Kathryn Davenport, Kat, Sandra Hoff, Karen M, Mary Nickell, Vanessa Rivington, Darlene Riggs, Jill Tatum, Helena George and Anne Kavcic.

# THE "BODY AT A BOARDING SCHOOL" COCKTAIL

The Champagne Cocktail was initially a 'morning bracer' but it was so good that enthusiasts carried on drinking it throughout the day. On Broadway, it was known as 'Chorus Girls' Milk' and the future King Edward VII, who was fond of many a chorus girl, was such a keen Champagne Cocktail drinker that he is said to have invented his own version, the Prince of Wales, with some American whiskey and a piece of then very luxurious pineapple.

The drink became popular in the United Kingdom in the first years of the 20th century. Its simplicity made it an easy drink to prepare and serve at events such as theatre premieres or... picnics! You can find references to it in a thousand books and films including 'Casablanca' and 'An Affair to Remember'. It is also quite flexible and is commonly drunk with cognac, by those looking for a stronger hit – though my French in-laws prefer it with a peach liqueur. This is the classic recipe which is believed to have been created by Edward VII himself, possibly on the first ever royal visit to the States...

**1 1/2 oz. (4.5 cl) whiskey**

**1 oz. (3 cl) Champagne**

**1 small piece of pineapple**

**1 dash Angostura bitters**

**1/4 tsp (0.125 cl) Maraschino liqueur**

**1 tsp (0.5 cl) sugar (or simple syrup)**

You pour the bitters over the sugar, then add the whiskey, liqueur and pineapple. Shake it with crushed ice and then strain it in a cocktail shaker, before adding the champagne last of all. I imagine that the prefects in the book were mixing a simpler version, but this sounds delicious!

The idea for the cocktail pages was inspired by my friend and the "Lord Edgington Investigates..." official cocktail expert, Francois Monti. You can get his brilliant book "101 Cocktails to Try Before you Die" at Amazon...

If you're looking for a modern murder mystery series with just as many off-the-wall characters but a little more edge, try **"The Izzy Palmer Mysteries"** for your next whodunit fix.

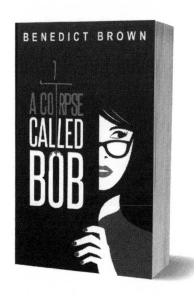

**"A CORPSE CALLED BOB"**
(BOOK ONE)

Izzy just found her horrible boss murdered in his office and all her dreams are about to come true! Miss Marple meets Bridget Jones in a fast and funny new detective series with a hilarious cast of characters and a wicked resolution you'll never see coming. Read now to discover why one Amazon reviewer called it, **"Sheer murder mystery bliss."**

# ABOUT ME

Writing has always been my passion. It was my favourite half-an-hour a week at primary school, and I started on my first, truly abysmal book as a teenager. So it wasn't a difficult decision to study literature at university which led to a masters in Creative Writing.

I'm a Welsh-Irish-Englishman originally from **South London** but now living with my French/Spanish wife and presumably quite confused infant daughter in **Burgos**, a beautiful mediaeval city in the north of Spain. I write overlooking the Castilian countryside, trying not to be distracted by the vultures, hawks and red kites that fly past my window each day.

When Covid 19 hit in 2020, the language school where I worked as an English teacher closed down and I became a full-time writer. I have two murder mystery series. There are already six books written in **"The Izzy Palmer Mysteries"** which is a more modern, zany take on the genre. I will continue to alternate releases between Izzy and Lord Edgington. I hope to release at least ten books in each series.

I previously spent years focussing on kids' books and wrote everything from fairy tales to environmental dystopian fantasies, right through to issue-based teen fiction. My book "**The Princess and The Peach**" was long-listed for the Chicken House prize in The Times and an American producer even talked about adapting it into a film. I'll be slowly publishing those books over the next year whenever we find the time.

**"A Body at a Boarding School"** is the second book in the "Lord Edgington Investigates…" series. I'm about to start work on the third novel and there's a novella available free if you sign up to my readers' club. If you feel like telling me what you think about Chrissy and his grandfather, my writing or the world at large, I'd love to hear from you, so feel free to get in touch via…

**www.benedictbrown.net**

# WORDS YOU MIGHT NOT KNOW!

I like to hint at antiquated language in the text without overloading my readers with it and here are some of the rarer terms I included. A **colloquy** is a conversation. **Oxonian** comes from Oxford and particularly the distinguished university there. **Bally** is a very soft euphemism for bloody. **Bandalore** is the old-fashioned word for a yo-yo – which was itself only trademarked in America in 1932 but originally came from a Philippine word. **David Garrick** was a famous actor and theatre owner. **To peach** means to reveal information on another person – to snitch or inform in modern English. **Grutching** means to complain – a bit like the more modern term grouching. The word **kidsman** has essentially been replaced by the term Fagin, as it implies an adult who recruits children for criminal activities. A **bursar** is the person who deals with a school's accounts. Oh, and **barley sugars** are an older (yet more politically correct) name for a Chinese or Indian burn in which kind-hearted school children would twist the skin on another child's arm in opposite directions. I can still remember the feeling and don't wish to repeat it.

A **panopticon** – which Chrissy himself doesn't know the meaning of – is an interesting concept which I learnt about at university, reading Michel Foucault on a literary theory course. It's a kind of prison in which the inmates are observed at all times without knowing for sure if they are actually being watched. This gives the guards an "invisible omnipresence" and makes it less likely for prisoners to cause trouble. Foucault used this in his book on penal systems as a metaphor for modern society as a whole making us docile and civil – so that's something to think about!

Some readers have told me they wish that there was a guide to British terms, but I'm so used to them that I'm afraid they're difficult for me to single out – I'll make more effort as I'm writing the next book and record them as I go. **Bobbies** are an obvious one as they come up often and the word implies any low-ranked police officer. The father of the British police force was Sir Robert Peel – hence the slang terms bobbies or peelers!

And finally, I found out that the verb *exit* is in fact singular in Latin and so the word **exeunt** was also adopted into English for when more than one person leaves a place. It's only used in the theatre and the law these days, but I thought it was old-fashioned and pretentious enough for an Oakton Academy pupil to employ, so I put it in my book.

It's amazing how many terms came into common usage in 1926 (the year after these books are set!) Very often when I look up words in an etymological dictionary, I come across entries from that year. These include "the colouring book", "clementines", "car park", "To strut one's stuff" and "Hollywood" standing in for American movie making in general. I have tried very hard to avoid anachronisms in language but have no doubt that some slip through. On my very last edit, I discovered that the word "scam" is only from 1963 and "come up with" is from the thirties, so swiftly removed any mention of them.